WHAT HAPPENED IN THE WOODS

PHIL M. WILLIAMS

AETHON THRILLS

WHAT HAPPENED IN THE WOODS
©2025 Phil M. Williams

This book is protected under the copyright laws of the United States of America. No part of this publication may be reproduced, stored in a retrieval system, or transmitted, in any form or by any means, without the prior permission in writing of the publisher, nor be otherwise circulated in any form of binding or cover other than that in which it is published and without a similar condition including this condition being imposed on the subsequent purchaser. Any reproduction or unauthorized use of the material or artwork contained herein is prohibited without the express written permission of the authors.

Aethon Books supports the right to free expression and the value of copyright. The purpose of copyright is to encourage writers and artists to produce the creative works that enrich our culture.

The scanning, uploading, and distribution of this book without permission is a theft of the author's intellectual property. If you would like to use material from the book (other than for review purposes), please contact editor@aethonbooks.com. Thank you for your support of the author's rights.

Aethon Books
www.aethonbooks.com

Print and eBook formatting: Kevin G. Summers. Cover art: Steve Beaulieu.

Published by Aethon Books LLC.

Aethon Books is not responsible for websites (or their content) that are not owned by the publisher.

This book is a work of fiction. Names, characters, places, and incidents are the product of the author's imagination or are used fictitiously. Any resemblance to actual events, locales, or persons, living or dead is coincidental.

All rights reserved.

Also by Phil M. Williams

WHAT HAPPENED IN THE WOODS
DEATH DO US PART

Want to discuss our books with other readers and even the authors?

JOIN THE AETHON DISCORD!

Author's Note

Dear Reader,
 If you're interested in receiving two of my popular thriller novels for free and/or reading many of my other titles for free or discounted, go to the following link: http://www.PhilWBooks.com.
 You're probably thinking, *What's the catch?* There is no catch.
Sincerely,
Phil M. Williams

Chapter 1

Before

They strolled home from school on a cracked and heaving sidewalk, the concrete losing the battle with the tree roots. They held their phones in their hands with no fear of dropping or losing them, as their removal would be like losing an appendage.

"It's the first freaking day, and I'm already over this shit," April said.

"I'm thinking about dropping out," Brandi replied, walking next to her best friend.

"For real?"

"What's the fucking point, you know?" Brandi's GPA was below 2.0.

"You can't drop out. That's some trailer-trash shit."

Brandi shrugged. "I'm just saying. I could get a GED."

"*I* might drop out if I don't get a *freaking* car," April said, as robins chirped in the trees above them.

"Or a boyfriend."

"I'm not going for another high school boy. They are literally losers."

"Big facts, but I wasn't thinking about high school boys."

April stopped in her tracks and put her hands on her hips. A ray of sun cut through the oak canopy, making her tan legs appear golden. "Spill the tea, bitch."

Brandi faced her friend. "There's nothing to spill."

April rolled her eyes. "You're such a little liar. Who is he?"

Brandi's phone buzzed with a notification from IG. While she checked the direct message, April checked her phone, neither girl needing to explain the interruption. It was another direct message from some guy telling Brandi how hot she was and asking where she lived. Brandi had posted a selfie of herself in the outfit she still wore—tiny jean shorts and a tank top—which she'd titled *Last First Day of School*. She'd already collected nearly 1,000 likes, 100 comments, and dozens of DMs from the post.

Brandi looked up from her screen. "Another loser."

April looked up from her screen, a crooked smile on her lips. She had posted a similar first-day-of-school picture with her tiny shorts and tank top. "Some rich guy offered to fly me to Miami for the weekend anytime I want."

"Sounds sus."

"He's for real. I stalked his IG. He drives a G-Wagon. Has a house near the beach."

"Are you gonna go?"

April giggled. "Maybe. I don't know."

"That's bananas."

They continued to stroll on the sidewalk.

"If I go, I was thinking about telling my dad that I'm staying at your house," April said. "You don't care, do you?"

Brandi shook her head. "As long as your dad doesn't come over to check on you."

"*Shit*. He might."

As they neared the entrance to their trailer park, Brandi asked, "You wanna go to One Stop? Get an iced coffee?"

"It's like a mile from here," April replied.

"It's not that far. C'mon."

"You're buying, bitch."

"Fine." Brandi knew she wasn't buying because she only had

two bucks in her pocket. She didn't care about the iced coffees. She was hoping to see a certain someone who frequented One Stop.

Along the way to the store, a Mustang honked at them, the driver likely admiring their attire.

"What do you think would happen if I waved at the next guy that honks?" April asked.

"Don't," Brandi replied.

April grinned. "Let's find out. These creepers honking at us could totally go viral." April recorded from the roadside.

Shortly thereafter, a lifted pickup rumbled by, the driver laying on the horn.

The guy in the passenger seat stuck his head out the window and said, "Damn."

April waved at the truck, off camera. The brake lights flashed, and the truck pulled over on the shoulder.

"Oh shit," Brandi said.

The man in the passenger seat said, "You girls are lookin' fine. Come over here."

April stepped toward the truck, still recording.

Brandi grabbed her friend's hand and tugged her in the opposite direction. "C'mon, April. Don't be crazy."

The two girls bolted towards the nearby townhouse neighborhood.

The man in the passenger seat called out, "Where you goin'?"

They stopped running near a gang of mailboxes. They were breathing heavy and giggling at the same time. April checked the video on her phone.

"Did you get it?" Brandi asked, smiling.

"You know I did. I bet this gets like a million views," April replied.

"You're a crazy bitch."

"That's why you love me."

They left the townhouse neighborhood, finally reaching One Stop. Brandi checked for his car in the parking lot, but it wasn't there.

The disappointment must have been written on Brandi's face because April asked, "What's wrong with you?"

"Nothing," Brandi replied.

They went inside the convenience store, the bell jingling as they opened the door. As they filled their plastic cups from the iced coffee machine, Brandi asked, "How much money you got?"

April frowned at her friend. "You're such a bitch."

Brandi smirked. "You know I never have any money."

April paid for their drinks, and they exited the convenience store, sipping their sweet coffee concoctions. Brandi's heart raced at the sight of a black BMW with shiny chrome wheels.

April stopped. "Oh my God. He's here."

"Who?" Brandi asked, playing dumb.

April pointed at the BMW. "Damon. The hottest freaking criminal ever."

Brandi bit her lower lip. "You know him?"

"Not personally, but everyone *knows* him."

Brandi exhaled, relieved that she could still claim her crush for herself. After all, she'd had a conversation with him. Twice. The first time, he'd been hovering over the coffee area inside One Stop, blocking the straws, so she'd asked him for one.

He had replied, "I'm sorry, baby. Here." Then he'd handed her a straw.

The second time, he'd seen her walking home from April's house, and he had pulled up alongside her and asked, "You need a ride?"

Brandi had been nearly home, so she'd declined, but they'd talked for five minutes or so. Him in his car, the window open. Her leaning over, dangerously close. Their conversation hadn't been about anything. It was mindless flirting. Him not believing that Brandi was seventeen, accusing her of lying, and then eventually telling her that she was too hot to be in high school.

She might've hooked up with him that day, but a black SUV had parked next to them, and the passenger window had motored down.

A weaselly man with big ears had grinned and said, "Jail bait, motherfucker."

Damon had chuckled and replied, "Fuck off, Eddie."

But Eddie hadn't fucked off. Damon had followed the SUV, cutting his conversation with Brandi short.

"Maybe he can give us a ride," April said.

Brandi still fantasized about their last conversation.

April nudged Brandi, jolting her from her daydream. "Hello?"

"Sorry. What?" Brandi asked.

"Maybe he can give us a ride."

"He looks busy."

"Whatever. I'm gonna ask him. I'm not walking all the way home."

April marched across the parking lot to his car and tapped on the window. Brandi followed her like a little puppy dog. Damon had parked near a billboard that read, "Blevins and Associates, because everyone deserves a good defense."

Damon powered down his window. "What's up, baby?"

April was right. He was the hottest freaking criminal ever. He was like a young Ryan Gosling with dark hair and more edge.

"Could you give me and my friend a ride to the Woods of Colebrook?"

Damon peered around April, catching a glimpse of Brandi, who gave him a little wave. The man winked back, then said, "Yeah, sure. Get in."

April sat in the front seat and talked his ear off. Brandi sat in the back, like their child. She normally scrolled on her phone in uncomfortable situations, but she stared at Damon instead, inspecting his sleeve tattoos. They were a woven mixture of hundred-dollar bills, skulls, guns, BMW symbols, and naked women. He glanced in the rearview mirror and smiled at Brandi, causing her to blush. April was oblivious as she went on about the injustice of being a baddie without a car.

Damon turned into their trailer park.

"It's 103 Crescent Woods," April said. Damon started to turn on Crescent, but April said, "Don't turn here. Go to the next street and park."

Damon frowned.

"If my neighbors see your car in our driveway, they'll tell my dad."

Damon lifted his chin. "I got you."

He parked on the next street along the curb.

"You wanna come over and hang?" April asked.

Brandi clenched her fists and thought, *Slut*.

The two girls walked the short distance to April's doublewide trailer. April instructed Damon to come a few minutes later so her nosy neighbors didn't see them together.

While walking, April asked, "You think I should hook up with him?"

Brandi lifted one shoulder. "I don't know."

April paced inside her trailer, near the front door, intermittently checking for Damon through the sidelight windows. When he appeared, April opened the door and ushered him inside. She led him to her bedroom, with Brandi trailing like a third wheel.

April twirled and said in a singsong voice, "This is my room."

April's bedroom was dominated by an unmade queen-sized bed with a half-dozen pillows on the floor. Everything was pink, teal, or white. A wooden cursive "April" was hung on the wall over her headboard. A full-size mirror hung next to her dresser, perfect for admiring herself. String lights hung from the ceiling.

Damon nodded. "I like your room."

"You gotta check this out," April said as she closed her blinds. Then she turned off the overhead light and flicked on the string lights.

"Nice," Damon said. He retrieved a Zip-Loc bag from the front pocket of his jeans. Inside were what appeared to be bright-colored gummy bears. He opened the bag and held it to April. "Pot gummies. You want some?"

"Yeah." April took a handful and popped them into her mouth.

"Easy, girl. Don't take more than five. They're strong." He held out the bag to Brandi. "You want some?"

Brandi took a few gummies, welcoming the escape. "Thanks."

Damon looked Brandi up and down. "No problem, girl."

Brandi popped the gummies into her mouth.

Damon leered at April, then Brandi. "How come you two don't have boyfriends?"

"Who says we don't?" April asked.

"Where are they, then?"

April giggled. "We don't have boyfriends. All the boys at school are so freaking immature."

Damon turned to Brandi. "What about you, shorty?"

"I don't have a boyfriend," she replied.

"You waitin' on a real G?"

Before Brandi could answer, April invaded Damon's personal space, placing her hands on his hips.

"Damn baby," Damon said, his attention returning to April.

April tilted her head upward, her lips pursed. Damon took the hint and kissed her open-mouthed. As they kissed, Damon's hands roamed over April's thin body. He picked her up easily and April wrapped her legs around his torso, their lips never parting. Brandi was frozen like a deer in headlights.

Damon tossed her on the bed, causing April to giggle. He took off his shoes and shirt and climbed onto April's bed. They resumed their making out horizontally. Brandi watched the muscles on his back, various tattoos moving as he rolled around with April. Brandi was about to leave, but Damon came up for air and reached toward her. "Come here, beautiful."

She tiptoed toward the bed, her entire body buzzing. April motioned with her head and eyes for her friend to leave the way she came, but Brandi didn't want to give him up. After all, she liked him first.

When Brandi reached the bedside, Damon grabbed her ass. "C'mon shorty. I got you."

A car or truck approached the trailer, the brakes squeaking as it parked in the driveway.

"*Shit*," April said as she hopped out of bed and hurried to the window. Her shorts were unbuttoned and her fly was down, exposing her pink underwear. April parted the blinds for a split second, then whipped around. "It's my dad." She rushed to her bedroom door, shut it, and locked it. Then she pointed to Damon. "You need to hide."

The front door opened and shut.

Damon grinned. "Where?"

April put her finger to her lips. "*Shh.*" She opened the closet and whispered, "In here."

Damon scooted off the bed without urgency.

"Hurry," April whispered. She shut Damon into her closet at the same time her door handle rattled.

The rattle was followed by a strong knock. "April? Open this door," her dad said.

"Coming," April replied, her voice high and cheerful. She opened the door.

Her dad stood in the doorway wearing a greasy jumpsuit, his name, Larry, embroidered on his chest. "What did I tell you about lockin' your door?"

"I was getting dressed."

Larry glanced at his daughter's outfit. "You didn't wear that to school, did you?"

"No. I just changed."

He glanced around the darkened room, the string lights twinkling overhead. "What are you doin' in here?"

"Homework."

Larry narrowed his gaze and scanned the room again. "I don't see any books."

April rolled her eyes. "Everything's online, Dad. We're working on our phones."

Larry peered over his daughter's shoulder at his daughter's friend. "That true, Brandi?"

Brandi held up her phone. "Yes, Mr. Kreiser."

He checked the room one more time, then said to April, "You shouldn't work in this light. You're gonna ruin your eyes. And don't lock this door." He flipped on the overhead light before leaving.

April shut the door, turned to Brandi, put her hand over her heart, and mouthed, *Oh my God.*

Brandi followed April to the closet. She opened the door to find Damon standing there with a grin. He grabbed April and pulled her into the closet, kissing her openmouthed.

When they separated, Damon undid his fly and pulled down his zipper. "Help me out before I go."

April glanced back at the door for an instant, then whispered, "*No*. You have to go. Like right now. My dad's seriously strict."

Damon sighed. "You owe me, girl." He zipped up his jeans.

April went to her window, unlocked it, and pushed upward, but it didn't move. She turned to Damon. "Can you help me?"

Damon went to the window and pushed, the aluminum frame grinding and squeaking as it opened. April's bedroom door blasted open.

Larry appeared. "What the fuck is goin' on in here?"

Larry and Damon locked eyes for an instant. Damon dove out the window head first, landing on the holly hedge, his body cracking the branches. Larry ran to the open window. Damon scrambled to his feet and sprinted from the scene of the crime.

Larry yelled through the open window. "If I see you again, I'll fuckin' kill you." With Damon out of sight, Larry turned his rage on April. "What the hell were you doin' with him?"

"Nothing, Daddy. I swear."

"How old is he?"

"I don't know. He's Brandi's friend. He asked for something to drink."

Larry smacked his daughter across the face. "Don't fuckin' lie to me."

April burst into tears.

Brandi ran from the doublewide trailer.

Chapter 2

After

Brandi sat in one of the sun-bleached lawn chairs behind The Tasty Chicken, rereading her final text string with Tyler.

Tyler: I can't do it anymore. You almost got me fired.

Brandi had been convinced that Tyler had been cheating on her with Becky, the receptionist at Dalton Concrete. Tyler worked there as a laborer. Brandi had seen Becky's name flash on his phone screen several times. Tyler had shown her the messages, which were regarding rain days, but Brandi had thought it was code, and that the two of them hooked up on rain days while she was at The Tasty Chicken. So, she had barged into Dalton Concrete primed for a confrontation. She had accused perky little Becky of being a slut before being escorted off the premises by one of the managers. Brandi still believed Tyler had fucked her.

Brandi: Just admit it

Tyler: You really are crazy.

Brandi: You really are a little bitch liar

Tyler: I'm done with this. I'll get my stuff tomorrow when you're at work.

Brandi: I hope that bitch Becky gives you HIV!!!!!!!!!!!!!!

Tomorrow was today, so Tyler and his dumbass friends were

probably moving his stuff out of her apartment at that very moment.

Her phone chimed. The screen read, Mrs. Cunt Calling. Brandi rejected the call. That was the other stupid ass thing Tyler did. He had this grand idea that Brandi should forgive Jack and Mrs. Hunt. When she rejected his dumbass idea, he looked them up and gave them her phone number. They had both tried to reconnect, but Brandi wanted nothing to do with them, and she had been seriously pissed at Tyler for interfering.

Her phone buzzed with a text.

Mrs. Cunt: Why aren't you here? What the H is wrong with you. He was your father. Call me back. I need to talk to you. I have a very important letter for you.

Brandi blocked her and thought, *She can go fuck herself.*

A black Tesla drove into The Tasty Chicken parking lot. The driver had his window down. He parked and stared at Brandi. Even from a distance, she could see that he was hot—in his mid-twenties, with dirty-blond hair, nice shoulders, and an athletic arm resting on the window frame.

She checked her clothes, suddenly feeling self-conscious in her black pants and blue Tasty Chicken polo.

The back door of the restaurant opened. Her manager stuck his fat head outside and said, "Break's over, Brandi."

She stood from the lawn chair and followed Dusty inside, giving him the middle finger behind his back.

After the lunch rush, Brandi manned the lone open register. The middle-aged woman paid with a twenty for her nine-piece bucket of fried chicken, biscuits and gravy, and sodas. Brandi handed her four dollars and twenty-two cents in change. The woman dumped the coins into the clear plastic donation bin for The Children's Hospital of Philadelphia. Then she added a single dollar, doing it very slowly, making sure Brandi saw her selfless act of generosity.

The woman gawked at Brandi, waiting for recognition.

After an uncomfortable silence, the cashier said, "Thank you," without enthusiasm.

The woman returned a tight smile, took her food, and left.

Brandi thought, *They tip everywhere except fast food. It's bullshit. I need money more than a fucking hospital.*

The next customer shuffled forward, his eyes on the menu above her head.

"Welcome to The Tasty Chicken. May I take your order?" Brandi said in monotone.

The man didn't reply but mumbled to himself like a tard, still gawking at the menu.

Brandi wondered how many times she had uttered that phrase since she had started working at The Tasty Chicken almost two years ago.

The man finally ordered and paid. His slow order and the single open register caused a backlog of five customers. Like most people, the slowpoke didn't leave any money for The Children's Hospital of Philadelphia. Brandi had more respect for the customers who *didn't* donate.

The next four customers were quick. The fifth customer was the last, as no new customers had joined the line. The old man ordered a chicken sandwich, fries, and a medium drink. He paid with a twenty from a fat roll of cash. Brandi gave him back eleven dollars and fifteen cents. When he reached for the donation box, she expected the man to drop the coins inside and maybe one dollar, but he kept his change and slipped the ten-dollar bill into the box instead.

Brandi expected the man to seek her approval, but he simply took his food and shuffled to the dining area. She stared at the donation box. It was pretty full, and one corner of the ten-dollar bill peeked from the piggy bank-like opening. Brandi looked around. She was alone. No customers, and she was the only cashier. She glanced at the ten-dollar bill, looked around one more time, then swiped the bill and shoved it into her pocket.

Then Brandi scrolled IG on her phone while she waited for another customer.

Shortly thereafter, Dusty appeared at her side.

Brandi shoved her phone into her pocket. Tasty Chicken employees weren't allowed to use their phones during work.

"I need to talk to you in my office," Dusty said, his double chin jiggling like a chicken wattle with each syllable he spoke.

"I'm the only cashier working," Brandi replied.

One of the cooks emerged from the back.

Dusty gestured to the skinny young man. "Aaron can fill in."

Brandi followed Dusty to his office. The manager wore his khakis over his big belly, exposing his white socks.

"Shut the door and sit down," Dusty said.

Brandi shut the door and sat across from Dusty at his metal desk. "I just looked at my phone for a second. There weren't any customers."

Dusty tapped on his laptop screen. "I want you to watch this." He turned the screen to Brandi.

It was her from about ten minutes ago. She watched as the old man shoved a ten-dollar bill into the donation box. After looking around twice, Brandi swiped the bill and shoved it into her pocket.

Dusty turned the screen back to himself and paused the video. "Did you see yourself stealing money from the donation box?"

Brandi crossed her arms over her chest. "I didn't steal anything. I was just pushing it in better."

Dusty shook his head. "I've been watching you—"

"That's creepy."

"Because I suspect this isn't the first time you've stolen here."

"I've never stolen anything in my entire life."

"I have camera footage that refutes that statement. I also suspect you've been stealing from your coworkers. As you know, we've had several team members complaining of money missing from their purses."

"This is bullshit. I never took anything."

"You're fired, Brandi."

She glowered at her boss. "You can't do that. I didn't do anything."

Dusty sighed; his shoulders slumped. "I don't know why you care. You obviously don't like this job."

"Nobody does. But I need a job."

"You have a choice. You can quit, and I'll mail your final check, or you can fight this, and I'll be forced to go to the police with the video you just saw. It's your choice."

Brandi stood abruptly. "Fine. This job fucking sucks anyway." She knocked over the chair on her way out.

Chapter 3

Before

Brandi ran down the street, her sneakers slapping the asphalt. At the street corner, Damon waited in his BMW. He beeped his horn. She jogged to the driver's side window.
"Need a ride?" Damon asked.
"I can walk. My house is right around the corner," Brandi replied.
"I don't mind drivin' you. Get in."
Brandi sauntered to the passenger door, climbed inside, and sat in the leather bucket seat. "I love your car."
Damon pressed on the accelerator unnecessarily hard, chirping the tires, and pinning Brandi into her seat. With the rapid acceleration, they passed the girl's street.
"My house is back there. On Briar Woods," Brandi said, pointing behind her.
"I wanna show you somethin' first," Damon replied.
Brandi furrowed her brow.
"Don't worry. It's not far."
Damon turned onto the main road, driving away from Franklin City, the nearest small city. Brandi watched him while he drove.
He glanced at her. "You like what you see?"
Brandi blushed and looked away.

"Don't worry about it, baby. I like what I see too."

She turned back to Damon. "You do?"

"You're hotter than your friend."

She blushed again. "No way. Everyone thinks she's really pretty."

Since they'd become best friends in middle school, Brandi had always been the less hot version of April. They had similar styles, but Brandi shopped at second-hand stores. They both had long, wavy hair, but April had blonde highlights, and Brandi was a basic brunette. They both had pretty faces with blue eyes, but April had good makeup. Brandi usually went without, or sometimes used her best friend's leftover makeup. They were both petite, but April was a little taller.

Damon reached over and put his hand on Brandi's bare thigh, sending a jolt of electricity through her body.

"You got it goin' on, shorty. I know what I'm talkin' about." He cracked a crooked smile.

Brandi beamed.

Damon turned off the highway and drove on a country road for several miles. He eventually turned off the road and drove behind an abandoned warehouse. He carefully navigated the dilapidated parking lot, avoiding large potholes, before parking in the rear, concealed by the warehouse behind them and the woods in front of them.

"You wanted me to see this?" Brandi asked.

"Naw, baby." Damon unbuttoned his jeans and pulled down his zipper. He lifted his butt off his seat and pulled his pants and boxer briefs down to mid-thigh, exposing his penis. "I wanted you to see this."

Damon parked his BMW several trailers down from Brandi's house. He placed his hand on Brandi's thigh. They leaned toward each other and kissed over the center console.

When they separated, he said, "You ever need another ride, lemme know."

The girl simpered and exited his BMW. Damon drove away. She watched his car disappear from view.

"Hi, Brandi."

The girl turned to the familiar voice. It was Hanna walking her Boston Terrier, Charlie. She was a mutual friend of Brandi and April, although she was closer with the latter.

Brandi waved to her. "Hi, Hanna."

Hanna sauntered over, her Boston Terrier in lockstep. "What are you doing?"

"Nothing." Brandi bent down and petted the dog. Charlie wagged his stubby tail and wiggled his chubby body.

"Is April in trouble again? I texted her, but she hasn't texted me back yet."

"I don't know." Brandi bent down, gave Charlie another pet, and said in an excited baby voice, "Who's a good boy? Who's a good boy?"

Charlie wiggled in delight.

"I bet she's in trouble," Hanna said.

Brandi stood. "I should go."

They said their goodbyes.

Brandi trudged to her rusty, single-wide trailer, with the weedy lawn and the dirty windows. It had been her great-grandmother's house. The girl had been living with her mother in the trailer since her parents had divorced when she was five years old.

She entered the trailer. A sweet chemical smell hung in the air. Brandi knew that smell. Meth. A ratty couch sat along the far wall of the living room. The tan carpet was stained and threadbare in high-traffic areas. The bracket from the television still hung on the near wall, but the television had been sold long ago. A large plastic bag of crystal meth sat on the coffee table. A single square of the dropped ceiling sat on the couch. Brandi glanced at the hole in the ceiling. Her mother's boyfriend was a meth dealer, and often stashed product in their trailer. Most of their arguments revolved around Brandi's mother using his stash.

Snoring came from her mother's bedroom. Brandi went to her mother. She slept on a bare mattress without a frame or a box spring. A meth pipe sat on the floor, just out of her mother's reach, the bowl burned black from use. Her mother's mouth was open, exposing her black teeth. Her thinning blonde hair was pulled back in a ponytail. Her face held the deep wrinkles and leathery skin of a much older woman. Her crop top and booty shorts were of a much younger woman. Brandi watched her mother's chest, breathing a sigh of relief at the noticeable rise and fall.

A tattoo of a scorpion perched on her right shoulder. It was a tattoo that held no personal significance or artistic merit. According to her mother, "It was just some crazy shit I did."

Brandi left her mother's side and went to the kitchen. She opened the fridge. It was mostly empty, which didn't surprise her as it hadn't worked for at least a year. But sometimes, the junkies and dealers who frequented their trailer left some food in the fridge. Brandi searched the cabinets, finding a mostly empty jar of peanut butter and a plastic spoon that appeared relatively clean.

She went to her room with her dinner. The free lunch she got was the only thing she liked about high school, even though she complained about it to April, telling her how disgusting it was. But she still ate every morsel. Her room was as barren as her mother's, with a single mattress. She did have a comforter and a pillow, but no sheets. She sat on her mattress, her pillow cushioning her back against the wall, scrolling TikTok videos and eating peanut butter.

Brandi's mother wouldn't and couldn't work. Their meager income came from child support, which mostly fueled her mother's drug habit. The phone service was the one bill her mother tried to pay, although even that was hit or miss. Consequently, sometimes her phone worked. Sometimes it didn't. It worked at the moment, so she took advantage of it while she could.

She watched beautiful women doing their makeup and talking

about how to marry the rare, high-value man and how to avoid the many losers.

A crash came from the front door, followed by heavy footsteps. Brandi rose from her bed, her heart pounding in her chest. A man dressed in black and carrying a rifle appeared in her doorway.

He aimed his rifle at her, the red dot dancing on her chest. "Get on the fucking ground! *Now!*"

Brandi stood stunned and shaking like a leaf.

Another man in black entered her bedroom and threw Brandi to the ground, wrenched her hands behind her back, and handcuffed her.

Chapter 4

After

Brandi smacked the steering wheel of her old Hyundai and screamed, loud enough that a nearby customer turned and looked. She backed out of the parking spot, put the car into Drive, and mashed the accelerator, chirping the front tire. She drove to the nearby Starbucks.

She bought an iced coffee with the ten bucks she had stolen and settled into a chair outside, on the patio. As she sucked her coffee through a straw, she thought about her father's funeral. *Why do I even care? We haven't even talked in like two years. It's not like he was even in my life.* Brandi slumped her shoulders. *What am I gonna do?* She stared at her iced coffee. *Maybe I could get a job here. It has to be better than The Tasty Chicken.*

A black Tesla drove by the Starbucks. It was the same hot guy that she'd seen at The Tasty Chicken. Brandi watched him park at the back of the lot, near the Under Armour store.

To distract herself from death and unemployment, Brandi opened TikTok on her phone and watched funny dog and cat videos.

She didn't notice when Mr. Tesla approached her table and said, "Excuse me."

His cologne wafted into her nostrils before Brandi looked up from her phone. He was tall, at least six feet tall.

"I'm sorry to bother you. I'm a model scout, and I was wondering if you were signed to a modeling contract?"

Brandi burst into laughter. "You can't be serious."

"I *am* serious. You have a fresh face. There's something special about you."

Brandi shook her head. "That's literally bullshit."

Mr. Tesla laughed, showing his perfect teeth, his blue eyes sparkling. "You're skeptical. I totally get it. And you should be skeptical. You don't know me." He grabbed a business card from his wallet. "My name's Colton, by the way. Here's my card."

She took the black glossy business card that read, "Colton Ellis, Owner, Platinum Models, Inc." The website and his phone number were listed at the bottom.

"I manage thirty-eight women, and they are *all* doing very well for themselves. My lowest earner makes over ten thousand dollars a month."

Brandi flipped over the business card in her hand. The reverse was blank.

"What's your name, if you don't mind me asking?"

"Brandi."

"It's nice to meet you, Brandi," Colton said, holding out his hand. They shook hands.

"What kind of modeling do they do?" she asked.

"Mostly online, social media, and subscription."

Brandi scowled. "*Subscription?* You mean OnlyFans?"

"OnlyFans is just a platform. What you do on the platform is up to you. I personally prefer that my models *don't* do any nudes. Some of them do, and they make more money initially, but it kills them for brand deals later."

Brandi inspected his shiny business card. "I don't know."

Colton flashed his palms. "No pressure, but if you're interested, I have a shoot coming up in a few weeks that I think you'd be perfect for. It pays two thousand dollars for a day's work, and you get to keep the clothes."

"What kinda shoot is it?"

"You'll be modeling a variety of clothes around this beautiful cabin. It's mostly jeans and sweaters, but there are a few bikini shots. Hopefully, you're okay with that."

Brandi stared at the tabletop. "I'm not a model."

"I think you could be, and I've been doing this for a long time."

Brandi raised her gaze to Colton. "A long time? You look really young."

The man grinned. "I'll take that as a compliment. I've been working in social media marketing since I was sixteen. I'm twenty-six now. I know what it takes to be successful, and I can honestly say, you have what it takes."

"What if I'm not successful?"

"You'll still earn two grand for a day's work, and you'll still get to keep the clothes. But really, two thousand dollars is nothing for you. With your face, I know I can pitch you to some really big brands."

Brandi nodded. "Can I think about it?"

"Of course. The shoot is scheduled for June 28th, which is a Friday. I would need to know at least a week before that."

"That's almost three weeks from now."

"Eighteen days to be exact." Colton cocked his head. "Is that a problem?"

"I lost my job. I could use the cash sooner."

Colton retrieved his wallet, produced five one-hundred-dollar bills, and handed the cash to Brandi.

"I'm not sure I wanna do this yet," she said.

"It's okay. Keep it either way."

Brandi took the cash. "Thank you."

"If you decide you want to do the shoot, just call me."

Chapter 5

Before

The social worker, Gloria, parked in front of an old farmhouse. Brandi expected it to be a long trip, but it wasn't that far from her mother's trailer. She hadn't seen her grandmother since she was five, but she'd been living so close the whole time. Gloria had said, "You're lucky she's so close. You don't even have to change schools."

Brandi trudged behind Gloria to the front door, a trash bag filled with her clothes in one hand and her phone in the other. The front door was open, but the screen door stopped the insects. Before Gloria could ring the doorbell, a tall, stocky woman stepped onto the porch, the screen door slapping the door frame behind her.

"Good afternoon," the large woman said.

The social worker smiled and said, "Hello, Mrs. Hunt. I'm Gloria Sandoval. We spoke on the phone."

The adults shook hands while the girl checked her phone. April still hadn't replied to the dozens of texts Brandi had sent since her mother was arrested. Brandi figured April's dad must have confiscated her phone after finding Damon in her bedroom.

Mrs. Hunt stared at Brandi for a long beat, then asked Gloria, "Is that all she has?"

"I'm afraid so," Gloria replied.

Mrs. Hunt narrowed her eyes at Brandi's short shorts, then she said, "Do you remember me?"

Brandi shook her head, now scrolling on IG. But that was a lie. She remembered her ugly face, with her perpetually downturned mouth and lazy eye. She remembered being spanked by the big woman for stealing a cookie from her cookie jar when she was five.

"Well, I'm your grandmother. You can call me Grandma or Mrs. Hunt. That's up to you."

"Okay, *Mrs. Hunt*," Brandi replied, her gaze glued to her phone.

Mrs. Hunt frowned, opened the screen door, and waved the girl inside. "Come on. Let's get you settled."

Brandi stepped into the farmhouse. Mrs. Hunt turned from the social worker.

"I have to verify her living conditions," Gloria said.

Mrs. Hunt turned back to Gloria and opened the screen door. "Knock yourself out."

Gloria didn't stay long. Just long enough to see that Brandi had a bedroom, bathroom, and food. Every room had some depiction of Jesus or a cross.

Once Gloria was gone, Mrs. Hunt led Brandi outside. Goats and chickens roamed a green pasture enclosed by electric fencing and two small sheds. Mrs. Hunt turned off the electric fence and showed Brandi the sheds. The girl tiptoed into the pasture, careful not to step in shit. Chickens and goats swarmed Mrs. Hunt, squawking and bleating.

"I don't have any treats," the old woman said to the animals.

She opened one of the sheds, which had nesting boxes, roosting bars, and a floor covered in straw and chicken shit. The air was musky with the animals and manure.

"Every morning, you'll have to collect and clean the eggs," Mrs. Hunt said, showing Brandi the nesting boxes.

But the girl still scrolled IG.

"Give me that."

Brandi looked up and held her phone tight to her body. "No. It's mine."

Mrs. Hunt motioned with her fingers. "Give me your phone."

"No. You can't take my phone."

Mrs. Hunt clenched her jaw. "I can and I will."

Brandi shoved her phone into her back pocket. "Please. I'm paying attention."

"Your phone won't work much longer without someone paying the bill, and from what I can tell, you're addicted to it. Give it to me. *Now.*" Mrs. Hunt held out her hand.

"I'll call Gloria. Tell her to take me someplace else."

Mrs. Hunt shook her head. "There is no other place. This is it." Mrs. Hunt spoke through gritted teeth. "I might be old, but I'm pretty sure I can overpower *you*. I bet you barely weigh a hundred pounds."

Brandi put her hands on her hips. "I'm one-fifteen, and if you touch me, I will fuck you up, old lady."

With the speed of a viper, Mrs. Hunt grabbed Brandi's left wrist and yanked her forward, nearly knocking her off her feet. Then, she twisted the girl's wrist, sending shooting pain up her arm and causing her to screech.

In a calm voice, Mrs. Hunt said, "With your other hand, grab your phone, and hand it to me."

The girl did as she was told, and the woman let go of her wrist.

Brandi snatched her arm and stepped back. "What the hell's wrong with you?"

Mrs. Hunt slipped Brandi's phone into her pocket, shaking her head. "You will *not* use that kind of language. Do you understand me? If you want respect, you have to earn it. If you want me to treat you like an adult, you need to learn how to act like one."

"Whatever. My mom's gonna get outta jail soon anyway."

"In the meantime, you're under my roof, and you *will* abide by my rules."

Brandi crossed her arms over her chest. "Whatever."

Mrs. Hunt went on with her instructions as if nothing had transpired between them. "As I was saying. You'll have to collect and clean the eggs every day. It's important that the eggs are spotless because I sell most of them. You'll have to refill the feeders every three days, fresh water every day, and you'll have to clean out the bedding every week."

A white goat with curved horns and a white beard nudged Brandi's leg, causing her to yelp.

"Don't worry about him. He won't hurt you," Mrs. Hunt said.

Brandi petted the goat's neck and back, and the animal nuzzled against her leg in return. She smiled for a split second, the first time since her mother's arrest. Then she remembered she was still angry.

"Don't get too attached," Mrs. Hunt said. "The goats are for meat. He'll be butchered this fall, along with most of the herd."

Brandi glowered at her grandmother, thinking, *I'd like to butcher your fat ass.*

Mrs. Hunt showed Brandi the goat shed and the chores she needed to perform for the herd. They left the pen. The white goat followed Brandi, stopping just short of the fence. Once they were out of the pen, Mrs. Hunt turned on the electricity.

"Don't forget to turn on the electric fence. Otherwise, you'll be running around trying to catch goats and chickens."

Mrs. Hunt led Brandi back to the house and into the kitchen. The large woman left her muck boots at the back door and instructed the girl to do the same with her sneakers.

"We'll have to get you some work boots tomorrow," Mrs. Hunt said.

The woman then showed Brandi the kitchen again. "I serve breakfast at 7:00 a.m. sharp. I expect your chores to be done before breakfast, so you will be expected to rise at 5:30 every morning, including weekends and holidays. The animals don't understand weekends and holidays. They shouldn't suffer because it's Saturday. You'll have a reprieve from chores tomorrow, as you need work clothes, but after that, your chores must be done every day, no excuses. I expect you to make your own lunch for school and on the weekends. I won't be giving you any money, but there's plenty of bread and lunch meat. Dinner is served at 6:00 p.m. sharp. I expect you to clean up the dishes after dinner every night. If you're not here at the appointed time, you don't eat. Do you understand?"

"Yeah," Brandi replied.

"Proper English, young lady. Yes, Mrs. Hunt."

"Okay."

"No. Not okay. Yes, Mrs. Hunt."

"Yes, Mrs. Hunt," Brandi repeated while rolling her eyes.

"I don't appreciate the sass, young lady."

"I didn't do nothing."

"*Anything*. You didn't do anything."

"Whatever."

Mrs. Hunt glowered at Brandi. "One final thing about the kitchen." She touched the jar on the counter. "This is my cookie jar. You are welcome to have one cookie after dinner if you eat all your vegetables, and that's it. Do not steal cookies. Stealing is sinful. This cookie jar is a good test of willpower and virtue."

Brandi thought, *I bet she eats way more than one cookie.*

Mrs. Hunt led the girl upstairs, the wooden steps creaking under her weight. The old woman stopped at the hall bathroom and said, "Like I told Gloria, this bathroom is yours. I expect you to keep it clean. Cleaning products are in the kitchen under the sink. If you don't keep it clean, you'll be cleaning my bathroom too.

Brandi shuddered at the thought.

"Do you understand?" Mrs. Hunt asked.

"Yes, Mrs. Hunt."

"Good."

Mrs. Hunt continued to the guest bedroom next to the bathroom. She entered the small room with a single bed, a wooden dresser, and a wooden desk that resembled something from an old schoolhouse. An alarm clock sat on the bedside table. A creepy crucifix with Jesus bleeding from his hands, feet, and head hung on the wall, along with several framed prints of horses. Brandi's trash bag full of clothes sat on the bed. The only comforting thing in the room was the stuffed animal on the dresser, which resembled a golden retriever puppy.

Brandi went to the dresser and picked up the stuffed animal.

Mrs. Hunt gestured to the bedroom. "This is your room and your space. I will give you your privacy, but don't give me a reason to revoke that privacy. Like your bathroom, I expect you to keep your room clean and tidy. Cleanliness is next to Godliness." Mrs. Hunt stepped across the bedroom and put her hand on the desktop. "You can do your homework here. I expect all your homework to be done immediately after school. No procrastinating. Do you understand?"

Brandi slumped her shoulders. "Yes, Mrs. Hunt."

"I know this is a big change for you, but rules and discipline are not your enemy. Without rules and discipline, you won't reach your God-given potential. You will *waste* your precious life. You won't get an education, and you won't have a career that you can be proud of. You'll be working at some fast-food restaurant for minimum wage, or you'll be on the streets working as a lady of the night. That's no kind of life."

Brandi hugged the stuffed puppy.

Mrs. Hunt stepped closer to her. "Your father bought that for your sixth birthday."

The girl tilted her head. "How come he never gave it to me?"

"Your mother sent it back."

Brandi narrowed her eyes. "Don't talk about her."

"I was simply telling the truth. Things are not always as they seem."

"Really? It *seems* like I haven't seen you or my dad since I was like five, and you live really close. It *seems* like you're a big fat hypocrite."

Mrs. Hunt nodded, her face blank. "Hypocrite. Good to know that you have a decent vocabulary. If I'm a hypocrite, God will judge me. Your contact with me, or rather your lack of contact, was out of my hands. You should talk to your parents about this."

"*Parents?* What parents? My mother's in jail, and my dad..." Brandi shook her head and set the stuffed animal back on the dresser. "You know what I remember about my dad, *your* son?"

Mrs. Hunt crossed her arms over her ample chest. "I'm sure you'll tell me."

Brandi put her hands on her hips. "I remember him punching my mom in the face and breaking her jaw. She had to eat out of a straw. You gonna tell me that didn't happen?"

"That was unfortunate."

"*Unfortunate.* It wasn't *unfortunate.* It was *abuse.* Your son is an abusive piece of *shit.*"

Mrs. Hunt blinked rapidly, the insult landing as intended. "Language, young lady."

With a smirk on her face, Brandi said, "I was simply telling the truth."

"Well, maybe your father can show you that he's not that man anymore."

"He's not even here."

"He's coming home in about six weeks. He's retiring, so he'll be able to make up for lost time."

Brandi huffed. "I don't want anything to do with him."

"We'll see." Mrs. Hunt grabbed the trash bag full of clothes and started for the door.

"What are you doing? Those are my clothes."

Mrs. Hunt pivoted to Brandi, still holding the trash bag. "While you're under my roof, you'll dress like a proper young woman of integrity and virtue." Mrs. Hunt pointed at the girl's short jean shorts and tank top. "You look like a hussy."

Brandi held out her hands. "A *hussy.* What does that mean?"

"A hussy is a lewd woman with loose morals." Mrs. Hunt lifted the trash bag for a beat. "If these clothes are like the ones you're wearing, you need a new wardrobe."

"What am I supposed to wear then?"

"There are a few things in your dresser. We'll get everything you need tomorrow." Mrs. Hunt held up one finger. "One more thing. I expect you to pray every night before bed, and we go to church every Sunday. Your spiritual life is as important as your earthly life." Mrs. Hunt left the bedroom.

Brandi called out, "I want my phone back."

Chapter 6

After

Brandi entered her apartment, her mail in hand and her purse over her shoulder. She scanned the living room. The television was gone. The La-Z-Boy too. The only thing left was the used couch and coffee table she had bought at Goodwill. She checked the bedroom. Her shoulders slumped. She had hoped Tyler wouldn't take everything, but his bedroom set was gone. Her clothes sat on the floor. He did leave her mattress and her golden retriever stuffed animal.

Brandi went to the fridge and retrieved a diet soda. The fridge was nearly empty. Apparently, Tyler had taken the food he had purchased too. She set her purse, the mail, and the diet soda on the coffee table. She plopped on the couch, opened her soda, and flipped through the mail. She opened the rent bill. *I can't afford this without Tyler.* Even with the five hundred bucks she got from Colton, she was short by almost two hundred dollars. Brandi took a swig of her soda and sat back on her couch. She stared at the holes in the wall where Tyler had installed his television. *They're gonna take that out of my security deposit. Shit.*

She grabbed her cell phone and Colton's business card from her purse. She typed his website into the browser on her phone: PlatinumModels.com. The site was surprisingly professional, with many beautiful women modeling stylish clothes in exotic locales. C. Howard Ellis was listed as the president of the company, but there was no picture of the young man. Brandi figured the omission was purposeful, as his age would be a negative in the business world.

She sent a text to Colton.

717-555-6321: This is Brandi. I want to do the shoot.

Chapter 7

Before

The alarm clock blared at 5:30 a.m. Brandi was jolted from a deep sleep, the golden retriever in her arms. She silenced the alarm after smashing several buttons. Brandi hadn't set the stupid thing and had no intention of rising before the sun. She covered her head with the comforter and drifted back to sleep.

Brandi was jolted awake again, this time by large hands shaking her.

"Wake up," Mrs. Hunt said. "You have chores."

"Leave me alone," Brandi replied, hugging her stuffed animal.

"You have three seconds to get up. One... two... three."

Brandi didn't move.

Mrs. Hunt pulled the girl's body from the bed, dumping her on the floor with a *thud*.

"Ow." Brandi stood from the hardwood floor, rubbing her head. "I hit my head."

"I told you that chores start at 5:30 a.m. sharp. Get dressed. I'll meet you outside." Mrs. Hunt left the bedroom.

Brandi dressed in her new work clothes. Canvas pants and a long-sleeve shirt. She slipped on her new boots. They were stiff and uncomfortable. She resembled a little man.

The girl clomped down the stairs in her stiff boots and exited the back door where Mrs. Hunt waited for her.

"I'll supervise this first time, but after this, I expect you to work independently like an intelligent person," Mrs. Hunt said.

Mrs. Hunt watched Brandi collect the eggs and refill the feeders and waterers. Even though the bedding wasn't due to be changed, Mrs. Hunt made her shovel the straw and shit mixture to make sure she knew how to do it.

As Brandi worked the pitchfork, she wondered, *Is there a wrong way to shovel shit?*

Once Mrs. Hunt was satisfied that Brandi understood her duties, the old bag left to make breakfast. While shoveling the goat pen, the white goat nuzzled her. She petted the goat, asking, "Who's a good boy? Who's a good boy?"

The goat jumped on a bale of hay stored in the shed. Then he hopped and climbed to the top of the stacked bales, about six feet in the air. The goat bleated from his perch.

"What are you doing up there?" Brandi asked. "You definitely need a name." She thought for a moment, then she giggled to herself. "How about Billy?"

Billy bleated again.

"Billy it is."

After her chores, Brandi showered and dressed for school. She tried on several of the dresses her grandmother had purchased for her. They were all equally ugly, so she settled on a plaid print dress that hung to mid-calf.

"Breakfast is ready," Mrs. Hunt called out from the kitchen.

Brandi went to the stairwell and called back, "Coming."

Then she snuck into the old bitch's bedroom to find her phone. The bedroom was dominated by a queen-sized sleigh bed. The walls were covered in floral wallpaper and pictures of Jesus. *The fat bitch probably thinks about him when she fingers herself.* Brandi opened and closed the dresser drawers. She grabbed a pair of cotton underwear, unfolded it, and held it up to the light streaming through the windows. They were massive, big enough to fit two Brandis inside. The girl burst into laughter.

"What's so funny, young lady?" Mrs. Hunt asked, standing in the doorway.

Brandi sucked in a breath and turned to her grandmother, hiding the underwear behind her back at the same time. "Uh. Nothing."

Mrs. Hunt stepped to Brandi, towering over her. She held out her hand. "May I have my underwear?"

Brandi dipped her head and handed the underwear to her grandmother.

Mrs. Hunt folded her underwear. "I am overweight, but I do not deserve to be mocked for it. You're better than that." Mrs. Hunt put her underwear back in her drawer and faced Brandi. "What are you doing in my room?"

"Nothing," she replied, not making eye contact.

"Lying is a sin, and I won't tolerate it in my house."

Brandi met her grandmother's gaze. "I'm *not* lying. I was just looking around."

"What were you looking for?"

"*Nothing*. I was just looking. You didn't tell me I couldn't go in your stupid room."

Mrs. Hunt sighed. "You were looking for your phone."

Brandi crossed her arms over her chest. "So what. It's mine."

"Your breakfast is getting cold."

"I don't want any breakfast."

"Fine. Get your school supplies, and I'll meet you in the truck. Don't forget your lunch. It's in the fridge." Mrs. Hunt left her bedroom and descended the stairs.

Brandi went to her room and grabbed the backpack containing various supplies that her grandmother had purchased yesterday. She descended the stairs into the kitchen. Her stomach rumbled at the remnant smell of bacon and eggs. She gazed out the kitchen window at her grandmother giving the goats and chickens her breakfast. Brandi grabbed her lunch from the fridge. She checked the kitchen window again, but her grandmother was gone. The cookie jar beckoned Brandi. The pickup truck started, the engine rumbling. She opened the jar, revealing chocolate chip cookies with a few pieces of bread to keep them soft. Brandi looked around, then grabbed three cookies and shoved them into her brown lunch bag.

On the way to school, Brandi stared from the passenger window of the old pickup truck.

Mrs. Hunt sniffed several times. "Do you have something to tell me?"

"Why would I have something to tell you?" Brandi replied, still staring from the window.

"Do you know what integrity is?"

Brandi shrugged, watching farms and the forest.

"Integrity is being honest and having strong moral principles. Your integrity is all you have in this world. Doesn't matter if you're rich or poor. Pretty or ugly. Without integrity, you're nothing."

Brandi turned to her grandmother. "Just 'cuz you said it doesn't make it true."

Mrs. Hunt turned on the two-lane highway toward the high school. "That's what someone without integrity would say."

Brandi scrunched her face. "Who the hell are you to judge me?"

"I'm not judging you. I'm judging your behavior. Did you or did you not steal my cookies?"

"*Cookies*? You're bitching about cookies. I did your stupid chores, and you're mad that I took a couple cookies. You should be thanking me. You don't need any cookies."

Mrs. Hunt glanced at Brandi, then back to the road. "It's not about the cookies. It's about your lack of integrity."

"Whatever." Brandi grabbed her lunch bag and retrieved the cookies. "Here's your precious cookies." She threw them across the cab at her grandmother. They all hit Mrs. Hunt. Two landed on the bench seat. One landed in her lap.

Mrs. Hunt didn't react to Brandi's outburst.

"You're such a hypocrite. You stole my phone. Where's your integrity, *Mrs. Hunt?*"

"Your phone is in the glove compartment," Mrs. Hunt said as she pulled into the Franklin High School parking lot.

Brandi opened the glove compartment and found her phone in a Ziploc bag smashed to smithereens. "What the hell?" The girl held up the Ziploc bag, various phone parts inside.

"If you were an alcoholic, it would be irresponsible of me to have alcohol in my home. Since you're a cell phone addict, I knew you would stop at nothing to recover your phone. This was the only way to give you the best chance at recovery."

Brandi gaped at her grandmother. "You are *literally* crazy."

Mrs. Hunt parked her truck in the line of drop-off vehicles. "I'll be here at 3:00 p.m. sharp to pick you up."

Brandi grabbed her backpack and her lunch, exited the truck, and slammed the door behind her.

Chapter 8

After

Brandi waited outside of her apartment complex, her backpack in hand and filled with her toiletries, makeup, and a change of clothes. She wore jeans and a T-shirt and was quite comfortable. It was already in the seventies that morning.

The black Tesla approached. Brandi waved at Colton, but he drove past. Thankfully, he parked down the road, about fifty yards away. She shouldered her backpack and fast-walked to the Tesla.

Colton exited the driver's side door. "Hey, Brandi."

The young woman waved. "Hi, Colton."

"Sorry. I was zoning out and I drove right by you."

"It's okay." Brandi tried to open the door, but there was no handle.

"You have to push one end of the handle and then pull."

Brandi pushed on the embedded handle in various places, finally causing the door to pop open a few inches. She pulled the door open, removed her backpack, and climbed inside. Colton climbed inside too. His cologne smelled earthy and woodsy. It reminded her of springtime in the woods.

"Sorry. I've never been in a Tesla," Brandi said, setting her backpack at her feet.

"No worries. It is a little different." Colton handed her an envelope. "That's the rest of your deposit."

Brandi took the envelope. "Thank you." She glanced at the hundred-dollar bills, guessing it was five hundred as they had agreed upon, but she didn't want to be rude by counting it in front of him, so she shoved the envelope into her backpack.

"I'll give you another thousand when we're done. Cool?"

Brandi smiled. "Cool."

Colton flicked a lever on the steering column, putting the car into drive, then he drove onto the highway.

"It's so quiet."

"Electric motors are quiet. It makes a spaceship noise when I back up, for safety."

"That's wild." Brandi touched the edges of her bucket seat. I like the interior too. I love leather."

"It's actually synthetic leather." He glanced at her and grinned. "Probably for the vegans."

Brandi giggled. Then she examined the dashboard, which was barren except for the large tablet screen. "Where's all the stuff? You don't have any buttons or anything."

Colton gestured to the tablet screen. "Everything's done on the screen, and on these levers." Colton pointed to the levers on the steering column, taking his hand off the wheel for a moment.

"That's so lit. Where does the key go?"

Colton flashed a grin. "You don't need a key." He touched his cell phone on the center console. "My phone is my key. The car automatically recognizes my phone so I can just get in and drive, and when I'm done, I can just park and walk away. The car automatically turns off and locks."

As Brandi watched Colton talk, she noticed the scar on his lip from cleft palate surgery. His little imperfection made him that much more perfect.

They had been driving for over two hours when Colton turned onto a gravel road and drove them deep into the Pennsylvania forest. Brandi scanned the surrounding trees. She hadn't seen another car in a while.

"How far is this place?" she asked.

"We're almost there," Colton replied.

Brandi tried to check Instagram, but she couldn't connect to the internet. "My phone's not working."

"There aren't any cell towers nearby."

Her heart rate increased. She shoved her phone into her pocket. The cabins along the gravel road were fewer and farther between. "Does anyone live out here?"

"Not full-time. The cabins are for hunters mostly."

"Is that what you use your cabin for?"

"No. I use it for pictures, obviously. Nature is better than the best studio."

Brandi nodded.

Colton glanced at her. "I come out here to get away sometimes too. It's beautiful, isn't it?"

Brandi pursed her lips. "What time do you think we'll be done?"

Colton checked the clock on the tablet screen. "Depends on the lighting and how long it takes for you to get ready and change clothes. I'd like to be done by five or six, so I can get you home by eight or nine."

"Okay." She wrung her hands in her lap.

He glanced at her again. "Are you okay?"

"I didn't realize it would be way back in the woods like this."

"You don't like the woods?"

"I had a really bad camping trip once. I've never been back since."

"You don't have to worry about camping. The cabin is really nice. It has electricity. Hot water. Nice bathrooms. The fridge is stocked. We'll be outside for the shoot, but you certainly won't be roughing it."

Brandi breathed a sigh of relief. "That's good."

Chapter 9

Before

Before the first bell, Brandi waited for April at her locker. Students trickled into the locker bank, dropping off their backpacks, and grabbing their first-period books. Cheerleaders hung homemade posters urging the Franklin Panthers football team to victory that Friday. April never showed.

She finally saw April at her locker before lunch. A cacophony of teenagers talking and rushing to lunch played in the background. A handful of boys in football jerseys pushed each other around, seemingly for fun.

Brandi marched to April. "Where were you this morning?"

April slammed her locker shut and gawked at her. "Oh, my God. What are you wearing?"

Brandi frowned. "I know. My psycho grandmother took all my clothes and gave me this ugly ass dress to wear. She fucking smashed my phone into a billion pieces."

April cackled.

Brandi furrowed her brow. "What are you laughing at?"

April pointed at Brandi's dress and said, "I love that for you."

"Why are you being a bitch? My mother's in jail. I'm literally living with a crazy woman. I don't need you acting like this."

"Like what?"

"What's going on with you?"

April lifted one shoulder. "What's going on with you?"

"I already told you. What is wrong with you?"

April narrowed her eyes. "I know what you did."

Brandi held out her hands. "What are you talking about?"

"Damon. Hanna saw you with him."

Her stomach churned, but she tried to show a calm exterior. "So."

"You fucked him, didn't you?"

Brandi flinched.

Several students turned to watch the argument.

"I knew it," April said. "I can tell by your face."

"I didn't do anything," Brandi replied.

"You're a shitty liar."

The eavesdropping students smiled and whispered among themselves.

Hanna approached them.

April brushed past Brandi, smiling and meeting Hanna. The new best friends strolled to lunch together, as if Brandi meant nothing.

Brandi trudged to the bathroom, avoiding eye contact along the way. Two bougie bitches freshened their makeup in the mirror. She went into an empty stall and closed the door. She sat on the toilet lid, put her head in her hands, and cried as quietly as she could.

The bougie bitches at the mirror giggled.

Brandi sniffed, wiped her eyes, and stood from the toilet. She emerged from the stall with her jaw set tight. She marched to the girls at the mirror. "What the *fuck* are you laughing at?"

The girls startled and stepped away from Brandi. One of them said, "Nothing. *Sorry.*"

Brandi swiped the girl's purse off the counter, knocking it on the floor. "Take your shit and get the fuck outta my face."

One of the girls grabbed her purse, and they hurried from the bathroom, leaving Brandi alone. She washed her face and all trace of her tears. Then she grabbed her lunch from her locker and marched to the cafeteria thinking, *Fuck April*.

Brandi strutted to the lunch table that she'd sat at with April, Hanna, and a dozen other girls with her head held high. A few of the girls saw her coming and whispered to each other, immediately spreading the news of her arrival. Her confidence wavered as she sidled up to her friends. Nobody looked at her.

April said to the table, "Don't you hate lying bitches who can't keep their legs closed?"

"They're so nasty," Hanna said, her eyes on April.

"I agree," said another former friend.

Another former friend gave Brandi the side-eye. "You mean that thot?"

Brandi's former friends stifled their laughter. *Thot* stood for That Ho Over There.

"Fuck all of you," Brandi said. "You don't know shit."

As she walked away, her former friends burst into laughter.

Brandi found a lonely table in the corner of the cafeteria. She thought about her mother, wondering when she'll get out. She thought it would only be a day or two, like the last few times she was arrested for possession. Of course, this wasn't just possession. It was possession with the intent to distribute, a felony. But her mother wasn't the drug dealer. *Would it matter?*

She set down her turkey sandwich. Despite having little to eat that day, she lost her appetite. Tears filled her eyes. She bowed her head and wiped her tears, not wanting anyone to notice.

Chapter 10

After

Brandi watched from her passenger window as Colton drove them deeper into the wilderness. She wrung her hands in her lap, nervous that she hadn't seen a cabin for several miles.

"Are we getting close?" she asked.

Colton glanced at Brandi. "We're almost there."

A small cabin with a red door appeared on the right side of the road.

Brandi pointed. "Is that your cabin?"

Colton chuckled. "Thankfully, not. That's my nearest neighbor, although I've never seen anyone at that cabin."

Shortly thereafter, Colton turned off the main road onto a driveway that twisted through the forest to a two-story log cabin with a detached three-car garage. The cabin had a porch in front, dormer windows on the second floor, and a shiny metal roof.

Brandi gaped through the windshield. "This is really nice."

"Thanks. I like it."

"You bought it yourself?"

"It's a business expense."

They exited the Tesla. Brandi followed Colton inside. The living room was cavernous, with exposed wooden beams, a stone fireplace, a chandelier made from deer antlers, and black leather furniture.

Brandi rotated three hundred and sixty degrees. "Wow. This place is lit."

Colton chuckled. "Thanks. Are you hungry?"

"A little. Can I use the bathroom first?"

"Sure." Colton gestured to the hallway beyond the living room. "It's down that hall, first door on the left."

Brandi found the bathroom. She set her backpack on the floor and peed. When she was finished, she washed her hands and exited the bathroom. She peered down the hallway, noticing another door. The young woman crept down the hallway and tried to open the door, but it was locked with a deadbolt. It resembled someone's front door, but it was inside the house.

"Did you find it okay?" Colton called out from the opposite end of the hall.

Brandi walked to him. "Yeah, I was just exploring." She pointed her thumb over her shoulder. "What's in that room back there?"

"It's just storage. People break into these cabins, so I keep valuables in there."

Brandi nodded.

"I have some snacks for you in the kitchen."

Brandi followed Colton to the modern kitchen with stainless steel appliances and oak wood cabinets. Colton had arranged cheese and crackers, ham, fruit, carrots, diet soda, and water on the center island.

"This looks great. Thank you," Brandi said.

"It's a long ride. You must be hungry," Colton replied.

"You must be hungry too."

Colton nodded. "I'm starving."

They ate together on bar stools at the center island. Brandi went easy on the cheese, trying not to overeat. After all, she was supposed to be photographed in a bikini.

WHAT HAPPENED IN THE WOODS

While they ate, Brandi asked, "Is it hard to manage all your models?"

Colton smirked. "It can be challenging sometimes."

Brandi popped a grape in her mouth. "Like challenging how?"

"I've had to deal with jealous boyfriends who try to micromanage everything the model wears on a photoshoot."

"How do you deal with that?"

"I try to politely let them know that they aren't in control of the shoot, and if the model wants to be paid, she'll have to wear the clothes we've been contracted to model. My models are very beautiful, but their boyfriends are often insecure. It makes for a flammable situation sometimes."

"I could see that."

"Then when these toxic relationships inevitably end, I become the model's therapist." Colton ate a cracker.

Brandi sipped her diet soda. "Why don't you just tell them to hire a therapist?"

"I do encourage that, but if they want to talk to me, I can't just blow them off. That would hurt their feelings. Some of these women have had issues with substance abuse and even suicidal ideation. As beautiful as they are, many of them have had eating disorders too. I just want them to be healthy and happy. I know I'm complaining, but I care about them. I feel responsible for their wellbeing."

Brandi smiled small. "That's really nice."

After lunch, Colton led Brandi upstairs. There were three bedrooms—a master bedroom at the end of the hall and two guest bedrooms. He gave her a quick tour. The master bedroom was decorated with oak furniture and paintings of forest scenes. The king-sized bed had been constructed with wood that matched the exposed beams overhead. The two guest bedrooms were nearly identical, with pale-yellow walls framed with ornate crown molding and light oak furniture. Like the master bedroom, various forest-themed paintings hung around the room.

The guest bedroom nearest the stairs would double as Brandi's changing room. Clothes sat atop the queen-sized sleigh bed, along with various shoe boxes.

Brandi glanced at the blue bikini, her stomach buzzing with anxiety.

Colton pointed to the jeans and white blouse on the bed. "I was thinking we'd start with this outfit, and we'd take some pictures around the cabin." He opened the shoebox sitting nearby, exposing tan Ugg boots. "You can wear these shoes."

"How should I do my hair?" Brandi asked.

Colton analyzed her wavy brown hair. She usually kept it in a ponytail, but for the occasion it hung to the middle of her back and parted to one side.

"It looks pretty good," Colton said. "The style works. I think just brush the ends and you should be fine. There are brushes and hair sprays in the bathroom."

"What about my makeup?" Brandi asked.

"Your face is radiant without makeup, but you could use a little eyeliner, mascara, and some blush. Not too much though. Less is more. You're supposed to be an outdoorsy type girl."

"Got it."

"There's makeup under the sink in the bathroom if you need any."

Brandi nodded. "I brought some, but thanks."

"I'll wait for you downstairs." Colton shut the door as he left the room.

Brandi went to the en-suite bathroom. A tub with a shower sat at the far end. The bathroom was decorated like the bedroom, with pale yellow walls and a painting of a buck in the forest.

She rinsed her mouth and made sure she didn't have any food stuck between her teeth. Brandi did her makeup, using minimal product as Colton had instructed. Then she returned to the bedroom to change. She thought about locking the door, but there was no lock on the handle. She changed into the skinny jeans, white bra, and white blouse, half-expecting Colton to walk in. Part of her wanted him to walk in. She slipped on the brand new Ugg boots and went to the full-length mirror. Everything fit perfectly. Maybe Colton was right about her. Brandi brushed the ends of her hair and exited the bedroom. She found Colton in the living room. He stood from the couch and grinned. "You look beautiful."

Brandi blushed. "Thank you."

The young woman posed around the cabin: by the window, in the kitchen, in front of the fireplace, and on the rear deck. While shooting on the deck, Brandi asked about the massive box next to the house.

"Whole house generator," he said.

Colton was professional, instructing her on how to pose and praising her efforts. At first, Brandi had felt self-conscious, but as they worked, Colton made her feel more comfortable.

When they finished shooting around the cabin, Colton said, "We have two more sites I'd like to shoot. There's a lookout that's about a twenty-minute hike from here, and there's the waterfall, which is the bikini shoot. The waterfall is only a few minutes from here, but we should do that last because you'll get wet."

Chapter 11

Before

Brandi marched out the front door of Franklin High School, ignoring the pandemonium of seven hundred teenagers stoked for the football game and the subsequent weekend of freedom. As the crowd dissipated and the buses drove away, she spotted her grandmother's truck at the front of the pickup line.

Brandi turned around and went back into the school. With her heart pounding, she hurried to the back doors and exited onto the sidewalk. She cut through the sports fields to the rusty fence at the edge of the property. Brandi found a hole in the fence, just big enough for her petite frame to slip through.

On the other side of the fence, she wiped the rust and dirt off her dress. She hiked toward Franklin City, more specifically Clayton Corner, known for its drug activity. A gentle breeze ameliorated the warm sun. As she walked toward Clayton Corner, the city row homes became more dilapidated, with peeling paint, rusty roofs, and swirling lawn trash.

Near Clayton Corner, she found two men vaping and talking in front of a black SUV. She recognized the little man with big ears. She had heard Damon refer to him as Eddie once. The other man looked Italian. He was taller and stockier, with a goatee and acne scars on his cheeks.

Brandi approached the men. "Excuse me?"

They turned their attention to Brandi.

Eddie blew marijuana vapor in her direction. "What's up?"

"I was looking for Damon. You know where he is?" Brandi asked.

The two men glanced at each other, with lascivious smirks on their faces.

"Who wants to know?" the Italian man asked before taking another puff on his vape pen.

"Brandi. He knows me."

"I bet he does."

Both men laughed, marijuana vapor spilling from their mouths.

"I really need to see him," Brandi said.

"I bet you do," the Italian man replied.

The men laughed again.

Brandi reddened and pivoted to leave.

"Hold on," Eddie said.

The girl faced the men.

"I'll call him for you." Eddie fished his phone from the front pocket of his jeans, and called Damon. After a quick conversation, Eddie said, "Hang tight. He'll be here in fifteen minutes."

The men in the black SUV left, but, true to his word, Damon parked his BMW along the curb approximately fifteen minutes later. Brandi went to his driver's side window.

"What's up, baby?" Damon asked.

"I need a place to stay for a while," Brandi replied.

"What happened?"

"My mom got arrested, and I'm staying with my grandmother, but I can't stay there. I can't."

Damon looked her up and down. "How old are you?"

"Eighteen." She was seventeen.

"Then you can do whatever the fuck you want." He gestured with his chin. "Get in the car."

Brandi beamed and strutted around the car to the passenger door. A pickup truck raced toward them, the throaty V8 roaring.

Mrs. Hunt's truck skidded to a stop, inches from the BMW's back bumper. Damon hopped out of his BMW and stalked to the old pickup, his chest puffed.

Mrs. Hunt exited her truck, her lips curled into a snarl. Brandi watched, frozen in horror.

"What the fuck, old lady?" Damon said.

Mrs. Hunt ignored Damon, her attention on her granddaughter. "Get in the truck, Brandi."

"No." Brandi gestured to Damon. "I'm staying with him."

"Is that so?"

The girl cocked her hip. "Yeah, it is. So fuck off."

Mrs. Hunt faced Damon. "How would you like to go to prison for kidnapping a minor?"

"A minor? She's eighteen," Damon said.

Mrs. Hunt shook her head. "My granddaughter was born on June 25, 2004. You look too imprudent for math, so I will simplify it for you. Brandi is seventeen years, two months, and fifteen days old. She is a minor under my care, and if you so much as sniff in her direction, I'll have the cops on your doorstep quicker than you can say felony."

Damon showed his palms. "Whoa lady. I was just helpin' out a friend. That ain't no crime."

Mrs. Hunt exhaled. "That *isn't* a crime. You sound like an idiot."

Damon glared at Mrs. Hunt and gestured to the road behind her. "Then take her and get the fuck off my corner."

"Let's go, Brandi," Mrs. Hunt said.

The girl looked to Damon for help, but he still glared at her grandmother, the drug dealer and the grandma bear locked in a standoff. Brandi trudged to the pickup truck, climbed inside and slammed the door.

As they drove home, Mrs. Hunt commenced with the inevitable lecture. "What the H were you thinking?" She glanced from the road to Brandi.

Brandi leaned against the driver's side door, staring from the window, her body as far from her grandmother as possible.

"That man is bad news," Mrs. Hunt said. "He'll have you addicted to drugs. Before you know it, you'll be a lady of the night. Is that what you want?"

Brandi didn't respond.

Mrs. Hunt stopped at a red light, the brakes squeaking. She turned in her seat to Brandi. "Look at me."

Brandi turned her head slowly, a scowl on her face.

"You need to be smarter, young lady. You're at an age when adult men will start to notice you. But those men are no good. They'll take advantage of you. They'll use you up and spit you out with nothing to show for it but an STD and an out-of-wedlock child that they refuse to support. Do you understand me?"

Brandi snapped her tongue off the roof of her mouth. "Who are you to talk? Where's your husband?"

"I was married when I got pregnant."

The light turned green.

"Where is he then?" Brandi asked, one side of her mouth lifted in contempt.

A honk came from behind them, startling Mrs. Hunt. She faced forward, gunned the engine, and drove through the light. She gripped the steering wheel, her knuckles white.

"Where is he?" Brandi asked again, knowing she was poking a sore spot.

Mrs. Hunt pursed her lips. "He left me for a younger woman when I was pregnant with your father."

"I wonder why he left? You're so pretty and fun," Brandi replied, her words saturated with sarcasm.

Mrs. Hunt didn't reply.

Brandi returned to the window and smiled to herself.

It was silent until they drove past Walmart.

"Did you hear about what happened to the girl who worked at that Walmart?" Mrs. Hunt asked.

"I don't care," Brandi replied, still staring out the window.

"You should care. She was your age, and she just up and disappeared last month. And she's not the only one. There was another girl. Nineteen. She worked at the Arby's on Seventh Avenue. She disappeared six months ago. They still haven't found her."

Brandi turned to her grandmother. "So what?"

"It's a dangerous world, young lady. You can ignore reality—pretend that your poor decisions won't affect your life—but in the end, you won't be able to ignore the consequences of your poor decisions."

"Whatever." Brandi turned away from her grandmother and watched the roadside, contemplating running away.

Chapter 12

After

They hiked on a rocky trail through the woods, Colton leading the way. Cicadas buzzed around them. A woodpecker hammered at a tree. Sweat accumulated in Brandi's armpits —not because of the warm weather.

Colton glanced back at Brandi, then pivoted to her, waiting on the trail. "Are you okay? You look a little flushed."

She took a deep breath. "I don't like the woods."

"I'm sorry. Do you need to go back?"

"I'm okay. I just need to relax, get out of my own head."

"When I was little, I was terrified of the dentist. My mom found this old dentist who was really good with kids. He used to distract me by telling stories, and it made it a lot better. I wasn't so focused on the dental stuff, you know?"

"Are you gonna tell me a story?"

Colton chuckled. "Sure, why not?"

"Okay."

They strolled side by side on the trail. Colton told Brandi a funny story about the pranks he used to pull when he was a kid. They started innocent enough, scaring his parents by hiding and jumping out while wearing his Halloween masks. Colton pranked his friends with whoopie cushions, fake vomit, and fake poop. He had a fake pack of gum that gave people a little shock when they grabbed a piece.

Colton's biggest prank came against the gym teacher at his elementary school. Colton had been disciplined by Mr. Haslet for talking. He had been forced to run in place for twenty minutes while his classmates played dodgeball. The gym teacher was so mean that most of the kids in school hated gym, a subject which was usually loved.

But mean Mr. Haslet had a weakness. And that weakness was Colton's pretty teacher, Ms. Abner. Colton often saw them talking and giggling together, even though Mr. Haslet wore a wedding ring. Colton saved his papers that included Ms. Abner's handwriting. After a few weeks of saving papers and practicing, Colton could mimic his teacher's handwriting. Not perfectly, but well enough to pass Mr. Haslet's scrutiny.

Before school, Colton slipped a letter under Mr. Haslet's office door that contained three pieces of hard candy.

The letter read:

Sweets for my sweetie. Ms. Abner.

At gym class that morning, Mr. Haslet was in an abnormally good mood. When he smiled and laughed, he showed his blue teeth. Eventually, one of Colton's classmates asked him what was wrong with his teeth. This confused him. Colton figured nobody had ever asked him something like that, especially a student. He disappeared into his office. He shouted, and there was a racket. Colton imagined him throwing a chair.

Mr. Haslet returned, but his smile was gone. He didn't show his teeth for the rest of class. But Colton couldn't stop smiling about the teeth-staining trick candy he'd given his gym teacher.

Brandi burst into laughter.

Colton laughed too.

When her laughter subsided, she asked, "Did he ever find out it was you?"

Colton shook his head. "You're the only person I've ever told."

Brandi arched her eyebrows. "Really? Not even your friends?"

"They all had big mouths. I knew if I told anyone I'd get caught."

"That's so smart, especially for a little kid."

"I was a devious little guy."

They arrived at the lookout.

"We're here," Colton said.

They gazed at the bright green valley from the lookout. Cottony clouds floated above them. Brandi peered over the ledge at the jagged rocks roughly fifty feet below.

"What do you think?" Colton asked, his hands on his hips.

"It's very beautiful," Brandi replied.

"Are you still feeling anxious about being out here?"

Brandi simpered. "No. Your story did the trick."

"Good."

Colton took pictures of the pretty woman at the lookout, using the blue sky and the green valley as the backdrop. After the shoot, they hiked back toward the cabin, intent on Brandi changing into the bikini for the waterfall shoot.

As they strolled side-by-side on the trail, she said, "I'm a little nervous about the bikini pictures. I'm pretty white."

"Don't worry about that. Pale skin on a woman looks nice. Haven't you ever heard of Snow White?" Colton winked.

"You're good at this, you know?"

"Good at what?"

"Making people feel comfortable."

"No. I'm good at making *models* feel comfortable. You're a model now. How does it feel?"

Brandi beamed. "You think I'm a model?"

"I *know* you're a model. One with a bright future too."

Back at the cabin, Brandi changed into the blue bikini. It matched her eyes and flattered her petite figure. She turned and posed in the full-length mirror of the guest bedroom. She grinned into the mirror, imagining Colton's reaction, covered herself with the robe that had been laid on the bed, and slipped her feet into the flip-flops.

Brandi stepped downstairs, the flip-flops snapping against her heels. She found Colton in the kitchen, eating some crackers. He had changed too. He wore board shorts, slides, and a T-shirt. When he saw her, he set the box of crackers on the center island and approached Brandi.

"Can I take a look?" he asked.

Brandi swallowed hard. She untied her robe and dropped it to the floor, revealing her blue bikini and pale skin.

Colton's eyes bulged. "You look... you look stunning."

Brandi reddened and dipped her head. "Thanks."

Colton led Brandi to the waterfall. It wasn't far from the cabin. Brandi heard the *whoosh* of falling water before she saw it. Colton led her off the trail, toward the rushing creek. They stumbled down a steep embankment. Brandi held on to Colton's muscular arm as they went, her flip-flops not providing much traction. At the bottom of the embankment, they stepped to the middle of the creek, using several exposed rocks to stay dry.

They faced the waterfall. Water fell from twenty feet above, splashing into the circular pool, creating whitewater, before continuing downhill with the creek. Willow tree branches stretched over the water.

"Wow," Brandi said.

"I know," Colton said. "Like I said, nature is the best studio."

An awkward silence passed between them.

"You ready to do this?" Colton asked, eyeing Brandi's robe.

Brandi nodded. "Where do you want me?"

"Let's start on this rock. I'll take your robe and your flip-flops."

Brandi untied and removed her robe, while Colton leered like she was unwrapping his present.

He took her robe and flip-flops and set them on a creekside rock. He retrieved his camera from its case and took pictures of Brandi from the creekside, instructing her poses and encouraging her with flattery. Then he kicked off his slides and removed his shirt, exposing his sculpted upper body. It was her turn to leer.

Colton smiled and crept closer, stepping on the exposed creek stones. "I'll have to get wet too." He took a handful of closeup pictures. Then he said, "You ready to get in the water?"

Brandi dipped her toe into the pool. "It feels good."

"Go ahead and step into the water, but only up to your knees. Be careful. The rocks are slick."

The young woman entered the cool water. She waded into the pool up to her knees. She pivoted to Colton, who stood on a large rock. "Is this okay?"

"Perfect. Splash yourself with water, but try not to get your hair wet. I want some pictures with water beading on your skin."

Brandi bent down and splashed herself with cool creek water. The water caused her nipples to harden against her bikini top. She stood and crossed her arms over her chest.

Colton lowered his camera. "Is something wrong?"

Brandi glanced down at her chest. "I'm not sure if this is okay."

"If what's okay?"

She blushed and lowered her arms. "The cold water..."

Colton leered at her chest, then raised his gaze. "You're perfect for me."

She blushed again. "Okay."

Colton took more pictures, instructing the young woman along the way. "Now back up a little closer to the waterfall. Stop when the water gets to mid-thigh."

Brandi backpedaled, her toes feeling the round river stones. As she waded deeper, the stone bottom turned to soft muck.

"Stop there. That's perfect." Colton took more pictures. "Now I want you to get your hair wet. You can dip your head in the waterfall and come back. Just be careful. The water has a lot of pressure."

Brandi waded to the waterfall, the water level rising just above her chest. She dipped her head into the falling water carefully, not letting the water hit her square on her head. She ran her hands through her wet hair, slicking it back and off her face.

When she returned to her place, Colton took more pictures. He entered the water and took close-up pictures too.

"Go ahead and back up some more," Colton said. "Let the water come up to your stomach."

A cloud covered them, blocking the sun.

"Shit," Colton said, peering at the sky. "My lighting. Just hold tight. It looks like it's moving."

Brandi hugged herself, suddenly feeling cold in the shade and cool water.

The cloud finally passed and the sunshine returned.

"That's better." Colton resumed his pictures of Brandi with the waterfall in the background. Shortly thereafter, he said, "That's it. I have everything I need."

"Oh. That was quick," she replied, wading in the pool toward Colton.

"You're very easy to work with," Colton said. "Thank you. You were very quick to change and do your makeup and hair. Most models are much higher maintenance."

"Thank you."

"No. Thank you." Colton checked his watch. "We finished really early. It's not even three."

"That's good."

"I'd like to show you something cool if you don't mind."

"Okay."

"You stay there. Let me put my camera away."

Colton went to the creekside and set his camera on the rock, next to their clothes and shoes. Then he waded back into the pool to Brandi and held out his hand. The young woman took his hand, feeling a jolt of electricity at his touch. Colton led her to the waterfall. He said, "You have to swim under." Then he dove into the whitewater.

"Come inside," Colton called out over the *whoosh* of water.

Brandi did as Colton had done, diving and swimming under

the waterfall. She felt the pressure of the falling water as she swam under. She surfaced under a rock ledge, the water level to her chest, and the waterfall curtain giving them complete privacy.

"Pretty cool, huh?" Colton asked, creek water dripping from his dirty-blonde hair.

She nodded. "It's like we have our own secret spot."

"That's exactly what it's like." Colton inched closer.

Brandi watched him with unblinking eyes.

He placed his hands on her hips and stared down at her. Brandi tilted her head up, her lips pursed, giving him the go-ahead. He bent down to her, painfully slow. When their lips finally met, she pressed hard against his, her mouth opening and accepting his tongue. Her entire body buzzed. He pulled her tight against his body. Brandi jumped into his arms, her legs wrapped around him, the buoyancy of the water making this easy.

They kissed and groped and moaned their approvals. Colton removed Brandi's bikini top and sucked on her nipple. She tilted her head back, groaning. The man untied and removed Brandi's bikini bottom like he had experience. She was naked but concealed and touched all over by Colton and the cool water at the same time. She rubbed herself against his shorts, feeling the outline of his erection as he kissed her neck.

They turned in the water so he was facing the stone wall, and Brandi faced the curtain of water. She opened her eyes and saw something dark through the water curtain—a figure on the stepping stones maybe.

Brandi stiffened and said, "I think I see someone."

Colton drew back from her neck. "What?"

"I think someone's out there. Look."

Colton turned to the water curtain just as the dark figure moved, disappearing from view. "I don't see anything."

"It just moved," Brandi whispered.

"I rarely see anybody out here. It's pretty secluded."

Brandi unhooked her legs from Colton's waist, placing her feet into the muck. "Somebody's out there. Can you go check? I'm literally freaking out."

Colton exhaled. "All right. I'll check it out." He touched the end of her nose. "Wait for me." Colton dove under the waterfall curtain and waded to the creekside.

Brandi squinted through the curtain, seeing a dark blob doing something roughly where they'd stashed their clothes. She figured Colton was putting on his shirt and slides to check the nearby trail. He disappeared from view. Brandi scanned the rock wall, searching for her bikini. She searched the water too. It was gone. *Did he take it? What did he do with it?* She felt around the water, figuring her bikini must've gotten caught in the waterfall and spit out into the pool somewhere.

Brandi hugged herself, suddenly feeling cold without Colton's body heat. She waited for what felt like ten minutes.

A dark blob appeared on the creekside, where they'd left their clothes. She waited, expecting Colton to take off his clothes and to wade back to their secret spot. But the dark blob didn't move. It just stood there. A wave of sadness passed over Brandi. *He realized it was a mistake to hook up with me.* She squinted at the blob, willing Colton to come to her. *I'm so stupid. I never should've said anything.*

Still the blob didn't move.

She called out into the water curtain, "Colton. Colton. Colton!"

Still the blob didn't move.

She wondered if Colton could hear her behind the *whoosh* of water.

Brandi held her breath and swam under the water curtain. When she surfaced, she saw a man standing in front of the rock where Colton had stashed her robe and flip-flops. He was tall, with a salt and pepper beard, heavy on the salt. He wore a bucket hat, sunglasses, and a fanny pack.

"Hi there," the man said with a shit-eating grin.

Chapter 13

Before

THE NEXT SIX WEEKS WERE AN ENDLESS ROUTINE OF CHORES, meals, school, church, and homework. There was a television in the living room, but it was dominated by Mrs. Hunt and her cop shows. If there was any daylight after Brandi's homework and dinner, she spent her time outside with the animals, which was exactly what she did this evening.

Brandi sat on a hay bale, watching the goats graze and the chickens peck at weeds and insects. She thought about her mother. Thankfully, her defense attorney had brokered a deal with the DA to reduce the felony charge of possession with the intent to distribute, to misdemeanor drug possession, but because of her prior convictions, the judge sentenced her to ten months in prison, including her time served in the Franklin Jail. All of this meant she'd be home on July 10, next year. Brandi felt like they were both doing time.

Billy, the white goat, spotted the girl and galloped her way, bleating and jumping when he got close. He hopped on the hay bale with Brandi and lay next to her, his body against hers.

Brandi petted the goat's head and neck. "Hey Billy. How's your day been?" She paused, waiting for a response that never came. "I had a shit day as usual. I'm on day eight of my experiment, and still, nobody's noticed."

Brandi had stopped talking at school, wondering if anyone would care. After eight days, the answer is no, nobody gives a shit.

"I was literally thinking about running away today. It's hard enough here with Mrs. Hunt watching me like a hawk. What's it gonna be like when my dad shows up? How am I supposed to act? Am I supposed to be like, 'Hi Dad, I love you?' I don't even like him. Shit, I don't even know him." Brandi sighed. "What do you think?"

Billy bleated.

Brandi's father was due to arrive at the farmhouse very soon. He was driving up from Fort Liberty, North Carolina.

Brandi petted Billy. "Is it pathetic that my only friend is a goat?"

The goat bleated again.

She grinned. "That was harsh."

The roar of an engine came from the driveway. Brandi figured it was her dad's vehicle. The engine idle ceased. Doors opened and shut. Mrs. Hunt's voice punctuated the silence. Her pitch was higher and more excited than the girl had ever heard. She almost sounded nice. Brandi thought about going inside to meet him, but she didn't know what to say to him. After all, she hadn't seen him in twelve years. Besides, *he* should approach *her*, not the other way around.

Brandi sat outside for an hour, waiting for her father to come outside and make an effort, but it never happened. It was nearly dark now, but Cardi B was still pecking around the pasture. Brandi had named the Red Star hen Cardi B because she was the diva of the flock, always the last to go in the coop at night. She marched to the diva and scooped her up before she could run, petting her as she carried her to the coop.

"You don't want me to leave you out here," Brandi said. "You'd become someone's dinner."

Cardi B clucked and tried to wiggle from Brandi's grasp.

"I'm trying to help you," Brandi said, still with a good grasp on the chicken. Brandi set her in the coop and locked the door. A simple latch wasn't good enough, as raccoons had the intelligence and finger dexterity to open latches.

Brandi went inside, not sure whether to feel relieved or insulted that her father didn't come outside to see her. Mrs. Hunt sat with a muscular man at the kitchen table. As soon as Brandi shut the door, the man stood from his seat. Her father was tall and clean-shaven, with short brown hair and a strong jaw. He resembled an action figure.

"Hello, Brandi," he said with his head bowed.

"Hi," she replied.

An awkward silence passed between them.

Brandi addressed her grandmother. "I'm tired. I'm going to bed."

"Don't forget to say your prayers," Mrs. Hunt said.

Brandi nodded and left the kitchen. She bowed her head at church when prompted and pretended to pray before bed, but she didn't believe any of it. Brandi went upstairs, showered, and put on her pajamas. While getting ready for bed, she replayed her interaction with her father. It was weird. She knew he was her father, but he was a total stranger.

She grabbed her puppy stuffed animal and crawled into bed. She retrieved the book from her bedside table, *Raising Chickens*, and cracked it open. With limited television, no internet, or a phone, she checked out books from the school library. As a bonus, the librarian let her eat her lunch in the library, as long as she was careful around the books and didn't advertise it to others. It beat the hell out of eating alone among hundreds of her classmates. As she was reading about broody hens, she drifted off to sleep.

Shortly thereafter, she was awakened by a banging on her wall, the wall she shared with her father's room. Groaning and grunting came from the room. He called out, "No. Don't shoot!"

Brandi hugged her stuffed golden retriever and drifted back to sleep.

The next morning, Brandi shoveled the chicken coop bedding into a wheelbarrow.

"Don't bend over like that," her father said.

Brandi startled, then pivoted to him. "What?"

"You'll hurt your back bending over like that."

"I'm fine."

"Because you're young, but you won't be young forever." He held out his hand. "Let me show you."

Brandi handed the pitchfork to her father.

He expertly scooped and dumped the bedding into the wheelbarrow, bending his knees slightly yet keeping his back mostly straight. "Use the length of the pitchfork to your advantage." He handed the pitchfork back to Brandi.

She copied his technique, instantly noticing improved ease of motion and the ability to scoop more material.

"That's better," her father said.

"Thanks," she said over her shoulder.

"Your grandmother told me about your drug dealer friend."

"So."

"She told me about your attitude too."

Brandi stopped shoveling and faced her father. "So."

Her father narrowed his eyes. "That's over now. Your grandmother is too old to be dealing with a disrespectful teen. From now on, if you have a problem, talk to me."

"I could use a phone."

"For what? To post sexually suggestive images on Instagram? To connect with your degenerate friends? You don't have the maturity for a phone."

Brandi shook her head. "You don't know shit. I need a phone to call my mom."

Her father nodded.

She went back to shoveling the soiled straw. "As soon as my

mom gets out, I'm done. You and *Mrs. Hunt* can shovel your own shit."

"I'm not afraid of hard work, and neither is your grandmother. You're the one who needs to develop a work ethic."

Brandi huffed. "Who are you to tell me anything? I don't even know you. I don't even know what to call you."

"What would you like to call me?"

"I'm *not* calling you Dad."

He winced for a split second. "Fair enough. My name's Jack."

Chapter 14

After

The water level bobbed just above Brandi's breasts. "Who are you?"

"I'm Roger. And who might you be?"

"None of your business."

Roger smirked, eyeing the top of the young woman's breasts. "That's not fair. After all, you know my name."

"What are you staring at?" Brandi expected Roger to be embarrassed.

But he grinned and asked, "What do you think I'm staring at?"

Brandi bent her knees, the water covering her shoulders. She called out, "Colton! Colton! I need help!"

Roger glanced over his shoulder. "I don't think anyone's out here."

"Colton! Colton!"

"I think we're alone."

Brandi glared at the man. "You need to get outta my face before my boyfriend comes back, you fucking creep."

"That's not a very nice thing to say. I haven't done anything to you. I was simply enjoying the waterfall when you appeared like a mermaid."

Brandi clenched her fists under the water, but said in a calm tone, "I need you to leave so I can put on my robe."

"That's incorrect. You are free to do as you wish, just as I am free to do as *I* wish."

Brandi scanned the area. "Colton! Where are you? I need you!"

Roger sighed. "I hate to be the bearer of bad news, but there's always the possibility that your boyfriend's never coming back."

A chill snaked down Brandi's spine. "Did you see him?"

Roger chuckled. "I don't think there ever was a boyfriend. I think you're making him up."

"Get the fuck away from me, or I'll call the police."

He retrieved a cell phone from his fanny pack and glanced at the screen. "Unfortunately, there's no cell service here. Otherwise, I'd call the police for you."

Brandi spoke through gritted teeth. "Leave me the fuck alone."

"I'd rather not. It's not every day that a man comes across a beautiful young woman in the woods, a woman who is so... vulnerable."

Brandi glanced at her robe and flip-flops on the rock behind him.

Roger noticed her gaze and sauntered to the rock.

"Don't touch my stuff," she said.

He touched her robe and leered back at her. "What will you do about my misbehavior?"

The hair on the back of Brandi's neck stood on end. She opened her mouth to speak but nothing came out.

Roger put the robe to his nose and inhaled, maintaining eye contact with Brandi.

"You're fucking gross," she said.

"Smell is a lot more powerful than people realize," Roger replied. "A smell can drive a man crazy with desire, or it can disgust him. Would you like to guess what your smell does to me?"

Brandi scanned the area again. She called out, "Colton! Help me! Somebody help me!"

Roger shook his head. "Again, I hate to be the bearer of bad news, but nobody's coming."

"You don't know that. Someone could come any minute."

Roger shook his head again, cradling her robe like an infant. "I don't think so. I've been in these woods hundreds of times. I can count on one hand the number of times I've seen another person. People prefer their comfortable homes and their Wi-Fi."

"Colton. Colton!"

"You're wasting your breath. Colton's gone."

"Where did he go?"

"He's in a better place."

"Did you hurt him?"

Roger cackled. "There are people in these woods to worry about, but not me. I would never hurt anyone. I'm a lover, not a fighter."

"Then leave my robe and walk away. I'd like to get dressed."

Roger smirked. "I bet you would."

Brandi remembered something that her dad taught her. She heard his voice in her head. *If you do get yourself into a situation that you can't avoid or run from, you have to be smart. If you're strong, act weak. If you're weak, act strong. Don't be afraid to use anything as a weapon. A rock. A hot beverage. Sand in the eyes. There are no rules in this situation.*

"It's your move, my little mermaid," Roger said.

"What do you want from me?" she asked.

Roger licked his lips. "What do you think I want from you?"

Brandi swallowed hard. "If I give you what you want, will you leave me alone?"

Roger set her robe back on the rock and faced Brandi again. "How do you know what I want?"

"I don't know. I just do."

"I'd like you to tell me what I want, just to make sure there are no misunderstandings."

Brandi waded toward Roger, bending her knees so her body remained submerged. "I think you want me... like sexually."

"I need you to be more specific."

Brandi cleared her throat. "I *um*, think you wanna fuck me."

The outline of his erection was visible through his khaki shorts. "I need more details."

"I think you... want me to give you a blowjob," Brandi said in her sexiest voice.

Roger put his right hand in his pocket, rubbing his erection. "Tell me more."

Brandi waded closer to Roger and the creekside, bending deeper at the knees to keep her body underwater. Her hands grazed the bottom, touching various smooth stones. Her gaze flicked to the large rock where her robe sat. "I think you'd like to bend me over that rock and fuck me from behind. *Hard*."

Roger exhaled, his hand fluttering in his pocket. "Tell me how much you want me."

"I want you... *so bad*." Brandi grabbed a baseball-sized rock. She inched closer to the shore, exposing her shoulders to the air, then her breasts.

Roger sucked in a breath.

Brandi rose from the pool, slowly, letting rivulets of water slip down her shiny skin. Her heart thumped in her chest. Her right hand was behind her back, but he didn't notice. His unblinking eyes were locked on her naked body, his hand still fluttering in his pocket.

On the rocky shore, he came to her, hands first. As he grabbed her breasts, Brandi swung her right arm like a hook, cracking Roger on his left temple with the round rock and sending him down for the count.

She rushed to her robe, fumbling the garment with shaky hands before finally slipping her arms through and cinching the robe at her waist.

Roger groaned and grunted, rising to one knee, blood covering one side of his face.

Brandi slipped on her flip-flops and ran for her life.

Chapter 15

Before

Over the next week, Brandi ignored Jack and Mrs. Hunt to the best of her ability, responding to them only when absolutely necessary and then limiting her responses to yes or no.

At breakfast, she ate her scrambled eggs while Jack and Mrs. Hunt talked as if Brandi wasn't there.

"I'm hoping I won't need another table next weekend." Mrs. Hunt sipped her coffee.

"You think you'll be able to pre-sell all the goat meat in two days?" Jack sipped his coffee.

"I did last year. Rich people from Harrisburg love homegrown meat."

They were discussing the farmer's market table that Mrs. Hunt had rented for the upcoming weekend.

Brandi thought about Billy, knowing his days were numbered.

Mrs. Hunt glanced at the clock on the stove. "It's time to go, Brandi."

Jack stood from the kitchen table. "I'll take her to school."

Brandi grabbed her backpack and her lunch and left with Jack. They didn't talk on the way to school, until Jack passed the turn for Franklin High School.

She pointed and said, "You missed the turn."

"You're not going to school today," Jack replied. "You're going to Lycoming to see your mother."

"Really?"

"Don't mention this to your grandmother."

Surrounded by farms, State Correctional Institution Muncy appeared more like a women's college than a prison, although there were high fences with razor wire around the lifers and violent offenders confined to maximum security. Brandi's mom, Kathy, was housed in medium security, along with the bulk of the inmates.

Jack and Brandi met Kathy in a colorful room filled with round tables and chairs, vending machines, and a play corner complete with a purple carpet and bins filled with various toys. Female inmates met with their friends and family at the tables and played with their kids in the play corner. A female guard patrolled the room.

Brandi hugged her mother. Kathy was still skinny, but she felt more solid. When they separated, the girl noticed that her mother's face was less gaunt too. Her hair was darker, her roots growing out on her blonde-in-a-box dye job.

"You look good, Mom," Brandi said.

Kathy frowned and gestured to her maroon pants and maroon button-down shirt. "I hate these clothes." Kathy turned her ire toward Jack. "It's been a long time."

Jack nodded. "It has. You look well."

Kathy rolled her eyes. "Don't bullshit a bullshitter."

"Why don't we sit?" Jack gestured to an empty table.

Brandi sat next to her mother, and Jack sat across the table.

The girl placed her hand atop her mother's. "How are you doing?"

Kathy lifted one shoulder. "It's prison. How do you expect I'm doin'?"

"I wish I could get you outta here."

"You and me both." Kathy sneered at Jack. "I bet you and your bitch mother are happy."

Brandi retracted her hand.

Jack clenched his jaw for an instant. "My mother has nothing to do with this."

"Bullshit. She never accepted me," Kathy replied.

"It gives me no pleasure to see you in prison, but maybe this is what you need to get clean."

Kathy huffed. "Look at you on your high horse." Kathy addressed Brandi. "Don't let him fool you. He's an abusive liar. Remember what he did to me?"

"There's no need to bring up the past. I'm here for Brandi; that's it."

Kathy laughed, but she didn't sound happy. "Oh, you're here for Brandi. That's surprisin', since I raised her on my own. Now you think you can swoop in, and act like father of the fuckin' year."

The female prison guard made a bee line to their table. "Kathy? Everything okay?"

Kathy answered with a racist rendition of a southern slave. "Oh, yes, Massa. I be good. Please, Massa, don't whip me."

Several black inmates gave Kathy the side-eye.

"Keep it down, and watch your language," the guard said. "There are children here."

Once the guard left their table, Kathy whispered to Brandi. "Your father's a cold-blooded killer. Did you know that? Ask him how many people he killed."

"Your daughter came to see *you*, not to talk about me," Jack said.

"She has a right to know."

"This isn't the time or the place."

Kathy mimicked Jack, using a stuffy man's voice. *"This isn't the time or the place."* Kathy cackled, then turned serious, pointing at Jack for emphasis. "I might be a drug addict, but you're addicted to war. You're a *psycho* killer."

The female guard appeared at the table. "Let's go, Kathy. Your visit's over."

Kathy glowered at Jack. "I'm done with this piece of shit, anyway."

"Do you want your visitation privileges revoked?"

Kathy pushed her chair back from the table and stood abruptly. "You think I give a fuck?"

The female guard grabbed Kathy by the elbow and led her out of the visitation room. A few inmates clapped at her removal. Tears filled Brandi's eyes.

Brandi didn't talk on the two-hour drive back to Franklin.

When they were nearly home, Jack asked, "Are you hungry?"

"No," Brandi replied, staring out the passenger window.

"We have a few hours to kill."

"Drop me off at school then."

Shortly thereafter, Jack parked his SUV in front of Franklin High School.

Brandi turned in her seat to her father. "I don't want you to pick me up."

Jack nodded.

The girl snatched her backpack from the floor and pointed at her father. "You're the reason she's like this."

"She's like this because she's a drug addict," Jack replied.

Brandi shook her head. "No. I remember what you did to her. I saw her in the hospital, all messed up."

Jack replied as if Brandi hadn't called him out. "You need to wake up early tomorrow. We're leaving at 6 a.m. I expect your chores to be finished before then."

"What the hell are you talking about? I'm not going anywhere with you."

Jack stared through Brandi and said, "It's not a request."

"Whatever. My mom's right. You *are* a piece of shit." Brandi exited the SUV, slamming the door behind her.

Chapter 16

After

Brandi scrambled away from the waterfall, up the embankment, her flip-flops slipping on soil and tree roots. At the top of the slope, she looked over her shoulder. Roger lurched toward the embankment. Brandi bolted along the rocky trail like a deer, high on adrenaline. Her toes gripped the flip-flop strap to keep the footwear on her feet. Along the way, she called for Colton and scanned the forest for his body. She hoped he was injured and not dead. But she never saw or heard from him.

As she neared the cabin, she checked over her shoulder. Thankfully, she didn't see anyone chasing her. Brandi rushed to the Tesla, wheezing, her hands shaky. She tried to open the door, but it was locked. She hurried inside the cabin, entering through the side door, and locking the deadbolt behind her. Brandi called out for Colton, but the house was dead silent.

Brandi searched the kitchen and living room for Colton's phone, which she knew doubled as the key to his Tesla. She didn't find the phone, so she hustled upstairs and checked the master bedroom, scanning the top of the dresser, the bedside tabletops, and the desk by the window. She rifled through dresser drawers and desk drawers and peeked into the closet. The dresser and closet were filled with hunting gear, everything perfectly ordered and/or folded. The desk drawers held neatly arranged office supplies.

After the master bedroom yielded nothing, she peered into the second guest bedroom, checking the dresser top and end tables, but there was no phone. Brandi returned to her room, intent on dressing and grabbing her phone. She thought if she ran down the road far enough, she would either find a nonpsychotic human being to help her or she'd find cell service. But her backpack, purse, and phone weren't on the bed where she'd left them, and neither were the clothes she had modeled earlier. She opened the closet, but it was empty. She checked the dresser drawers, but they were all empty too.

She thought about what Colton had said about people breaking into cabins. *Is this some kinda weird burglary?* Brandi sucked in a sharp breath, remembering what Roger had said. *There are people in these woods to worry about, but not me.*

A door opened and shut downstairs.

Brandi's eyes bulged. *I locked the door. Didn't I? But I didn't check the other doors.* She surveyed the bedroom. The door was open, but she didn't bother to shut it, as that would make noise, and there was no lock anyway. So she crept to the closet and shut herself inside. She sat in the dark, the only light, a sliver from the gap under the door. She scooted back against the wall. *This is a stupid hiding place. All they have to do is open the closet.* Brandi thought about going to the master bedroom to hide behind the hunting gear.

But it was too late. Heavy footsteps climbed the stairs. Brandi squeezed her eyes shut, trying to listen over her pounding heart and shallow breathing. The steps continued closer, *thumping* the hardwood at a leisurely pace. *Maybe it's Colton?* The steps stopped at what she thought was the doorway to her room. Then they moved closer.

Brandi watched the gap under the closet door, sweat accumulating under her arms and at the small of her back. The light shapeshifted, molding to the shadow of whoever stood there.

Brandi held her breath, expecting the closet door to swing open, but the light returned in full, and the footsteps receded. She listened as the steps left the room and ambled down the hall, likely checking the other bedrooms. Brandi exhaled a sigh of relief.

A minute later, the footsteps grew louder, walking down the hallway, back toward Brandi's room. But the intruder had to come back that way to access the stairs. Brandi clasped her hands together and prayed for the first time in her life. *Please, God, make them leave. Please. I need your help.*

Instead of repelling the intruder, her prayer seemed to draw him to her, like a magnet.

The sliver of light under the closet shapeshifted again. The intruder stood silent for a long moment. Then, the steps receded again. The box spring squeaked. She imagined Roger sitting on the bed. Two thumps came from the wood floor. She imagined him taking off his hiking shoes and getting comfortable. But the box spring squeaked again, as if the intruder had risen from the bed. There was rustling. Metal clanged together. Brandi imagined a belt buckle, but it could be many things. A zipper buzzed, followed by a lighter rustling.

The footsteps approached, stopping and standing in front of the closet door for the third time. Brandi held her breath again, sure that her pounding heart would give her away. The door whipped open, flooding the closet with sunlight, temporarily blinding Brandi. The intruder grabbed her by the ankle, dragged her into the bedroom, and let go. As her eyes adjusted to the light, she recognized Roger with his half-bloody face, bucket hat, salt and pepper beard, and sunglasses, but other than that he was naked.

Roger inched closer to Brandi with his hands held out and his penis erect. "Relax. I won't hurt you."

Brandi waited until he was within striking distance and kicked upward at his groin, but Roger turned his body, her kick glancing off his thigh. Brandi scrambled to her feet and tried to run, but Roger grabbed her by the neck and slammed her against the wall, her head making a divot in the drywall. Brandi slid down the wall in a daze, the room spinning.

Roger went to the bedside table and grabbed something, but Brandi's vision was too blurry to see what it was. Roger returned to Brandi and bent over her crumpled body. She felt a pinch to her neck. As her vision sharpened, she saw what he was holding. It was a syringe which he tossed out of reach. She tried to stand up, but Roger forced her on her back and straddled her, holding her by her wrists.

"This is for your own good," he said.

Brandi screamed and bucked and kicked, but he was too heavy. Her world dimmed, her vision darkening at the edges. She tried to kick, but her legs felt so slow and weighty. He let go of her wrists. She tried to move but she couldn't. She tried to scream, but nothing came out. He untied her robe and opened it. Roger sat back on his haunches and admired Brandi's naked body.

"You really are gorgeous." Roger spread her legs apart and knelt before her. "Don't worry about my head. Head wounds tend to bleed a lot. I have a concussion, but I'll be fine. I know it was an accident."

Someone entered the room. Brandi tried to turn her head, but she couldn't. Her vision was very dim. *Is it Colton?*

But Roger didn't seem to notice or care about the other person. His gaze was locked on her as he said, "I'll give you exactly what you need. I'll be the best you ever had."

Footsteps approached. Someone stood next to her head. Then it leaned over into Brandi's dim view. The face was stone white. The eyes were black as coal, and the mouth was a black zipper.

Then everything went black.

Chapter 17

Before

Brandi followed her father on a narrow trail. He wore a large camouflaged backpack. Leaves crunched under their feet and fluttered to the ground. Trees were in various stages of undress, some mostly barren, while others still held yellow, red, or brown foliage. Despite the early hour, it was already in the fifties, with sunbeams filtering through the canopy.

"Where are we going?" Brandi called out.

"It doesn't matter," Jack replied over his shoulder. "You're here to learn."

"Learn what?"

Jack stopped and faced his daughter. "What if you were out here by yourself?"

"I would walk back to the road, hitchhike or something."

Jack exhaled. "What if you were lost in the woods?"

"This is stupid. I've been up since 4:30. Can we go?"

"No."

"I'm tired."

"Everything that happens is either improvable, survivable, or not. If you can improve your situation, then do it. Complaining only makes it worse. If you can't improve your situation, but it's survivable, then endure it. Complaining only makes it worse. If it's not survivable, then die with honor. Complaining only makes it worse."

Brandi rolled her eyes. "What does that even mean?"

"It means no complaining under any circumstances. It never helps."

"Whatever."

"The first rule of survival is to find shelter. We can either find a natural shelter, enhance a natural shelter, or build a shelter. Keep your eyes open for anything that looks like a possible shelter."

Brandi didn't point out any possible shelters, although she noticed several. But Jack noticed them, giving the girl an unsolicited lecture on each type. The hollow tree was cozy and hobbit-like, but filled with insects, spiders, and possibly snakes, although they didn't see any snakes.

They explored a rock formation that offered several options for shelter—a simple overhang, as well as various crevasses and holes that could be covered with branches. These rock shelters had their downsides too, as there was the ever-present danger of falling rocks. Like tree hollows, they were excellent habitats for snakes and spiders. Pathogens could be found in the rock dust, as rodents often used these shelters.

They found a cave near the rock formation, which appeared to be the best shelter. Jack shined his flashlight inside. They walked about thirty feet into the cave, descending a few feet as they went.

"Do you feel that?" Jack asked.

"The air feels cool," Brandi replied.

"That's right. If you go below ground a few feet in a cave, you'll get a stable temperature of about fifty degrees. Caves are dangerous though." Jack turned his flashlight back the way they came. "Caves can collapse. If that entrance was sealed, we'd be buried alive."

Brandi sucked in air, the oxygen suddenly feeling thin.

"The air can be pretty stale too," Jack continued. "It's best to stay near the mouth of the cave." Jack shined his flashlight deep into the dark. "And you might be sharing the cave with apex predators like bears."

Brandi's stomach churned, expecting a bear to appear from the darkness.

Jack shined his light on the cave floor, exposing piles of black dirt. "See that?"

"What? The dirt?"

"It's bat shit." Jack shined his light on the ceiling, where hundreds of bats slept upside down.

Brandi gasped and covered her head with her hands, sure the bats would swoop down and attack her hair at any moment. "Oh my God. Can we leave?"

As they returned to the mouth of the cave, Jack said, "The bats won't attack you, but their droppings are toxic and they can transmit diseases."

When they emerged from the cave, Brandi sucked in a deep breath of fresh air.

"I prefer to use the landscape to help construct a shelter," Jack said. "Natural shelters are usually already occupied."

They continued exploring the forest. Jack talked about finding the right place to build a shelter. Ideally, it was in a flat, dry place, not in danger of falling rocks or limbs.

They encountered the *whoosh* of rushing water as they hiked deeper into the forest. Wherever they were, they were totally alone. The trail led to a creek about twenty feet wide, with rocks of varying sizes protruding from the water.

Jack turned back to Brandi. "Watch the wet rocks. They're slippery. It's important to stay dry when you're in the woods, especially your feet." Jack zig-zagged from rock to rock like he'd done it a million times.

Brandi carefully stepped from rock to rock, nearly slipping twice before making it across with dry feet.

About one mile from the creek, they came across a large overturned oak tree. Jack climbed atop the tree and jumped on it to make sure it was stable. He climbed down and said, "This would make a good spot for a shelter."

"Where? On top of the tree?" Brandi asked.

"No, underneath it."

"There's not much space." There was only about three feet between the tree and the ground.

Jack shrugged off his backpack, grabbed a folding shovel, and handed it to Brandi. "We'll have to dig. Being below ground will make it much warmer in the winter."

Brandi rolled her eyes. "Can't wait to hang out here in the winter."

They dug a six-by-ten rectangular hole about three-feet deep under the fallen oak. It was backbreaking work that took hours, but Jack worked like a machine. Once the hole was dug, Jack could walk under the tree without stooping too much.

After the digging, Jack asked, "You ready for lunch?"

"I'm starving," Brandi replied, reaching into her backpack and grabbing the lunch she'd prepared for herself.

"It would probably take you about a month to starve to death. You have plenty of stored fat and protein."

"I didn't mean it literally."

"Details matter." Jack retrieved his bagged lunch and water bottle from his backpack.

They ate their lunches atop the fallen oak.

"I want you to think about the prevailing wind," Jack said.

Brandi spoke with her mouth full. "What does that mean?"

"It's the predominant wind direction."

The girl swallowed a bite of her peanut butter and jelly sandwich. "You mean like where the wind is blowing?"

"Which direction it's likely to blow the most often."

"It seems like it's been blowing from that way, but not very hard." Brandi pointed to the west.

"So where do you think we should put the door to our shelter?" Jack asked.

"On the east side?"

"Exactly. If we put the door on the west side, we would be constantly fighting the wind. Details matter."

After lunch, they collected large straight branches from the nearby trees and leaned them against the fallen oak, which served as the main ridge of their shelter. Once they had collected and set enough branches for the walls, they tied them together, using skinny willow branches and mature honeysuckle. According to Jack, the willow branches were ideal, but honeysuckle would also work if willow wasn't available. Once the branches were tied together, they collected smaller pine branches filled with needles to fill the gaps. They also used sod and mud to fill the gaps, the material conveniently coming from their earlier digging.

Jack stood back and wiped his hands, admiring the shelter. "Looks good."

"Can we go home now?" Brandi asked.

Jack frowned at his daughter. "We have to insulate the interior. And we need someplace to sit and sleep."

"I'm not sleeping out here."

"We're not sleeping out here tonight, but it's important to finish what you start."

They built a three-by-six frame with thick branches that resembled the start of a tiny log cabin. Between the logs, they installed pine branches in a herringbone pattern. They installed more pine branches over the floor and walls, covering the mud, insulating the interior, and making it smell nice.

Jack sat on the makeshift bed. "What do you think?"

Brandi lifted one shoulder. "I think we did all this work for nothing."

Chapter 18

After

Brandi's eyes fluttered and opened. A ceiling fan rotated above her. She had a dull headache. Sunlight filtered through the white curtains. Her mouth felt cottony and her bladder was full. She lifted the comforter and checked her mostly naked body, not recognizing her cotton underwear. Her vagina felt sore, like it did when she and Tyler used to have crazy sex. She reached between her legs, probed herself, searching for signs of dried semen, but everything felt clean. She sniffed her fingers, and they smelled like soap. She lifted her arm and smelled her armpit, which also smelled like soap. Her hair was clean too, smelling like shampoo. Brandi scanned the room, recognizing the pale-yellow walls and the forest-themed paintings.

It came back to her in pieces. She remembered the great day she'd had with Colton. They had been making out under the waterfall. *We must've had sex. Did we do drugs? Where is he?* She pictured the curtain of water behind the waterfall. A blurry figure appeared. *Colton went to check it out.* Brandi's stomach lurched. *He never came back.* She remembered diving under the waterfall and emerging to find a man watching her. *What was his name? Roger.* She remembered knocking him out with a rock and running back to the cabin. *Then what happened?*

Brandi shook her head, like she was trying to shake loose the memory. She closed her eyes, remembering someone breaking into the cabin. *There was no good place to hide.* She remembered hiding in the closet and Roger finding her. Tears welled in her eyes. She touched her neck, remembering the prick. She pictured Roger opening her robe, spreading her legs, and kneeling before her. Tears slipped down her face. Brandi turned over and hugged her pillow, sobbing.

After a few minutes, her sobbing subsided. She wiped her face with the comforter. Brandi figured it was over. She had been raped but she was alive, which was better than whatever happened to Colton. *I need to get the hell outta here.*

Brandi sniffed back mucus and exited the bed. She wobbled and grabbed the oak bedpost to steady herself. When the room stopped spinning, she noticed clothes on the dresser top. She went to the clothes, but she'd never seen them before. They were neatly folded and appeared brand new. Brandi dressed in the khaki pants, belt, white sports bra, white long sleeve T-shirt, and wool socks. She slipped her feet into the hiking boots and tied them. She glanced at the shut bedroom door, thinking about checking the hallway, but she was too scared to face it yet. Instead, she crept to the window and parted the curtain. Colton's Tesla was parked in the driveway, just as it was the day before. From the angle of the sun, she figured it was around one or two in the afternoon.

She went to the en-suite bathroom. Her entire body buzzed with anxiety as she peed. *Is he still here? Is he waiting for me downstairs? I can't stay here. I need to get help.* She washed her hands. A brand-new toothbrush and toothpaste sat on the counter, along with a glass. Brandi chugged three glasses of water, trying to quench her thirst and rid her mouth of that cottony feeling. After the water, her mouth still felt dirty, so she opened the new toothbrush and brushed her teeth. She returned to the bedroom and went to the door.

Brandi grabbed the handle, took a deep breath, and opened the door as quietly as possible. She peered right and left, checking the hallway. It was empty. She crept downstairs, her heart pounding. The aroma of brewing coffee wafted into her nostrils. She surveyed the living room. Nobody was there. She spied the spread of breakfast treats on the center island.

Her stomach rumbled, her hunger overtaking her fear. She tiptoed to the kitchen, her head on a swivel, expecting Roger to jump out any second. A breakfast feast was arranged neatly on the center island: muffins, pastries, and fresh fruit. *Who the hell did this?* She wondered if Colton had a service or something, and maybe they were there while she was sleeping. She devoured a blueberry muffin, savoring the rush of carbs. She grabbed another and took a big bite.

As she chewed her muffin, she saw a masked man peeping through the back window. Brandi squeaked like a mouse and ducked behind the kitchen island with a serious case of déjà vu. The white mask, black eyes, and black zipper for a mouth, jogged a memory from yesterday. That man, or at least someone in that mask, had been in the room with Roger.

Brandi crawled to the end of the kitchen island and looked through the living room to the front door. Her heart raced as she rose to a sprinter's stance, her head still below the kitchen island. She thought, *You can do this.* She raced to the front door, her boots stomping the hardwood. She wished she wore running shoes instead of stiff hiking boots.

At the front door, she undid two deadbolts, her hands jittery. She opened the door and dashed outside. She sprinted as fast as she could on the winding gravel driveway. Heavy footsteps came from behind. Brandi glanced over her shoulder, seeing the masked man about forty yards behind her, running with a rifle in his hands. Apart from the mask, he wore camouflaged hunting gear. She pushed harder, making it to the main road and seemingly extending her lead on the psycho.

Brandi turned left on the main road and continued to run, her breathing labored. Somehow, the masked man exited the woods about fifty yards ahead of her and darted into the road, blocking her path. This caused her to turn right toward the woods. She crashed through blackberry brambles at the forest edge, the thorns scratching at her pants.

Once she was past the brambles, the forest floor opened up, and she ran deeper into the woods, heading away from the cabin. Brandi dashed, ducking low branches and jumping over fallen trees. As she went, her heavy breaths turned to wheezing, and her legs burned. She glanced over her shoulder, but she didn't see anyone chasing her. She slowed to a jog, trying to catch her wind and her bearings.

A flash of red appeared in the distance. Then it disappeared behind a tree. She slowed to a walk, scanning the forest, not sure if it was a friend or a foe. A dog barked, buoying Brandi's spirits and causing her to jog toward the barking. Like a mirage in the desert, a hiker with a dog appeared. The dog tugged at his leash toward Brandi. The small man wore a red T-shirt and a backpack.

The hiker waved and called out, "Are you looking for the trail?"

Brandi waved back while jogging and called back, "I need help."

They met between two large oaks.

"I need help," Brandi said through labored breaths.

The golden retriever barked and tugged at his leash.

Brandi backpedaled, eyeing the dog.

"Don't worry. He's friendly. He's just excited." The hiker tugged on his leash. "Relax boy." The dog calmed. "Are you okay?"

A lump formed in Brandi's throat. She shook her head. Tears filled her eyes. "There's someone chasing me. I think he's trying to kill me."

"Oh my God." The hiker scanned the forest. "We need to call the police." He retrieved his cell phone from his pocket and swiped on the screen. He sucked air through his teeth. "There's no service."

A gunshot cracked, startling them. Brandi and the hiker turned to the gunfire. The man in the mask appeared with a rifle less than one hundred yards away from them.

"Did he just shoot at us?" the hiker asked, incredulous.

"We have to go!" Brandi said.

"Let's take the trail."

They scurried through the woods, the hiker leading them to a rocky trail. They continued on the trail, seemingly deeper into the wilderness.

After running for several minutes, Brandi tired and slowed to a jog. She called out to his back, "I need to slow down."

The hiker slowed, glanced back at Brandi, and said, "Me too."

The dog panted alongside the hiker, on his leash.

"Where are we going?" Brandi asked, also panting.

"I saw a cabin about three miles from here," the hiker replied over his shoulder, also breathing hard. "I'm pretty sure people are staying there."

"I think I need to walk for a bit." Brandi slowed to a walk.

The hiker waited for Brandi. "So do I."

They hiked tight together on the narrow rocky trail, catching their wind, the dog on the leash behind the hiker.

The hiker held out his hand. "I'm Matt."

She shook his sweaty hand. "I'm Brandi."

Matt was only slightly bigger than Brandi, who was quite petite. His eyes were too small, and his hawklike nose was too big. His scraggly beard covered his weak chin.

"It's nice to meet you," he said. "I wish it was under different circumstances."

"Me too." Brandi glanced back at the golden retriever, thinking about the stuffed animal her father had given her. "What's his name?"

"Scout."

"Where were you going when we ran into each other?"

"I wasn't leading the way. Scout was. He's really good at finding people. Last summer, we found this hiker who was lost in the woods for like two days. He saved her life. So, when he pulls me some way, I let him."

"He's a hero," Brandi said.

Matt smiled, showing the gap between his front teeth.

"Can I pet him?"

"Be my guest."

They stopped on the trail. Matt let go of Scout's leash, and the dog rushed to Brandi. She petted his yellowish-tan fur, peering into his dark, watery eyes. Scout wagged his fluffy tail as Brandi gave him the attention he craved.

"He's a sweet boy," Brandi said.

"He loves people," Matt replied.

After a much-needed break in the tension, Brandi said, "We should probably run again if you're not too tired."

Matt nodded. "You're right."

Over the next couple of miles, they alternated between jogging and fast-walking, Matt and Scout leading the way. As the trail turned a sharp corner, she lost sight of Matt.

He cried out in pain. Brandi found Matt writhing on the ground, holding his ankle. Scout stared at his owner, unconcerned.

"Are you okay?" Brandi asked.

"I twisted my ankle," Matt replied.

"Can you walk?"

"I have to try. It's not too much farther."

"I'll take your backpack." Brandi took his backpack, which was light.

She helped him to his feet. Matt stood on his good leg, groaning from the effort.

"You can lean on me," Brandi said.

They shuffled slowly, Matt limping along, leaning on Brandi for the next half-hour or so.

"There's the cabin," Matt said.

"Where?" Brandi asked.

Matt pointed to another trail. "It's hidden by the trees, but it's down that trail about sixty yards." They turned onto the other trail.

As they shuffled along, Matt pointed to the ground. "See the ATV tracks. Somebody's here."

As they followed the ATV tracks, Brandi had a bad feeling deep in the pit of her stomach. Matt's injury reminded her of a stunt her father had pulled once. And it seemed too secluded for a cabin. *I don't know this guy.* But around the bend, the cabin appeared among the trees, just as Matt said it would.

Chapter 19

Before

"Can we go now?" Brandi asked, standing in her newly built survival shelter.

Jack stood from the makeshift bed, his bucket hat brushing against the roof. "All right. We can go, but I have something to show you on the hike back."

They took a circuitous return trip, stopping at a waterfall along the way, with a fifteen-foot drop and a small pool of churning water. Red leaves floated in the pool like a bathtub of rose petals.

"How much farther?" Brandi asked. "My feet are killing me."

"What did I say about complaining?" Jack replied.

She rolled her eyes.

Jack put his hands on his hips and faced the waterfall, framed by maples with flaming red leaves. "Isn't it beautiful?"

Brandi lifted one shoulder. "I guess."

"Your mother and I used to come here."

"For what?"

"To be somewhere beautiful together that nobody else knew about."

"My mom doesn't hike."

Jack's shoulders slumped. "She used to be a different person."

Brandi took her water bottle to the swirling pool, unscrewed the cap, and plunged it into the cool, clear water.

"What do you think you're doing?" Jack asked.

She turned from the pool to her father. "I'm thirsty. Am I not allowed to have water?"

"Go ahead."

She brought the water bottle to her lips.

"If you want dysentery," Jack added.

Brandi lowered her water bottle. "What's dysentery?"

"Basically, bloody diarrhea, which could kill you in a survival situation."

She gestured to the waterfall. "If that water's not clean, then no water's clean."

"Most of what makes water dangerous isn't visible. A stream like this can become contaminated by runoff from heavy rains, dead animals rotting in the water upstream, or feces. If you have to drink from a stream, check to see if there are fresh animal tracks and swarms of insects nearby. If other living things are drinking the water, it's likely you can too, but it's always a risk."

"So you can't drink any water in the woods?"

"There's a risk with everything you do. The lowest-risk water would be the source of a natural spring. This creek goes for miles and miles upstream. That's a lot of area to be contaminated."

"How do you find the source of a natural spring?"

"On the way back, look for areas with bright green grass"—Jack gestured to the surrounding hills—"and maybe a very small stream coming from one of these hills."

As they hiked the narrow path, Brandi surveyed the forest for greenery. She pointed to a lowland area with a lot of green moss. "What about there?"

"Let's check it out." After investigating, Jack said, "This is probably just a wet lowland area. If you look upslope, you don't see any pattern of greenery connecting to this patch. Let's keep looking."

They returned to the narrow path and continued their journey back to civilization. Brandi still searched for greenery, motivated by her thirst. Eventually, she saw a patch of dark-green grass uphill from the trail.

She pointed at the grass. "What about there?"

"Good eye. Let's check it out."

As they neared the green patch, they noticed a very shallow stream of water flowing next to the grass.

"There it is," Brandi said.

"We still need to find the source," Jack replied. "It's a very shallow stream, so we probably won't have to walk far to find the source. Go ahead and follow the stream uphill. You lead the way."

Brandi did as she was told, following the shallow stream. As they hiked uphill the stream became smaller and smaller.

"How far do I go?" she asked.

"As long as you see surface water, keep going," Jack replied.

They walked uphill another thirty yards, following the water with their eyes and ears.

"I don't see or hear it anymore," Brandi said.

"Look at this area. Do you see any green grass?" Jack asked.

"No."

"Does the ground feel soft and spongy?"

"No."

"Then we probably passed it. Let's go back downhill a little."

They hiked slowly, searching for signs of the spring.

"I think it's coming out from under this rock," Brandi said, pointing.

"I think you're right." Jack removed his backpack, bent down, and cleared a few small stones from the area. He pointed to a small creature. "See that salamander?"

Brandi also bent down and spotted the little lizard-like creature. "I see it."

"If you see salamanders or crayfish, it means the water is likely clean because those animals are sensitive to pollutants." Jack grabbed a folding shovel from his backpack and handed it to Brandi. "Dig a hole right where the water's coming out."

Brandi dug a hole, the spring filling it immediately. Jack placed a few rocks above the hole.

"I'm trying to slow down the spring so it doesn't churn up so much sediment," Jack said.

"What do we do now?" Brandi asked.

"We just have to wait a few minutes for the sediment to clear."

When the sediment cleared, Jack said, "I think it's good to drink."

Brandi filled her water bottle with the clean, cool spring water. Then she guzzled the entire bottle. "Is this the best water you can get?"

Jack smiled. "Probably."

Chapter 20

After

As they neared the small stone cabin, Brandi's heart sank. No ATVs likely meant nobody was there. She pounded on the front door anyway. Scout stood next to her, wagging his tail. Matt peeped into the front window, putting most of his weight on his good leg. Nobody answered.

She pivoted to Matt. "Shit. They're gone."

"Maybe not," Matt replied. "It's very possible that they're still out hunting. I saw two guys on ATVs come from this cabin like two hours ago. I doubt they left. It's Saturday."

"Does your phone work here?"

"I doubt it, but I'll check." Matt grabbed his phone from his pocket and swiped the screen. He shook his head. "Still no signal."

"What do you wanna do?"

"I don't think I can walk anymore today." Matt leaned against the stone cabin. "My ankle is killing me."

"What if I kept running on the trail? Would I eventually find help?"

"I don't know. It's about fifteen miles until you reach civilization. You'd never make it before dark. I think we should hide out here. The guys on the ATVs could be back any minute."

Brandi's legs were tired from running and hiking, and she was hungry and thirsty. "You're probably right." She jiggled the door handle. "I wish we could hide in the house. I feel so exposed out here."

Matt tried to open the front window. "Window's locked."

"I'm gonna check the other windows." Brandi walked around the stone cabin, checking the windows and the back door. Scout followed her, wagging his tail. She found an unlocked window, opened it, and crawled into the cabin. Scout barked. She spoke to the dog through the open window. "Go to the front door, boy. I'll let you in."

Brandi shut and locked the window. She surveyed the one-room cabin with a fireplace, a single bed, a couch, a wooden chair, and a cooler. A few half-melted candles perched around the cabin. Deer antlers decorated one wall. Beer cans hanging from the tabs decorated another. A coating of dust covered everything. She walked to the front door, unlocked the deadbolt, and opened the door.

"Nice job," Matt said.

Scout bounded inside.

Brandi helped Matt to the couch. He slumped on the couch with a groan, keeping the pressure off his bad ankle. She returned to the front door, peered outside, then shut and locked it.

She joined Matt and Scout in the sitting area. Matt elevated his bad ankle on the coffee table, using a couch cushion underneath for comfort. Scout lay on the bear skin rug. Brandi sat in the wooden chair next to the cooler and across from the couch. She leaned forward and scrawled a *B* in the dusty coffee table. "It doesn't look like anyone's been here in a long time."

"Guys don't dust. Check the cooler," Matt replied.

Brandi opened the cooler. She placed her fingertips in the ice water. "Bottled water and beer. The ice isn't totally melted."

"That's a positive sign that they're coming back," Matt said.

Brandi grabbed a water for herself and another for Matt. She tossed the plastic bottle to him. She opened her water and drank half of it. "Do you have a bowl for Scout?"

Matt fished in his backpack and produced two silver dog bowls, but Scout had already stood from the rug and put his head into the cooler, lapping up the icy water.

"Could I have a beer too? To ice my ankle."

"I think it would work way better if you put your foot in the ice water," Brandi said.

"Good idea."

"Before I put my nasty foot in there, can you fill Scout's bowl?"

Brandi dipped Scout's bowl into the icy water and set it on the floor. Scout drank from his bowl. Brandi removed the bottled water and beer from the cooler, placing the beverages on the coffee table. Then she helped Matt out of his boot, and the hiker removed his sock himself. Brandi filled Scout's bowl one more time before Matt plunged his foot into the cooler water.

He winced. "Damn that's cold."

Brandi sat back on the wooden chair and snagged her water from the coffee table. Scout padded closer to her. She finished her water, then reached over her chair and petted the dog.

Matt dug in his backpack and retrieved two protein bars and a large Ziploc bag filled with dog food.

Scout barked at his food.

"You want a protein bar?" Matt asked.

"Yeah," Brandi replied.

Matt tossed her a protein bar.

She caught it two-handed. "Thank you." She eyed the dog food. "You want me to feed him?"

"Please. Give him about a quarter of what's in the bag."

Brandi fed Scout, then returned to her chair. She opened the protein bar and took a bite. She gestured to Matt's backpack and spoke with her mouth full. "Got any weapons in there?"

Scout ate his food.

Matt reached into his backpack and retrieved a folding shovel and a Buck knife.

"Do you have a gun?" Brandi asked.

"I'm not really a gun guy," Matt replied.

"We might need that knife."

Matt packed the shovel and knife into his backpack. "Let's hope not."

Scout curled into a ball.

"Where's your car? Is it far?" Brandi took another bite of her protein bar.

"It's about twenty miles from here. I was planning to hike all weekend. Fifty miles in total. I'm training to hike the Appalachian Trail from Maine all the way to Georgia." He took a big bite of his protein bar.

"How far is it?"

Matt chewed and swallowed. "About 2200 miles."

"Wow. That's a crazy long way to walk."

Matt nodded. "I plan to stop in a few towns along the way. They have shelters for hikers too. It's not like I won't rest."

"You must really like hiking." Brandi took another bite of her protein bar.

"I like being away from... everything." Matt took another bite of his protein bar.

"What are you trying to get away from?"

Matt shrugged and looked away. "My life I guess."

"Well, my life totally sucks, but I literally can't wait to get back to it."

Matt chuckled. "I guess I can understand that. Being chased by a psychopath in the woods would do that."

Brandi giggled. "Big facts."

They ate their protein bars in silence for a while. Brandi grabbed another water, downing half of it. Scout settled on the bear skin rug at her feet.

"So, what do you do, like for work?" Brandi asked.

"I used to have a really good job. I worked in IT at Google," Matt replied.

"Used to? What happened? Did you get fired?"

Matt exhaled and nodded. "About eight months ago, I found

out that my wife was having an affair." He grimaced and added, "With my best friend."

Brandi cringed. "That's literally the worst."

"I was really depressed after I found out. I wasn't doing well at work, and they fired me."

"That really sucks."

Matt sighed. "It does."

"I can see why you like to get away from everything."

"What about you? How did you get into this mess?"

"It's a really long story."

"I'm not going anywhere, but it's okay if you don't want to share."

Brandi told Matt the story from the beginning, leaving out the part where she was likely raped.

"I'm so sorry, Brandi," he said.

She swallowed the lump in her throat. "It's not your fault. I'm sorry I got *you* into this mess."

Matt shook his head. "Don't be sorry. I'm glad Scout found you. And don't worry—we'll get out of here."

Brandi forced a smile. "Thanks."

Chapter 21

Before

For the second Saturday in a row, Brandi followed her father into the woods. In just a week, she noticed the increase in leaf litter and the opening of the canopy overhead, with many more barren trees. It was also much cooler, in the low forties that morning.

"It's cold," Brandi said.

Jack glanced over his shoulder and replied, "What did I say about complaining?"

"Makes me feel better," Brandi mumbled to herself.

Jack stopped and faced his daughter on the trail. "Do you know why it makes you feel better to complain?"

The girl lifted one shoulder. "I don't know."

"It's because you have a victim mentality, but I want you to have a warrior mentality."

Brandi frowned. "What does that even mean?"

"It means you're situationally aware, not just in the woods, but everywhere you go. It means you can assess and handle situations before they become problems. If the problem's unavoidable, it means you can devise a plan to deal with the problem efficiently. And if all hell breaks loose and you have multiple major problems, you have the mental toughness to triage and solve your most pressing problem first."

Brandi rolled her eyes. "Sounds extreme."

"Is it? What's your most pressing problem right now?"

She hugged herself. "I'm cold."

"Let's get moving then. Once we get to camp, I'll show you how to make a fire."

They hiked to the survival shelter they had built last weekend. Jack set his backpack inside the shelter, and returned with his two folding shovels.

Brandi dropped her backpack and groaned. "More digging?"

"There's that victim mentality," Jack replied.

Brandi scowled and took her shovel.

They dug a circular pit near their shelter entrance. Then, they collected and lined the pit with stones. Finally, they collected what Jack called tinder, kindling, and firewood. Tinder was dried leaves and dried pine needles. Kindling was small sticks, and firewood was thicker logs, which was the hardest to find.

By the time they dug and lined the fire pit and collected the burn materials, the temperature had risen into the fifties, and Brandi was no longer cold. *A bunch of work for nothing.*

But Jack continued with his fire-building lesson, showing Brandi various firewood stacking arrangements based on the intended use. They settled on the log cabin arrangement, good for sustained heat over a long period of time. After she arranged the tinder, kindling, and firewood to Jack's specifications, she asked for matches.

Jack handed her a piece of steel with a handle that was attached to another piece of steel by a little chain.

"What's this?" Brandi asked.

"It's a flint fire starter," Jack replied. "It's yours. You can use it as a key chain. As long as you have that in your pocket, you can start a fire anywhere."

"I've never had to start a fire in my entire life."

"Now you do."

Jack showed Brandi how to create sparks with the flint block and her steel striker. "Try to light the tender."

She scraped the steel striker across the flint block, creating a spark, but nothing happened.

"Keep trying," Jack said.

Brandi continued striking the flint until the tender lit. "It worked."

"Blow on it. It's about to go out."

She tried to blow on it, but it was too late. The flame was gone. She added some more tinder and tried again. This time, she was able to create a sustained fire.

Brandi stood back from the fire with a grin on her face, watching the flames dance.

"Good job," Jack said.

"What's next?" Brandi asked.

"Have you ever been in a fight?"

The girl tilted her head. "Like a real fight, with punching and stuff?"

Jack nodded.

"A few times."

"What happened?"

"Last year, this bitch was talking shit, so I grabbed her by the hair and threw her on the ground. She tried to get up, but I kicked her in the stomach."

Jack frowned. "Do you think it's right to assault someone because of what they said?"

Brandi shrugged. "She was talking all that shit. She wanted the smoke."

Jack turned from the fire and faced his daughter. "I don't want you fighting unless it's in self-defense or defense of another. You understand me?"

Brandi pursed her lips. "Yeah."

"But if someone attacks you, all bets are off."

She turned from the fire and faced her father. "What does that mean?"

"The first rule of self-defense is to run away. That goes for anyone, regardless of their size and self-defense ability. The best way to survive an attack is to run from danger."

"What if you can't run?"

"Then you have to fight to survive, even if it means killing your attacker."

Her eyes widened, thinking about what her mother had said about Jack being a cold-blooded killer.

"I'll show you. Come on." Jack walked away from the fire to a flat, open area.

Brandi followed her father.

"Punch me as hard as you can in the stomach," Jack said.

"What?" she asked.

"Punch me as hard as you can." He tapped his stomach. "Right here. Go on."

Brandi wound up and punched Jack as hard as she could, but it did nothing.

Jack grabbed her by the wrist and said, "Try to get away."

Brandi tugged and pulled, but Jack controlled her with ease.

He let go and said, "Your attacker might be bigger and stronger than I am, which means if you can't run away, you're in serious trouble, unless you fight smarter."

Jack showed Brandi how to attack vulnerable body parts such as the major joints like elbows, wrists, and knees, as well as sensitive areas like the groin, eyes, and throat.

"What do I do if someone grabs my wrist like you did? I couldn't do anything," the girl said.

"Let's try it again in slow motion." Jack grabbed her right wrist. "Your instinct is to pull away, but if you pull away, it's easy for me to control you. Instead of pulling away, I want you to dip down with a strong athletic base, lean toward me, bend your arm, and try to touch my forearm with your elbow."

They did this in slow motion several times, the odd arm angle forcing Jack to let go each time.

"There's another wrinkle to this," Jack said. "Ideally, you want to rotate your arm so the skinny part of your wrist is facing the opening of my grip. This will make it easier for you to slip out. See if you can rotate your arm too."

They practiced, increasing the speed with each repetition. In time, Brandi learned the proper arm angle and body position to break the wrist hold.

"I want you to be able to do this purely from reaction and muscle memory," Jack said. "If you're attacked, you won't have time to think."

Brandi nodded.

They worked on several other scenarios. One started with Jack grabbing a fistful of Brandi's hair. The girl learned to fight her urge to pull away, instead grabbing Jack's arm with two hands, squatting and rotating her body, potentially breaking her attacker's arm. Brandi doubted she would have the strength to pull off the maneuver against someone as strong as her father, but she went through the motions over and over again.

The scariest scenario featured Brandi on her back, with Jack straddling her, his hands around her neck. This, according to Jack, was the last place she should ever be. Brandi could barely breathe with his weight on her stomach. He instructed her to first bring her elbows in tight to her body, then to focus all her energy on one side. He instructed her to grab his right wrist with a monkey grip, not using her thumb, to grab his right triceps with her left hand, and to hook his right foot. With this control, Brandi bridged her hips and rolled, moving her much heavier opponent off her and allowing her to escape.

Even after practicing many times, Brandi wondered if she could actually do this in a real-life situation. She knew her father wasn't using his full strength.

By lunchtime, Brandi was sweaty from the exercises and dirty from rolling around on the ground. Jack made sloppy joes over the fire for lunch. They sat on stones her father had rolled from ten feet away. They were heavy enough that Jack couldn't pick them up.

"We'll have to make some chairs," Jack said before taking a bite of his sloppy joe.

"This is so good," Brandi replied with her mouth full.

They ate in silence, listening to blue jays cawing and squirrels scampering about the dried leaves. Jack devoured his lunch in just a few minutes. Brandi was famished, but she still took twice as long to finish her food.

"You eat fast," she said, with brownish red stains at the corners of her mouth.

"Bad habit from the Army." Jack handed Brandi his handkerchief. "I forgot napkins."

She took his handkerchief and wiped sloppy joe from the corners of her mouth, then she handed it back. "Thanks."

Jack nodded.

Brandi wondered if he picked up other bad habits from the Army. Was her mother right that he was a killer? "You think someone would ever attack me? Like for real?"

"I hope not, but I've been around the world, and I've seen the worst atrocities you can imagine, often against women and children. In my estimation, violence against women is common enough that you should be prepared."

Brandi wondered if he wanted her to be prepared for men like him.

"It's not enough to learn some self-defense techniques," Jack continued. "It's far more important to be situationally aware. Don't do stupid things with stupid people in stupid places. You're bound to get a stupid prize. You understand?"

Brandi thought about the drug addicts and drug dealers her mother had entertained. "I think so."

"If you do get yourself into a situation that you can't avoid or run from, you have to be smart. If you're strong, act weak. If you're weak, act strong. Don't be afraid to use anything as a weapon. A rock. A hot beverage. Sand in the eyes. There are no rules to survival. You understand?"

Brandi nodded. "Did you learn to fight in the Army?"

"Mostly."
"Have you ever been in a fight?"
Jack nodded.
"Like in war?"
Jack nodded again.
"Is that why you have nightmares?"
Jack stood from his rock, his empty plate in hand. "You need more practice."
Brandi stood from her rock. "I can hear you in my room."
"I'm adjusting to the world."

Chapter 22

After

It was nearly dusk outside, and even darker inside the cabin. Matt lay on the couch, snoring. Scout lay on the bear skin rug at Brandi's feet. She stood from the chair and went to the front window. She gazed outside, into the fading light, seeing nothing but trees. *It's getting dark. Where the hell are these hunters?*

Brandi returned to the wooden chair. She thought about waking Matt and discussing their options, but he was sound asleep. *Maybe it's over. They know I'm with someone now. Maybe they're afraid. They don't know Matt. He could have a gun for all they know, or friends. Maybe they figured I'm too risky to fuck with now. It's not like I saw their faces. They could let me go.*

I should've kept going on the trail. I can't leave now. It's almost dark. Maybe Matt has a flashlight. Brandi moved the coffee table and lay next to Scout. She wanted to pet the dog for comfort, but she didn't want to disturb his slumber.

Brandi curled into the fetal position and closed her eyes, hoping to sleep through this nightmare. But her mind wouldn't let her go. Her dad was in her head again. *Details matter.* Brandi thought about the details of her predicament. *Roger's one of them. There's another man too. The one in the creepy mask. Roger stuck me with a needle. He drugged me obviously. I was out for like* twenty hours. Then what? They let me walk out of the house and run away. Why? Maybe I woke up earlier than they thought I would, and they weren't ready. But they set out clothes for me. And that spread in the kitchen. It seemed like they were totally ready for me, but they still let me run away.

Scout lifted his head and growled.

Brandi stiffened and opened her eyes, trying to adjust to the darkness. She petted Scout's head. "Shh."

The dog stopped growling.

Brandi glanced at the rear and side windows, but everything was nearly black. She peered out from the couch at the front windows. A white mask with black eyes and a black zipper for a mouth appeared in the left front window. She scooted back behind the couch, her heart racing. *Can he see in here?*

Careful to keep her head down, Brandi shook Matt and whispered, "Wake up. Wake up."

Matt mumbled something incoherent and opened his eyes.

Brandi put her finger to her lips, then whispered, "They're here. Get your knife."

Without leaving his prone position on the couch, Matt reached into his backpack and retrieved his Buck knife. He lay on his side, facing Brandi, his back against the backrest. He held the knife tight to his body, the blade still sheathed. She wondered if he had the courage to use it.

The front doorknob jiggled. Matt tensed. Brandi dug her nails into her palms. The deadbolt turned. The young woman had a disturbing thought. *What if the two guys Matt saw on the ATVs are the same guys who are trying to kill me?* Matt ducked his head, covering his face with his forearms. Brandi made herself small against the couch, hoping not to be seen in the dark cabin. The door creaked open, followed by a flashlight beam. Slow footsteps entered the cabin. The door shut. The beam of light circled the cabin, passing above them.

Brandi glanced at Scout, worried he might bark or growl, but his head was down, unconcerned about the intruder. The intruder crept closer to the couch, the floorboards groaning with each step, the flashlight beam exploring the cabin. The intruder lingered near the couch. The flashlight beam circled the room again. Brandi held her breath.

The intruder jumped beyond the couch and said, "*Boo,*" his light shining on Brandi, Matt, and Scout.

The dog barked.

On reflex, Brandi sprinted to the front door. She whipped it open, revealing another masked man. This man was gigantic, built like a bear. She screeched and pivoted. She pushed off her right foot, intent on running for the back door, but the big man reached out with his long arm and grabbed Brandi by the back of her collar. He yanked her off her feet like a ragdoll and deposited her on the hardwood with a *thud*.

Chapter 23

Before

Jack and Brandi hiked through the woods, headed to their camp. Jack carried his customary rucksack, but this time he also shouldered a .22 caliber rifle.

"We're in the woods every weekend," Brandi said, following her father. "I know this is your thing, but it's not mine."

Jack didn't reply.

Brandi shuffled through the leaf litter, the morning sun cutting through the mostly barren tree canopy. "I'm starving. How come we didn't have breakfast?"

Jack didn't acknowledge Brandi's complaints.

"I've been up since five doing chores. I need to eat. This is bullshit. I can't stay out here all day. We didn't even pack lunches."

Jack stopped and pivoted to his daughter. "*Enough.* What did I say about complaining?"

Brandi huffed. "Whatever."

"What is the most important skill needed to become a successful human being?"

"I'm guessing you're gonna tell me."

"Problem solving. Not just the ability to solve problems, but the wisdom to know which problems to solve and which ones to ignore."

Brandi held out her hands. "I don't understand."

"What's your biggest problem right now?"

"I don't know. My mom's in prison."

"Is that problem solvable?"

"She gets out when she gets out."

Jack nodded. "This problem is outside of your control, so focusing on it is draining you mentally, and making it difficult to solve problems you can control."

"Like what?"

"You're hungry, right?"

"Yeah."

"Hunger is one of the most important problems we have to solve as human beings."

Brandi placed her hands on her hips. "We could *easily* solve this problem by walking back to your car and going to a restaurant."

"What fun would that be?" Jack continued hiking on the trail.

She followed.

At the camp, Jack retrieved paper targets from his rucksack and tacked them to several trees. He led Brandi to a large rock, as big as an oven, and set his rifle on the rock. Then he retrieved a handgun from a holster that had been concealed by his jacket and set that gun on the rock as well.

"Treat every gun like it's loaded," Jack said. "Never point a gun at anyone unless you intend to shoot them." Jack picked up the handgun, the barrel pointed at the ground. "Keep your finger straight and off the trigger until you're ready to fire. Like this." Jack showed Brandi his index finger, which was straight and outside of the trigger guard. "And always be aware of what's beyond your target." Jack gestured to the targets he had tacked to the trees. "What do you think will happen if we miss those targets?"

Brandi scanned the area beyond the targets, which was uphill. "I guess we would hit another tree or the hill."

They worked for two hours, practicing the proper grip and stance for the weapons, loading and unloading, lining up the sights, breathing, and clearing malfunctions.

Brandi loaded fifteen 9mm rounds into the Beretta magazine as instructed. The last few rounds were difficult to insert, but she managed it. Then she inserted the full magazine into the handgun. Jack walked behind Brandi as they approached the targets. They both wore ear and eye protection.

"Keep your muzzle pointed down range," Jack said. "Range is hot. Make ready."

Brandi racked the slide, chambering a round. She spread her legs and bent her knees in an isosceles stance, bending forward just slightly. She gripped the handgun with two hands, her index finger straight and off the trigger.

"Three shots. Center target. Engage," Jack said.

Brandi aimed, lining up the front and rear sights, and pulled the trigger. Nothing happened. The girl turned to Jack, the gun turning with her.

"Watch that muzzle," her father said.

Brandi turned back to the target. "I don't know what I did wrong."

"You sure you didn't forget something?"

"The safety." Brandi flicked the safety with her thumb, exposing the red dot. Then, she reengaged the target. She pulled the trigger, anticipating the bang. When it came, the loud pop startled her, despite the ear protection. Her first shot hit the target, but barely. She was more accurate with the next two, but still off target.

"Watch your trigger control," Jack said. "You're pulling. That's why your shots are off target. Try pressing. Let's go. Three shots. Center target. Engage."

Brandi tried to exercise better trigger control, and her shots were more accurate. Not perfect bullseyes, but close.

"That's a much tighter group. Nice job."

Brandi shot over one hundred rounds with the Beretta, then she practiced shooting the .22 bolt-action rifle. She was more accurate with the rifle, and she liked the quieter shot of the .22.

By lunchtime, Brandi was feeling faint. "I really need to eat something."

"Let's go find something to eat," Jack replied.

Brandi carried the loaded rifle—with the safety engaged—as they crept through the forest. Jack said they were hunting for rabbit and squirrels since a .22 wasn't suitable for larger game.

While they searched for game, Jack led Brandi to other sources of food, teaching her what was edible. They ate chickweed, which tasted like lettuce. Even without dressing, the girl was happy to get something into her stomach. They ate a few wild grapes, but most were past their prime. The aronia berries were too bitter for Brandi, but she was hungry enough to eat a handful.

Jack led her to a grove of small trees with large leaves that appeared tropical. A sweet smell hung in the air. She stepped on something gooey. Pale-green fruits hung on the trees and many more lay on the forest floor.

Brandi grabbed one from the ground and showed it to Jack. "What's this?"

"That's the largest native American fruit, the paw paw," Jack replied. "These groves are few and far between. Your mom and I found this one a long time ago."

Brandi smelled the fruit, which was split, exposing the yellow pudding-like substance inside. "Can I eat this?"

"You can eat the yellow stuff."

Jack grabbed a fruit from the forest floor and sliced it open with his knife.

"How come you didn't pick from the tree?"

"The ones on the tree aren't ripe. They'll taste terrible."

Brandi ate the custard and spit out the large seeds. Paw paws tasted like nothing she'd ever had before. It was kind of like coconut and pineapple, but also not. It wasn't the best fruit she'd ever had, but she was famished, so she ate three of them.

Jack nudged her and pointed to a rabbit nibbling on henbit.

Brandi aimed her rifle at the gray rabbit. She pressed the button, disengaging the safety. She placed her finger on the trigger. The rabbit ate his meal, none the wiser, his little cheeks fluttering. Brandi's stomach turned with the creature in her sights. She fired over the rabbit's head, sending the little guy scurrying in the opposite direction.

"You missed," Jack said. "What happened?"

Brandi shrugged. "I think I forgot to line up the sights."

"That's all right. Next time."

On the way back to camp, Jack identified a cluster of mushrooms growing at the base of an oak tree. "That's hen of the woods. It's very tasty."

Jack cut a large cluster of the mushrooms and tossed them in his rucksack.

As they neared camp, Jack spotted another rabbit. He whispered to Brandi, "Take the shot."

She hesitated.

The rabbit started to scamper away, much to Brandi's relief. But Jack drew his handgun from his holster and shot the rabbit like he was an old western gunfighter. Brandi averted her gaze as Jack grabbed the carcass. They hiked back to camp with their rabbit and mushrooms.

Jack hung the carcass from an overhanging branch. He skinned, gutted, and butchered the animal, forcing Brandi to watch and participate.

"I don't like butchering animals either, but it's an important skill," Jack said.

They cooked the rabbit and mushrooms over the campfire. They ate in silence, Brandi devouring the tasty meal.

"What do you think?" Jack asked.

"I feel bad for the rabbit, but it's good," Brandi replied.

Jack nodded. "It's better to be at the top of the food chain."

Brandi swallowed some rabbit meat. "Obviously."

After their meal, Jack stood from his rock. "It's getting late."

Brandi stood from her rock.

"You think you could lead us out of here?" Jack asked.

Even though she had been to the camp three times, she still didn't know her way back. "I don't think so."

"I'll teach you land navigation at some point."

Brandi spoke in monotone. "Oh, joy. Can't wait."

Chapter 24

After

The big man slammed the front door and dragged Brandi by her collar across the floor to the middle of the cabin. She groaned, in a daze from the impact of her fall. The big man flipped on his headlamp, illuminating wherever he looked. He straddled Brandi, his headlamp blinding her and his weight making it difficult to breathe. He put his massive mitts around her neck, suffocating her.

Brandi slapped at the man, but her blows did nothing. She bucked and kicked, but he was an immovable object. Every cell in her body screamed for air. Her vision dimmed. She grabbed the man's right wrist and elbow and she hooked his leg. She tried to bridge her hips and roll, but he was too heavy. He let go of her neck and slapped her across the face. Brandi sucked in oxygen, wheezing, her cheek stinging. She turned her head, searching for help.

Matt knelt less than ten feet away, watching the attack. The other masked man had a gun to his head. Scout lay on the floor, unconcerned. The big man slapped her again, causing her to yelp. He reached into the sheath on his belt and brandished a Buck knife, similar to Matt's. Brandi's eyes widened, her gaze on the blade.

The big man grabbed her long-sleeve T-shirt, pulling and

wrenching the cotton in his fist. Then he slashed the shirt in one fluid motion, exposing her bra. He grabbed her sports bra and slashed again, cutting it off and slicing her bare sternum in the process. Blood seeped from the gash. The pain burned white hot. The big man raised his mask, just enough to expose his thin lips and crooked teeth. He bit her left nipple like a rabid animal, causing Brandi to screech. Blood seeped from her breast, the nipple partially detached. He grinned, his teeth stained red.

Then the big man sheathed his knife and lowered his mask, fully covering his face. He put his massive mitts around her neck, choking her again. She reached for his knife, touching the handle. Her vision dimmed again, her body in desperate need of oxygen. She tried to grasp the knife, to retrieve it from his sheath, but she didn't have the strength. She was nearly gone. Brandi didn't think about it, but somehow she knew she was dying. As her vision went black, he let go again, bringing her back to the light.

Brandi gasped for air again, tears streaming down her face, as her vision returned. The big man hit her. This time with his fist. The room spun from the impact. One side of her face throbbed.

"Go *easy*. I'm the one who has to pick up the pieces," said the man holding the gun.

Brandi recognized his voice. It was Roger. She didn't fight as the big man cut her pants and underwear off her body. He opened his fly. She turned away from the big man and his headlamp, making eye contact with Matt, who was still on his knees with a gun to his head. Matt was slack-jawed, his eyes wide open in terror.

The big man smacked Brandi and said, "Fight, you stupid cunt."

But she wheezed, still struggling for air.

"She can't fight if she can't breathe," Roger said.

The big man pointed at Matt. "Get him out of here."

"No. No. I need to stay with her. Please don't do this," Matt said.

"Shut the fuck up. And take the dog too."

Roger yanked Matt to his feet and forced him outside by

gunpoint. Scout followed without prompting. On the way, Roger said to the big man, "Show some restraint. I'd like to have another day."

With the back and forth between the men, Brandi's breath regulated and her strength returned. She grabbed the knife handle at his waist and removed it from the sheath. She thrust the knife at the big man's stomach, but he seized her wrist and twisted, causing her to drop the blade. He grabbed the knife and tossed it across the wood floor, out of reach.

A gunshot cracked outside, making Brandi flinch, then scream in anger. She bucked and squirmed, trying to get away from the big man, but her resistance only served to sexually excite him.

He used his penis as a weapon, slamming himself into her over and over again, each thrust causing Brandi to shriek. When she let go and stopped fighting, he slapped or punched her in the head, causing her eyes to water and her vision to blur. He needed the resistance to perform, so she chose the lesser pain, fighting so he could satisfy himself. It continued far longer than Brandi thought possible. She would've gladly chosen death over what she experienced on that cabin floor.

Chapter 25

Before

After breakfast on Saturday, Brandi dressed in her hiking gear, expecting another trip to the camp. She found Jack in the dining room, with the contents of a first aid kit spread out on the table.

"I thought we were going to the camp?" she asked.

"After this," her father replied.

Jack taught her the basics of first aid, teaching her how to clean and dress wounds and to stop bleeding. He taught her how to tie a tourniquet with a leather belt.

"Be careful with tourniquets," Jack said. "If you can stop the bleeding with direct pressure, that's better. You always run the risk of causing an amputation with a tourniquet. But if you apply direct pressure and they're still bleeding heavily, you'll have to use a tourniquet until you get help."

Brandi nodded. "What do you do if someone overdoses?"

"Call 9-1-1 immediately. Try to wake them up. There's a drug called Narcan. You can get it in a nasal spray. It reverses the effects of opioids and can help someone who isn't breathing."

"What if it's not opioids?"

"Narcan won't work, but it won't hurt the person either."

"What if they're still not breathing after the Narcan?"

"You'll want to administer CPR. If that's something you're interested in learning, I can find a CPR class."

Brandi nodded, thinking about her mother. "Okay."

After the medical training, they hiked to their camp in single file, with Jack leading the way. Brandi's breath condensed in the air. Their footsteps crunched dried leaves. The canopy was barren. Brandi thought, *Winter's coming.*

As they went deeper into the forest, Brandi imagined her mother being released from prison and being a different woman. She imagined her drug-free and having a job. She imagined spending time with her mother like they used to when she was young. She remembered how they used to crack up playing this old game called *Twister*. It was this rubber mat with circles of various colors. A spinner told them to put a foot or a hand on a particular color. Brandi's mom was so flexible and wiry. She was nearly unbeatable.

"Help!" Jack called out, jolting Brandi from her daydream.

He writhed on the ground fifty feet ahead of her. Brandi ran to him, her heart pounding. He gripped his calf, his hands and leg soaked with blood.

"Oh my God. What happened?" she asked.

Jack groaned. "I tripped and fell on a very sharp rock. It impaled my calf. It's bad, Brandi. I need to go to the hospital."

"Do you have your phone?"

He frowned. "It's in my truck?"

"Okay. I'll run back and get it. Wait a minute, I'm not sure I know the way."

Jack shook his head. "It'll take them too long to get here. I need you to tie a tourniquet. You need to take me to the hospital. I'm losing a lot of blood."

"I can't carry you!"

"One problem at a time. What do I need first?"

"The tourniquet."

"All right. Let's do it." Jack kept his hands on his bleeding calf, trying to hold back the tide of blood. "Take off my belt."

Brandi undid his belt and pulled it off. She made a loop with the belt and passed it down through the buckle, creating a double loop. "Tell me if I'm doing it wrong."

"That looks right."

Brandi put the double loop over his shoe and up his calf, above the wound. She expected the wound to gush blood when Jack let go, but it didn't. Brandi cranked the tourniquet until he said it was enough.

"Now what?" she asked.

"You'll have to let me lean on you, like a human crutch. Help me up."

Brandi grabbed her father's hands and helped him upright. Jack winced and stood on his good leg. He put his arm around Brandi's shoulders, and she put her arm around his waist. They left their backpacks behind, only taking Jack's car keys and wallet.

It was slow going as Jack hopped along the trail, supported by Brandi. She had her own struggles, as her father was very heavy. Her back and legs tired and throbbed in pain. Brandi worried that they wouldn't make it, but she kept her worries and complaints to herself. After all, she wasn't the one with the massive gash in her calf.

"One step at a time," Jack said.

Brandi repeated his mantra as they went. *One step at a time.* It felt like a million steps, but they eventually reached Jack's SUV.

She held out her hand. "Give me your keys."

It was then that Jack stood on his bad leg. "You did better in a crisis than I thought you would."

Brandi drew back from her father. "You're not injured?"

Jack shook his head.

"I saw the blood."

"Fake blood packets."

Brandi's face contorted as if she'd eaten a lemon. "You asshole! My back's killing me."

"I needed to see you react under stress."

"For *what?*"

"Because if you're ever in a life-and-death situation, I don't want it to be the first time you've experienced that type of stress. It's very hard to simulate the real thing."

"I wanna go home."

"We need to get the backpacks."

"I hate you." Brandi marched back into the forest.

Chapter 26

After

Brandi stirred and opened her eyes. The ceiling fan rotated overhead. The curtains were drawn, allowing sunshine to brighten the bedroom—the same bedroom as the day before. She turned her head and grimaced, pain radiating from her neck. She tried to sit up, but her entire body screamed in revolt.

She glanced under the comforter. She wore a new pair of underwear and nothing else. Her sternum and left nipple were bandaged, where she had been slashed and bitten.

The door opened, and Roger entered the bedroom, carrying pajama pants and a white T-shirt. He wore sunglasses but no hat. His salt-and-pepper hair was gelled and matched his beard. He was tall and thin, athletic but not bulky like the other guy. He wore jeans and a blue button-down shirt, with several buttons undone, exposing his tan chest that's likely seen the inside of a tanning bed.

"I thought I heard you," he said. "How are you feeling?"

Brandi narrowed her eyes.

"I know that was rough last night, but don't worry, it's my day, and I'll take good care of you." Roger set the pink pajama pants and the white T-shirt on the bed next to her. "These are for you."

Brandi glanced at the clothes.

"Are you thirsty? Hungry? You need help going to the bathroom?"

"Water," she said, her voice raspy.

Roger grinned. "Coming right up." He went to the bathroom.

While he left, Brandi put on the T-shirt.

Roger returned with a glass of water. He helped Brandi to sit up and he watched intently as she sipped her water.

Brandi glanced at the bathroom.

"You need to go to the bathroom?" Roger asked.

She nodded.

Roger put his arm around her, causing her to flinch. "Relax. I'm here to help." He put his arm around her again and helped her to her feet.

"I got it," she said.

Roger let go but stayed close, his hands out as if he expected Brandi to fall at any moment.

Brandi staggered to the bathroom, carrying the pink pajama pants, her legs like rubber. Everything felt sore, especially her neck, face, chest, and vagina. The young woman entered the bathroom, Roger following her, but she shut the door in his face.

"I'll be out here if you need any help," Roger said through the door.

Brandi set the pajama pants on the counter and stood before the mirror, leaning on the sink. Her face was swollen and black and blue. Her neck was bruised black with fingerprints. She turned from her reflection and staggered to the toilet. She sat and peed, feeling the burn, a little blood mixing with the urine.

She put on the pajama pants, her back sore as she bent over. She opened the door and shuffled forward. Roger rushed to her side and helped her into bed.

"I stitched your nipple last night," he said. "I used butterfly strips on your sternum. The cut wasn't that deep. I cleaned you too."

She sat up in bed, wincing, tears in her eyes. "Why are you doing this to me?"

"That wasn't me last night."

"Yes, it was. I heard you."

"I was there, but I didn't do this to you. Harold's a sadist. Do you know what that means?"

Tears slipped down Brandi's face.

"It means he enjoys hurting people," Roger said. "He doesn't know how to love like you and I do. He only knows pain and violence."

"I wanna go home."

Roger sat on her bedside and placed his hand atop hers. "Don't worry. It'll be over very soon. In the meantime, today will be a much better day. I do have one simple rule. Treat me with the same kindness and love that I treat you. As long as you accept and reciprocate my love and kindness, you'll have a wonderful day. I promise. How about some breakfast? You must be starving."

Chapter 27

Before

The day after Thanksgiving, Brandi and Jack were back at the camp. She hadn't said a single word to Jack since last Saturday, and his fake injury stress test bullshit. Jack didn't seem to get the hint, still expecting her to go to their stupid camp in the woods for another weird Army training class. Brandi wondered if he had severe PTSD or something.

"You need to protect yourself from predators," Jack said.

Brandi rolled her eyes, too annoyed to keep quiet any longer. "Like bears and wolves? That's stupid. We haven't seen a single predator out here."

Jack shook his head. "I'm talking about human predators, which you aren't very good at spotting."

Brandi crossed her arms over her chest. "What the hell are you talking about?"

"That scumbag drug dealer you tried to run away with."

Brandi huffed. "You don't even know him. You weren't even there."

"I don't need to be there. I know the type."

"Whatever."

"Do you know how many young girls are assaulted, raped, and murdered?"

"Isn't that why you're teaching me to fight and shoot?"

Jack shook his head again. "It's not enough to know how to fight and shoot. I knew plenty of men who could fight and shoot better than me, and they're dead. They're *dead*, Brandi. Do you understand me?"

Brandi nodded, but she had no idea what her father was talking about. She thought he was clinically insane.

"Whether you're in the woods or in an urban environment, you have to use the terrain to your advantage. Follow me." Jack walked outside of their camp and uphill. He stopped and faced Brandi. "Do you think it's better to be uphill or downhill from your attacker?"

Brandi stared at her father, who appeared massive with the extra height advantage of the slope. "Uphill?"

"Exactly. Follow me."

Jack left camp and hiked to the trail with his daughter in tow. He gestured to the trail. "If someone was chasing you, do you think it would be smart to use this trail?"

"I don't know. I guess," she replied.

He faced Brandi. "The answer is no. People will take the path of least resistance, meaning a predator will use trails before they walk through brush or through the unexplored wilderness. Use that to your advantage."

"Okay, fine. Got it."

Jack clenched his jaw. "Where are the predators in an urban environment?"

"I don't know."

"Damn it, Brandi. That's the problem. You *don't* know. Predators are in bars and clubs and any other place where women are consuming alcohol or drugs. What should you do about that?"

"Don't go to those places?"

"*Exactly*. Don't go to stupid places with stupid people doing stupid things. What happens if you do?"

"I win a stupid prize?"

Jack pointed at his daughter. "*Exactly*. Nobody wants a stupid prize."

They continued down the trail. Her father identified a section of trail that narrowed between two boulders. "This would be a perfect place for an ambush. Do you know what an ambush is?"

"It's like a surprise attack, right?" she replied.

"That's right."

They found a bamboo grove, and Jack cut a few pieces. "Bamboo is incredibly useful."

"What are we using it for?" Brandi asked.

"You'll see."

They hiked back to camp. Along the way, Jack identified different terrain, explaining the tactical advantages and disadvantages of trees and rocks and hills and holes. He talked about using natural camouflage.

"White is the easiest thing to see in the woods, except for maybe orange. Don't wear white. I don't know why any woman would ever wear white. You're immediately at a tactical disadvantage."

"I'm not trying to be mean, but this sounds crazy," Brandi said.

Jack glared at his daughter.

When they arrived at camp, Jack led her to their shelter.

He gestured to the wood-and-mud shelter, "I want you to imagine that you're living in this shelter, all alone in the wilderness. Imagine that you're tired and you need to sleep, but you're worried someone might kill you at night."

Brandi wrung her hands, the hair on the back of her neck standing on end. "I don't think any of this is gonna happen."

"Listen to me. I've seen what men can become. Think about the worst crime you can possibly imagine. Is it in your mind?"

The girl thought about being stabbed to death.

"Whatever that is, I've seen much worse."

Brandi swallowed. "I think we should go home."

"*No*. Not until you've completed your training. What do you do if you're tired, but you're worried about someone killing you in your sleep?"

"I have no idea."

"You set a trap for him. Your trap never sleeps. Your trap is always working for you." Jack grabbed the folding shovels from his backpack.

They dug several small holes of two different sizes in places Jack thought an intruder would likely step. As Brandi dug these holes with her father, she figured the worst that might happen to an intruder would be a sprained ankle.

But then Jack produced scraps of plywood, a box of long nails, smaller nails, and a hammer from his rucksack. Jack hammered multiple nails through a plywood scrap, using two large rocks as his workbench, and the gap between to allow the nails to protrude from the plywood. Then he placed the plywood with multiple protruding nails in the bottom of a hole.

Jack stood over the hole, his hands on his hips, admiring his handiwork. "If the predator steps in this hole, those nails will go right through his boot. You can spread shit on the nails too. Give him a nasty infection."

Brandi twisted her face in disgust.

Jack turned to his daughter. "You need to do the next one. I need to know that you know how to protect yourself."

She shook her head. "This is crazy."

"*No.* It's crazy that you walk around thinking you're safe. Nobody's safe. Especially not young women like you. Let's go."

Brandi hammered nails through a scrap of plywood.

"Make sure the nails are straight," Jack said. "If they're bent, it won't work."

With Jack hovering over her, Brandi duplicated her father's gruesome foot trap.

The nail traps were installed in the larger of the holes they dug, but Jack had something much more menacing for the smaller holes. Jack grabbed some glue from his rucksack. Then he collected a few small squares of scrap plywood, along with some smaller nails and his hammer.

"This next trap is a cartridge trap," Jack said. "If you have the materials, these are quick and easy to install and very effective at incapacitating the enemy."

Jack drove a nail through the middle of a piece of wood. He instructed Brandi to cut a few two-inch pieces from the bamboo he had collected. The girl's eyes bulged at the shotgun shell Jack retrieved from his pocket.

"What's that for?" Brandi asked.

Jack placed the shell inside the bamboo, making sure it fit. "You'll see." He glued the hollow piece of bamboo to the wood, upright, so the nail was perfectly in the center of the bamboo. He showed Brandi the bottom of the shotgun shell. "See that little circle?"

"Yeah."

"That's the primer. If you hit that hard enough, the bullet goes bang." Jack placed the shotgun shell inside the bamboo sleeve. "It's important that the nail is lined up on the primer, and the top of the shotgun shell is higher than the bamboo sleeve." He took the wooden square with the bamboo-encased shotgun shell to one of the smaller holes. He placed it at the bottom of the hole. The top of the shotgun shell was at ground level. Jack placed his foot over the hole. "If someone steps here, the shotgun shell goes bang, and the predator is no longer a threat."

"Why would anyone step in a hole? You can easily see it," Brandi said with her hands on her hips.

"That's why we have to conceal the traps."

Jack and Brandi covered the traps with sticks, leaves, moss, and other natural debris to conceal the holes. His preferred method was to create a web of small sticks over the holes, followed by moss or leaves that were held in place by the woven sticks.

As Jack admired the first concealed trap, he said, "It's very difficult to tell that there's a trap here, especially if it's at night or if someone's chasing you."

By the end of the day, they had six concealed traps scattered around the camp. Jack packed his rucksack.

Brandi glanced at the darkening sky. "Are we leaving?"

"It's getting dark," he replied.

"We can't leave these traps out here," Brandi said. "What if an animal steps in it?"

"They're not that stupid."

"What if *we* step in one by accident?"

"We're not that stupid either."

"I'm not coming back here then. I'm done."

"If the enemy comes into our camp—"

"Please, Jack." It was the first time Brandi had used his name. "You're scaring me."

Her father exhaled. "Fine."

Chapter 28

After

Brandi sat up in bed, with a tray in her lap, eating her breakfast of French toast, fresh raspberries, orange juice, and coffee. Roger sat on a chair he'd moved to her bedside.

He tapped a single blue pill into his palm, held out the medicine, and said, "Take this with your food."

She hesitated.

"It's just naproxen. It's a painkiller." Roger showed her the container of Aleve.

Brandi put the pill on her tongue and washed it down with orange juice.

He watched her eat. "How's your breakfast?"

She swallowed a bite of her French toast and scowled at Roger. "Did you kill Colton?"

Roger furrowed his brow. "Who's Colton?"

"My boyfriend. At the waterfall."

"I thought the boyfriend was a ruse to scare me. You actually have a boyfriend?"

Brandi set aside her half-eaten breakfast. "He wasn't *actually* my boyfriend, but that's not the point. Did you kill him? I need to know."

Roger shook his head, his mouth downturned. "Of course not. I could never kill anyone. I take spiders outside. I'm a healer and a lover, not a killer."

"Did Harold kill him?"

Roger glanced over his shoulder as if checking to see if someone was watching. "I can't say."

"What about Matt? The guy that was with me at the cabin."

"I'm not a killer."

"What about the dog?"

"I let it go."

She wrung her hands in her lap. "What's gonna happen to me?"

"Well, after breakfast, I thought we could watch a few movies and cuddle in bed. I think it would be nice for both of us to have a relaxing day. What do you think?"

"There's no TV."

"Let me worry about that." Roger stood from his chair. "I'll be right back."

While he was gone, Brandi ate her breakfast.

Roger returned, wearing plaid pajamas and his shades. He carried a flat-screen television and set it on the dresser. "I wanted to be more comfortable for our snuggle session."

She cringed and averted her gaze.

Roger left again and returned with a cardboard box. He extracted a DVD player and some cords from the box. Then he set the cardboard box on the bed next to Brandi.

"Go ahead and pick what you'd like to watch," Roger said.

Brandi peered into the box filled with DVDs. There were movies and television shows—comedies, dramas, romances, thrillers, and even a few horror flicks. She couldn't even look at the covers of the horror movies. She picked up the DVD *Marley and Me* starring Owen Wilson and Jennifer Aniston. She remembered seeing the movie with her parents before their divorce. Tears filled her eyes. She must've been four. She pictured herself sitting between Jack and Kathy with a bucket of popcorn, her feet dangling from the seat. Her mom was so beautiful, and her dad was so happy.

"That's a good movie," Roger said.

Brandi looked up from the DVD.

He gestured to the tray of breakfast dishes on the bed beside her. "Are you finished with breakfast?"

She nodded.

He reached over her and grabbed the tray. She flinched from his proximity. He set the tray on the dresser top, removed his slippers, and sat next to Brandi on the bed. She inched away from him.

He frowned at her. "Will this be a problem?"

Brandi held up the DVD featuring the happy blond couple and the puppy pulling at his leash. "Can I watch this by myself?"

Roger sighed. "I cared for you; tended to your injuries. I made you a beautiful breakfast. I arranged for this relaxing day, yet you're not returning the same kind and loving energy that I'm giving to you. Do you think that's fair?"

Brandi stared at the lavender comforter.

"I think we both know you're not being kind or loving. Would you prefer that I match your negative energy?"

She shook her head.

"Would you like to cuddle together and watch *Marley and Me*?"

She nodded, still staring at the comforter.

"I need you to look at me and give me a verbal response."

She looked at Roger and whispered, "Yes."

"Yes, what?" He held out his hands. "I have no idea what you're saying yes to."

"Yes." She swallowed the bile creeping up her throat. "I want to watch the movie with you."

He smiled. "Okay." He stood, took the movie from Brandi, and loaded it into the DVD player. Roger returned with the two remotes—one for the TV and one for the DVD player. He sat on the bed and scooted against Brandi, sitting next to her and sharing the pillow she used to cushion the headboard. Roger flipped on the television and DVD player. It took him a minute of pointing and clicking to get the movie going.

As the opening credits rolled, he asked Brandi to lay down with him. He instructed her on how he liked to cuddle. Roger lay on his back, his head propped with a pillow, while she lay on her side, hugging him, her head on his shoulder. He smelled like soap and deodorant. Brandi thought she might throw up on him, but she concentrated on the movie, remembering better days, and her stomach calmed.

She tried to lose herself in the movie, to forget about what had happened to her over the past two days. But her dad's advice popped into her head over and over again until she stopped ignoring him. *Details matter. Details matter. Details matter.* As Marley made messes on the flat screen, Brandi glanced at Roger's face. She saw a little of his dark eyes under his sunglasses. She wondered if she could identify him without his shades and without his beard. She thought about the details of the night before.

Terrible images flashed through her mind. She wanted to forget, but as her father said, *Details matter.* So, Brandi thought about what she'd seen and what she'd heard. *Harold's a sadist. He enjoys hurting people. He gets off on it. Roger's different. He doesn't wanna hurt me, but he will if he has to. He slammed me against the wall that first day. He wants to control me, but he wants me to want to do what he wants. The fucking creep wants me to love him. It's like he wants me to be his girlfriend or something.*

He said he didn't kill Colton. Is he lying? Maybe Harold killed Colton. When I asked him if Harold killed Colton, he said he couldn't say, which sounds like Harold did kill Colton. What about Matt? Roger said he's not a killer, but he took Matt outside and I heard a gunshot. None of this is helpful. I need to figure out how to get outta here. I need to know more about what they're doing to me and why. They literally drug me every night, and every morning I wake up in this room.

Roger laughed, his entire body shaking, as Marley scampered down the street pulling a table with his leash. Brandi winced and pulled back.

Roger turned to her. "Are you okay?"

"I think so."

"Did I hurt you when I was laughing?"

Brandi touched her chest, just above the bandage. "My chest is sensitive."

"Sorry about that." He motioned with his finger. "Come back. I'll go easy on the laughing."

She settled back into his nook and thought about what he had just said. *I'll go easy on the laughing. He said something like that last night to Harold. What was it?* She closed her eyes. *Go easy. I'm the one who has to pick up the pieces.* Brandi opened her eyes and thought about what that meant. *Roger didn't want Harold to beat me up last night because he wanted to have his fun today. Is that why they're doing this? Is this some kinda sick game? Is that why they let me go? So they can catch me?*

She gasped, remembering something Roger had said earlier. *Don't worry. It'll all be over soon.*

Roger turned his head to Brandi. "Are you okay?"

Brandi sat up, rubbing her neck. "My neck's hurting."

He sat up and paused the movie. "You want a massage?"

She suppressed her cringe. "Could I have something else to eat?"

"What would you like? Salty or sweet."

"Salty."

Roger stood from the bed with a grin. "You're in luck. We have chips."

"Thank you."

Brandi didn't care about the chips. She needed a moment to herself to think. When he left, she replayed what Roger had said in her mind. *Don't worry. It'll all be over soon.* Then she remembered something else Roger had said to Harold last night. *I'd like to have another day.* She tried to think through her dull headache. *Another day for what?* Then it hit her. *Roger wanted another day with me. He had the first day with me. The second day was with Harold. The third day is with Roger. That means Harold gets me tomorrow.* A chill ran down her spine. *Harold's gonna kill me tomorrow, but that's not even the worst part. He'll hurt me so bad that death will literally be a relief.*

Chapter 29

Before

Brandi darted through the forest, branches whipping her. She glanced over her shoulder. A man dressed in black chased her, close enough to hear his breathing. She ran faster, her legs and lungs burning. Then she stepped into a hole, and there was a *bang*.

Brandi gasped for air and sat up in bed.

"Wake up," her grandmother said, standing over her. "It's processing day."

"I don't want breakfast," Brandi said, knowing what they had to do that day.

"That's good because you already missed breakfast."

Brandi stood from her bed, wearing her pajama pants and a sweatshirt. "I'm not doing this."

"You don't have a choice." Mrs. Hunt left her granddaughter's bedroom.

Brandi brushed her teeth, her hands shaky. She changed into her work clothes and joined her grandmother and father in the pasture. It was overcast and cool, her breath condensing in the air.

The goats were still confined to their shelter. The hens pecked around the pasture, unconcerned.

"Bring one out here," Mrs. Hunt said.

Brandi shook her head. "I'm not doing it."

Jack went to the shelter. He returned with a single male goat, pulling him along on a leash.

Brandi breathed a sigh of relief that it wasn't Billy.

Jack and Mrs. Hunt wrangled the goat to his side. Jack held the front and back legs together. The goat screamed like a baby in distress. Mrs. Hunt drew a knife from the scabbard at her belt. She grabbed the goat's mouth and bent the head backward, exposing his neck. In one quick motion, Mrs. Hunt sliced the goat's neck from ear-to-ear. Blood gushed from the gash. The goat jerked violently, but Jack still held tight to the animal's legs.

Brandi turned away, her stomach in knots.

"He's done," Mrs. Hunt said.

Brandi peeked at the murder scene. Jack hefted the goat on his shoulder and carried it to the garage, where he would eviscerate and butcher the animal.

Mrs. Hunt brushed off her canvas work pants. She pointed to the shelter. "Get another one."

Brandi hesitated.

"Go on."

"I said I'm not doing it."

"I know what you said. It's not a request." Mrs. Hunt handed Brandi the leash. "Go on."

Brandi went to the goat shed, her legs like concrete. Billy bleated at Brandi and rubbed against her, but Brandi ignored her favorite goat and leashed another castrated male. She tugged the stubborn goat to Mrs. Hunt.

Mrs. Hunt wrangled the goat to the ground and held his legs. The goat screamed and bucked.

"I could use some help," Mrs. Hunt said.

Brandi was frozen.

"You're making it harder on him. Grab his legs."

The girl knelt and grabbed the goat's legs, struggling to keep him under control. Mrs. Hunt retrieved her knife, tilted the goat's head to expose the neck, and sliced his carotid artery in one quick motion. Blood spurted like a fountain from the animal's neck. Brandi averted her eyes. The goat kicked violently.

"Hold tight," Mrs. Hunt said.

After the longest twenty seconds of Brandi's life, it was over.

"Take this one to your dad," Mrs. Hunt said. "He'll teach you how to butcher."

The goat was too heavy for Brandi to carry, so they set the carcass in a wheelbarrow. Brandi pushed the wheelbarrow to the garage.

Jack stood in the middle of the garage, a skinned goat hanging from the ceiling, with a wheelbarrow underneath filled with guts, skin, and fur. He took the goat down and placed it on a large plastic table.

Jack taught Brandi the basics of butchering, showing her how to cut and saw the carcass into different cuts of meat. Brandi wasn't bothered by the butchering, as the carcass no longer resembled an animal. Brandi imagined Billy having his throat cut by Mrs. Hunt.

"You all right?" Jack asked.

Brandi raised her gaze to her father. "I don't wanna kill Billy."

Mrs. Hunt marched into the garage. "You don't have to kill Billy."

Brandi glanced at Mrs. Hunt, then said to Jack. "I don't want *anyone* to kill him."

"He's not your animal," Mrs. Hunt said, butting into the conversation.

"Please," Brandi said to Jack.

Jack addressed his mother. "We could spare him."

Mrs. Hunt shook her head, a scowl on her face. "That meat has already been presold."

"I'll pay for it."

Brandi watched Jack and Mrs. Hunt argue, her gaze going back and forth like she was watching a tennis match.

"It's not about the money," Mrs. Hunt said. "I promised someone goat meat, and if I can't deliver, that's my reputation."

"It's one customer," Jack replied.

"There's also the matter of caring for an animal that serves no purpose."

"He's my friend," Brandi said.

"I'll call the customer if you need me to," Jack said. "And I'll pay for his upkeep."

Mrs. Hunt glared at Jack. "You coddle her." She left the garage.

"Thanks," Brandi said to her father.

Chapter 30

After

Roger was mostly true to his word. If not for her soreness and the creepy cuddling, the day would've been pleasant, especially in comparison to her night with Harold. Brandi had been well fed, hydrated, and medicated. They'd spent the entire day watching television—*Marley and Me* followed by the first season of *Friends*.

It was nearly dusk when Rachel finally found out that Ross was in love with her, thus concluding the first season of *Friends*. As the end credits flashed, Roger pointed the remote and turned off the television. Then he turned his head to Brandi and pressed his lips to hers. Brandi stiffened but didn't resist. His hands roamed over her battered body. He at least avoided her wounded nipple, sternum, and bruised neck.

"Please don't," she said. "I'm still in pain."

He drew back and exhaled. "We were having such a good time. Let's keep everything consensual."

"Please. It hurts when you touch me. I'm literally sore everywhere."

Roger stood abruptly and left the room, slamming the door behind him like a petulant child. He returned with a syringe.

Brandi scooted to the opposite side of the bed.

"This is for your own good. I don't want to have to hurt you," Roger said.

She exited the bed. "Please don't."

Roger half-circled the bed, approaching Brandi with caution. "I could tell Harold that I don't want you anymore. I'm sure he'd be happy to take over."

Brandi backpedaled, her hands up in defense. "Please don't hurt me."

Roger inched closer. "I'm trying not to. Take the injection, Brandi. The alternative is far worse."

It was the first time he'd used her name. Was this significant? Brandi realized that it wasn't, that he probably checked her driver's license when they had stolen her purse. She held out her arm. Roger gave her the injection and led her to the bed.

Brandi lay on the bed, waiting for the drugs to take effect. It didn't take long for her limbs to feel heavy and her vision to blur. Roger sat on the bed next to her. He removed her pajama pants and white T-shirt. She didn't fight. Even if she wanted to fight, she couldn't move her limbs. Roger slid her underwear down her legs. A man with a mask walked into the room. He sat on the chair next to the bed. The last thing Brandi remembered before it all went black was Roger mounting her and the man in the mask pleasuring himself.

Chapter 31

Before

Just before lunch, Brandi set her Algebra II book inside her locker. She glanced to her right, spotting April and Hanna chatting and giggling. Since Brandi had been called out as a slut for sleeping with Damon, she'd been shunned by her former friends, and she hadn't tried to make new ones. She was a pariah with her Amish-like dresses, bad reputation, and bad attitude.

Brandi grabbed her lunch and left the locker bank, brushing past her old friends, and giving Hanna a little shoulder check.

"*Hey*," Hanna said.

"Bitch," April said.

Brandi pivoted and glared at April. "Come over here and say that to my face."

April ignored Brandi and said to Hanna, "Let's go. She's not worth our time."

The girls sauntered toward the cafeteria.

"That's because you're scared," Brandi called out to their backs.

"She's tryin' to fight," a nearby boy commented.

Brandi took her lunch to the library. She waved to the librarian. The librarian waved back.

Brandi left her lunch on a round table. The library was empty except for the librarian, which suited her perfectly. She went directly to the animal section and browsed for a while, settling on a book entitled *Fun Facts About Goats*. She returned to her table and ate her peanut butter and jelly sandwich while she read the book.

She read that some animal researchers believed goats were as smart as dogs and just as capable of building emotional relationships with humans.

Brandi thought about taking Billy for a walk after school. He didn't mind the leash when Brandi was at the other end of it. *He probably needs some extra attention, especially after his entire family was murdered.*

She returned to the book, trying not to think about the processing day. She read that goats were among the first animals to be domesticated, around ten thousand years ago. They're very resourceful eaters, able to find food almost anywhere. Goats could even eat tree bark, which is rich in tannins.

The girl had a disturbing thought. *I can't leave Billy alone with Mrs. Hunt. She might kill him while Jack and I are in the woods.*

"Brandi?"

She looked up from the book to see her counselor standing before her. Mrs. Long was short and round, with a curly mop of black hair.

"I didn't do anything," Brandi said, figuring that bitch Hanna told on her for bumping her in the hall.

"I know you didn't," Mrs. Long said. "I'd like to talk to you in my office for a few minutes, if you don't mind. You can bring your lunch."

She accompanied Mrs. Long to her office. They sat across from each other at the counselor's cluttered desk.

"We're at the midpoint of the second quarter today," Mrs. Long said, "and you currently have a 3.5 GPA. If you keep this up, you'll be on the honor roll." The counselor smiled, her eyes sparkling. "It's such a wonderful improvement. I'm so proud of you."

Brandi blushed. "Thanks."

"I know you've had it rough with your mom's arrest and living with your grandmother, which makes your accomplishment that much more impressive."

"There's nothing to do at my grandmother's. I can do my homework or stare at the wall."

"Well, you're doing great. Keep it up."

Chapter 32

After

Brandi woke in the pale-yellow room again, her mouth cottony and her mind fuzzy. Sunlight filtered through the curtains. She peeked under the purple comforter. Like usual, she wore a new pair of underwear and nothing else. Fresh bandages had been applied to her nipple and sternum. Her body was still sore, but it was slightly better than yesterday.

She exited the bed and dressed in the clothes that had been laid out for her—a white sports bra, white long sleeve T-shirt, khakis, a belt, wool socks, and hiking boots. The clothes appeared brand new, but the boots were scuffed, likely the same ones she'd worn two days ago.

Brandi went to the restroom and checked her bruised and battered face. It was a little less swollen than the day before, but she still looked terrible. She rinsed her mouth out and downed several glasses of water. She sat on the toilet and peed. It burned a little. The hair on the back of her neck stood on end as she thought, *It's Harold's day. He's gonna kill me. No, he's gonna torture me so bad I'll wanna die.* Tears filled her eyes. *Will they even let me run again? Do I even have a chance?* Tears slipped down her cheeks. *I can't do this anymore. I can't.* She wiped herself, stood, and flushed. As she washed her hands, she heard her father's voice in her head. *Details matter.*

"What details?" she mumbled to herself as she exited the bathroom. "Like how I'm gonna fucking die, and you're not here to help me." She searched the dresser drawers for clues. They were empty as usual. So was the closet. She went to the window, parted the curtains, and thought, *Another beautiful day in hell.* By the angle of the sun, Brandi guessed it was about 10:00 a.m. She noticed that Colton's Tesla was gone. *That means they must've killed him and taken his phone. I wonder what did they did with his car?*

Brandi checked under the bed and lifted the mattress, but found nothing. She rotated 360 degrees, scanning the room. She surveyed the ceiling, noticing the intricate crown molding. Tiny little circles were embedded in the molding at regular intervals, eight in total. *What is that?* Brandi stiffened and dropped her gaze. *They're cameras.* Brandi went to the bathroom, grabbed another glass of water for cover and glanced at the crown molding. Cameras had been installed in the bathroom too. *Are they watching me right now?*

If this is a game, it's fucking rigged against me. They're literally watching me. Maybe that's why they don't lock the doors. Brandi returned to the bedroom, pacing and thinking. *If they're watching me, how do they watch me in the woods? Maybe the cameras are for what they do to me.* She cringed at the thought.

If this is a game, I need to know the rules. All I know is I literally wake up in this room. They give me these clothes to wear. The same outfit every day. Why? Brandi glanced at her outfit. She remembered something her father had said to her. *White is the easiest thing to see in the woods, except for maybe orange. Don't wear white. I don't know why any woman would ever wear white. You're immediately at a tactical disadvantage.*

"Shit," she said aloud. *They wear camouflage and I wear a bright white shirt. Fucking bullshit rigged game.* Brandi clenched her fists, angry at the unfairness of it all. *They think I'm some stupid little girl that they can play with like a cat plays with a mouse.*

How else are they rigging the game against me? It can't just be cameras and my white shirt. The doors are probably unlocked, like they don't care if I run, or maybe they want me to run so they can catch me. Or maybe Harold wants me to run. He likes the chase. He likes the fight. It's his day. I didn't run from the house on Roger's days.

She thought back to day two, when she ran from the luxury cabin. She remembered seeing the man in the mask peering into the window. She exited the front door and sprinted on the driveway. She outran the man, or at least she thought she had, and then another one appeared out of nowhere, that caused her to turn into the woods. Then she met Matt, and one of the men tried to shoot them. *He had to be shooting at Matt because they could've killed me when they caught me, but they didn't.* Then they ran to the cabin, but the men in the masks found them again. *It's like they always know where I am and what I'm doing.*

It hit her like a bolt of lightning. She remembered something terrible her dad did to her. She thought she knew exactly how they were doing it and exactly what they were doing it with. The best part was that she might be able to prove it and use it to her advantage.

Brandi glanced at the cameras and meandered to the closet. She shut herself inside and pulled the string, lighting the single overhead bulb. She checked for cameras but found none. She took off her boots and all her clothes and set them in a pile on the floor. She felt her underwear and bra. Nothing was out of the ordinary, so she put them back on. Then she checked her socks and T-shirt. No issue there either, so she slipped them back on. Then she checked her khaki pants, nearly certain the pants would contain what she was searching for. After an exhaustive search, the pants were clean, so she put the pants back on.

The only thing left to check was her boots. She felt inside. She removed the insoles and checked underneath. She checked the underside of the tongue and toe. Then she felt the top of the tongue and the underside of the leather near the eyelets for the shoelaces. In that tight little space, she felt a circular piece of plastic. She ripped it out and inspected it in the light of the closet. Some of the glue was still attached to the plastic disc that was slightly larger than a watch battery. Brandi smiled and shoved the device into her pocket.

Brandi slipped her feet back into her boots, laced them, and exited the closet. She opened the bedroom door and stuck her head into the hallway, checking both ways. It was empty, as she expected. She tiptoed downstairs, her heart thumping. Just like two days ago, there was a nice spread of muffins, pastries, and fruit on the kitchen island.

She devoured a blueberry muffin, watching the windows, expecting to see a masked man appear. She shoved another muffin into her pocket and hurried for the back door. She opened the door and sprinted into the woods, taking the same trail that Colton and Brandi had used for the photoshoot. Her body protested the running, her soreness flaring, but after several minutes her muscles loosened and the pain subsided.

She stopped near the waterfall, removed her white T-shirt, plunged it into a puddle, and rubbed the shirt against the muddy bottom. She wrung out the water as best she could and put on the dirty brown shirt. Then she continued running on the trail until she reached the lookout.

Wheezing and perched on the ledge, Brandi reached into her pocket and retrieved the little plastic device. She tossed it off the cliff to the jagged rocks below.

Chapter 33

Before

Brandi and Jack hiked on the path beneath the barren trees, leaves crunching under their feet, and their breath condensing in the air. Billy walked alongside the girl. The goat tugged on his leash, interested in a small clearing with a patch of dormant grass, and green chickweed.

"C'mon," Brandi said, tugging Billy.

Jack pivoted to her. "I don't know why you insisted on bringing him. He's not a dog."

"Goats are as smart as dogs." Brandi tugged again, getting Billy back on the path. "See? He's fine."

Jack nodded and continued hiking.

Brandi and Billy followed a few steps behind.

They hiked for an hour, finally ending on a rocky ledge. Brandi and Billy stood alongside Jack, taking in the valley below. The whoosh of falling water reverberated through the valley. Sharp rocks pierced the rushing stream, causing bits of whitewater, before ending in a fifty-foot drop to a circular pool.

Jack glanced at his daughter. "What do you think?"

Billy tugged on his leash toward a patch of henbit.

"What are we doing here?" Brandi asked.

"I thought you'd like to see this."

What Happened in the Woods

Billy led Brandi toward the forest edge.

"Where are you going?" Jack called out.

"Billy's hungry." Brandi tied Billy to a tree near the henbit. He grazed on the winter annual weeds while she returned to Jack and the lookout. She removed her backpack and leaned it against a rock.

"Your mom and I used to come here," Jack said, gazing at the waterfall.

"It's nice," Brandi replied.

"It is." Jack removed his backpack, sat it on a large rock, and faced his daughter. "I know I've been hard on you. Your grandmother's been hard on you too."

Brandi pursed her lips.

"When you're a new recruit in the Army, they break you down, so they can build you into a disciplined soldier."

"You're trying to make me into a soldier?"

Jack shook his head. "No. I'm trying to make you into a disciplined, competent, and successful adult."

Brandi frowned. "How's that going for you?"

"I'm proud of you."

She blinked several times, her mouth ajar. "For what?"

"You're doing a great job caring for the animals. I see you reading all the time. Doing your homework. Mrs. Long called me and told me about your grades. You're on the right path, and I'm very proud of you."

Tears welled in Brandi's eyes. She hugged her father. Jack was stunned for a beat, then he wrapped his arms around his daughter. Brandi cried against his chest. After a moment, she sniffled and disengaged from her father before wiping her eyes with her sleeve.

An awkward silence passed between them.

Brandi sniffled again. "I'm kinda hungry."

Jack rifled through his backpack, happy to have a task. He produced two granola bars. Father and daughter sat next to each other on a rock, overlooking the valley, eating their granola bars.

When Brandi was finished with her snack, she said, "Can I ask you about something my mom said?"

Jack glanced at his daughter. "Depends on what it is."

Brandi looked away. "Then I doubt you'll answer it."

"Try me."

"She said you were addicted to war—that you're a psycho killer."

Jack stared into the distance. "My first combat action was in Iraq in '03. It was the beginning of the invasion. We were tasked with capturing any high-value targets that were trying to escape into Syria. We set up a roadblock on the highway near Tikrit. There was an SUV driving very fast. We fired warning shots, but they kept coming. So we lit this vehicle up. Killed everyone inside. I was on the .50 cal., so I did most of the damage." Jack hung his head. "When we checked the wreckage, we didn't find any evidence that they were combatants or high-value targets. Looked like a family. Two little girls in back. Probably their parents in front. All shot to shit."

A gust of wind howled, the cold air causing Brandi to shiver and hug herself. "What happened? Did you get in trouble?"

Jack shook his head. "More civilians are killed in war than combatants. That's the dirty secret about war. Generals and politicians call it collateral damage. People are just numbers to them. But for me, I think about that family every day."

Chapter 34

After

After tossing the little plastic device off the cliff, she pivoted to the trailhead. Brandi could go back on the trail toward Colton's cabin, which was a terrible idea for obvious reasons, or she could take the trail deeper into the wilderness. She remembered something her dad told her. *People will take the path of least resistance, meaning a predator will use trails before they walk through brush or through the unexplored wilderness. Use that to your advantage.*

Brandi ran off trail, hopefully perpendicular with the main access road to Colton's cabin. Her hope was to eventually meet up with the road, but several miles away from Colton's cabin and closer to civilization, or at least an occupied cabin. As she ran, she hoped she was headed in the right direction. She thought about how her dad had wanted to teach her land navigation.

She ran as far as she could, until nearly hyperventilating. She stopped and caught her breath, hiding behind a gigantic oak tree. Robins and blackbirds chirped and sang overhead. Cicadas buzzed, the drone seemingly surrounding her. A chipmunk scampered about. Most importantly, she didn't hear any voices or heavy footfalls. She smiled to herself and retrieved the muffin from her pocket. While she ate, she thought, *They'll think I literally killed myself, but they'll eventually figure out there's no body. They won't know where I am this time, but they'll come looking. I need to keep moving.*

Brandi stood and jogged through the forest, hoping her sense of direction was somewhat correct. Her legs tired after five minutes or so, but she didn't stop. She simply walked, creeping through the forest, listening for any signs that someone had gained on her.

Where the hell am I? She meandered, searching for an occupied cabin or the gravel access road. She swallowed, her throat and mouth dry. *I need water.* As she hiked, she searched for overly green and wet areas, hoping to find a spring. Shortly thereafter, she didn't find a spring, but she spotted a gravel road to her right. She hoped it was the access road.

Brandi crept to the edge of the woods, concealed by brambles, but watching the road, hoping to see a car. It resembled the access road. She waited for several minutes, but nobody came. *I need to keep moving.* She continued hiking near the edge of the woods, watching the road for vehicles. She still didn't see any vehicles, but she came upon a log cabin. She raced to the cabin, excited by the prospect of rescue. Her shoulders slumped, and tears filled her eyes as she gaped at the red door of the little log cabin. She was almost right back where she started, at the nearest neighbor to Colton's cabin.

"What the fuck?" she said to herself.

The cabin appeared abandoned. Colton had said that he'd never seen anyone there. She tried the front door, but it was locked. She peeped into the front window, checking out the one-room cabin with a kitchen, bunk bed, and sitting area. She spied the sink and thought, *Water.* Brandi checked the windows and the back door. Everything was locked. She found a softball-sized rock and broke a pane of glass, just above the lock on a rear window. She reached through the broken pane and unlocked the window. Even though it was unlocked, she struggled and grunted as she forced the window open.

What Happened in the Woods

Brandi crawled inside the window. She went to the sink and turned the spigot, but no water came. "Shit." The kitchen was quite spartan with a wood table, two chairs, a counter, drawers, a cupboard, and no electrical appliances. She opened a few drawers. One drawer was filled with mismatched forks, spoons, and steak knives. Another was filled with Ziploc bags. Another held random junk. She opened the cupboard over the counter and found two unopened bottles of water and some homemade deer jerky in a Ziploc bag. She opened another cupboard door and found a mostly full bottle of whiskey.

A dog barked in the distance, causing Brandi to startle. She crept to the front window and peered outside. Scout led Matt toward the cabin. She grinned and hurried outside, meeting them on the driveway.

"Oh my God. I thought you were dead." The young woman hugged Matt, her hands touching his backpack.

Scout barked and jumped on them both.

When they separated, Matt said, "I thought you were dead too. I thought Scout was taking me to your body."

Brandi glanced at the gravel road. The cabin was partially concealed by the trees but still visible from the road. "We should go inside. Someone might see us."

They entered the cabin. Matt shut the door behind them.

Brandi bent down and hugged Scout. She stood while Scout circled her legs. "I heard them shoot you. What happened?"

"They shot next to my ear." Matt touched his right ear. "I still can't hear right. Then they injected me with something, and I woke up in a root cellar in that cabin where we were. The hatch was under that bear skin rug. It was completely dark and terrifying. Thankfully, Scout was with me, but I thought we'd die down there. We were in there for a whole day. Then, when I woke up this morning, the hatch was open. Just like that. It doesn't make any sense."

"Did you call the police?"

"They took my phone."

Brandi's eyes widened. "Oh my God. They might be tracking you. Take off your shoes. That's where they put my tracker."

"I didn't think of that." Matt set his backpack on the floor. He bent down and unlaced his hiking shoes.

When he bent down, Brandi saw a handgun imprinted on the small of his back. Her mind churned, trying to make sense of it. Brandi gaped at Matt, thinking about running. He wouldn't be able to catch her with his shoes untied. But she was frozen like a deer in headlights, her mind refusing to believe the betrayal.

Matt stood and eyed the young woman. "What's wrong?"

Brandi backpedaled. She thought about running and diving through the open window or attacking Matt, and trying to take the gun. Her overthinking eliminated her options as Matt drew the handgun from the small of his back.

He aimed the gun at her chest, his grip awkward, and his hand trembling. "Don't move or you're dead."

Brandi thought, *I'm dead either way*.

Matt reached into the front pocket of his cargo pants and retracted a walkie-talkie. He held the gun in his left hand, the barrel shaking. He pressed the talk button and said, "I got her. She's in cabin number three."

Brandi recognized the Beretta 92 handgun. She tilted her head and glanced at the rear safety. The red dot wasn't exposed, meaning the gun was still on safe. She doubted there was a bullet in the chamber, and she doubted Matt was very comfortable with the weapon.

"We're on our way," Roger said through the walkie-talkie.

"Ten-four," Matt replied.

As Matt shoved the walkie-talkie back into his pocket, Brandi lunged and grabbed the barrel of the Beretta. Matt pulled the trigger, but nothing happened, as the gun was still on safe. She twisted the gun, crushing Matt's finger in the trigger guard and causing him to let go. He groaned and held his broken finger. Brandi aimed the gun at Matt, flicked the safety with her thumb, and racked the slide in one fluid motion. To her surprise, a 9mm bullet ejected from the chamber.

Matt grabbed the barrel as Brandi fired into his chest, emptying the magazine, the *pop* of the bullets reverberating around the cabin. Matt's fingers slid off the hot barrel as he dropped to his knees. Scout barked. An acrid smell from the propellant filled the cabin. Brandi backpedaled, shellshocked, as Matt slumped to his side. His eyes were vacant, and his chest didn't move.

Scout whined and sniffed his owner, waking Brandi from her stupor. *Roger and Harold are on their way.* She stared at the sweet golden retriever, distraught over his owner's demise. She swallowed hard and searched the floor, finding the bullet she had ejected from the chamber. She loaded the bullet into the magazine and racked the slide, chambering the round.

Brandi went to Scout and petted his head with her left hand, holding the gun in her right. Then she gripped the handgun with both hands and aimed the Beretta at the back of the dog's head. Tears filled her eyes. "I'm so sorry." She placed her finger inside the trigger guard, touching the trigger. Her finger shook. Tears streamed down her face. She removed her finger from the trigger guard and pointed the gun at the floor. "This is so fucked up. Think. There has to be another way."

She inspected Scout's legs, thinking of a way to disable the dog without killing him or maiming him for life. She thought shooting him in a paw or his front leg, but she thought the bullet would shatter his paw or his thin front leg, possibly beyond repair. She thought about using Matt's Buck knife, assuming it was in his backpack, but she thought the chances of failure were higher with the knife. She thought about how much the goats struggled when her grandmother slit their throats. It's not like she had another person to hold the dog in place. Brandi remembered butchering goats with her father. Their back legs contained good meat. She petted Scout and felt his hindquarters. She found a spot that she thought would disable the dog at least temporarily, but hopefully not forever.

Scout stood over Matt as Brandi staggered the dog's rear legs, so the left leg nearest her was stretched back, allowing access for her to aim at the inside of his back right leg. She aimed toward the back of upper thigh, hoping not to hit any major arteries, and hoping for the bullet to go through. Scout was compliant, ever the obedient dog, holding the pose for Brandi.

"I'm so sorry, boy." She squeezed the trigger.

Chapter 35

Before

Over the winter, Brandi and Billy continued to visit the woods, and Jack continued to teach her survival skills, with an emphasis on cold weather survival, shelter building, fire building, and hunting. Despite the frigid temperatures, the girl enjoyed the time with her father, while Billy became more and more doglike.

Over spring break, many of Brandi's classmates went to the beach or lounged around their houses, spending countless hours on social media, playing video games, or streaming videos. But Brandi was happy to hike in the woods with her father.

The trees were still barren, but light-green buds showed on the oaks, and yellow flowers bloomed on the forsythia. Brandi and Billy followed Jack as they hiked off trail, far from civilization, in woods that were unfamiliar. She dressed in her cold weather gear for the morning, but with the sun rising, she was already warm.

Billy eyed a patch of green grass and weeds near a fallen oak. He tugged on his leash.

"Billy's hungry," Brandi called out.

Jack waited for his daughter.

She gestured to the patch of grass. "He wants to go over there."

Jack checked his watch. "We should take a break."

The girl figured they had been hiking for around two hours.

They walked to the patch of greenery and the fallen oak. She let Billy off his leash to graze, confident that he wouldn't go far. He bleated and hopped toward the grassy patch.

Brandi set her backpack on the ground and touched the fallen oak, gauging the five-foot space under the massive tree. She tried to push the tree, but it was rock solid. "This would make a good place for a shelter."

Jack set his .22 rifle and his rucksack on the ground next to Brandi's backpack. He checked the tree too, climbing and hopping on the trunk. Jack climbed down. "Looks solid."

The girl surveyed the unfamiliar forest. She pointed at the green patches of grass and weeds snaking up the hill. "I bet there's a spring there."

"Might be. You remember how to find clean water?"

"How could I forget? We've found like ten springs."

Jack smiled. "You think you know your stuff, huh?"

Brandi smiled back. "I've had a pretty good teacher."

"I've had a pretty good student."

"What are we doing? You've never taken me out here. Are you gonna teach me land navigation?"

"Not yet."

"Then what are we doing? Endurance training? I feel like we've been walking a long way."

Jack fished a granola bar from his rucksack and held it out to Brandi. "You hungry?"

She took the granola bar. "Thanks."

"Your mom will be out in a few months."

"I know. Two weeks after my birthday."

"We can go see her on your birthday."

Brandi opened the granola bar wrapper. "I don't know."

"Have you thought about what you'll do after graduation?" Jack asked.

She spoke with her mouth full. "I have no idea."

"What about college?"

She laughed and spit bits of granola on the ground. "My GPA is 2.2."

Jack was stone-faced. "You've been on the honor roll the last two quarters."

"Too little, too late."

"Not for community college. Lots of people go to community college for one or two years, then transfer to a four-year school."

"What would I even study?"

"What would you like to do, as a career?"

Brandi shrugged. "I don't know."

"You're good with animals." Jack gestured to Billy grazing nearby. "You trained a goat to be a freaking dog."

"But what would I be? I don't think people need a goat trainer."

Jack chuckled. "You could be a veterinarian."

"Don't they have to go to school for a really long time?"

Jack nodded. "That doesn't mean you can't do it."

Brandi frowned. "School's expensive."

"Don't worry about that. I transferred my GI Bill to you before I retired."

"What does that mean?" Brandi took another bite of her granola bar.

"It means if you go to an in-state college, your tuition will be covered for thirty-six months, and you get a monthly housing allowance, so you won't have to work."

Brandi took a few steps away from Jack and the fallen oak. She faced her father. "You would pay for my college?"

"The GI Bill will get you through undergrad. Vet school would be a lot more. I have some savings, but probably not enough to cover it. I could take out a loan. If this is something you want, we'll make it happen." Jack moved closer to his daughter. "You don't have to be a vet, though. You can be anything. A doctor. A lawyer. An accountant."

"An accountant? No way. I'd be bored to death."

"Think about it, and let me know. It's good to have a plan."

Brandi nodded. "Did you always wanna be in the Army?"

Jack shook his head. "I didn't have any other options. I'm not smart like you."

"You used to teach soldiers. You have to be smart to be a teacher."

"They're a captive audience."

"Did you teach them the same stuff you're teaching me?"

"Not exactly, but there are parallels."

Brandi crumpled the granola bar wrapper and shoved the trash in her pocket. "What test was the hardest? Like what was the thing that a lot of soldiers failed?"

Jack rubbed the stubble on his chin. "During Selection—"

"What's Selection?"

"It's a four-week course to get into a harder six-month course called OTC, which stands for Operator Training Course."

Brandi grabbed her water bottle from her backpack.

Jack continued. "During Selection, we had a difficult land-navigation course."

"What made it difficult?"

"One test they had to pass required that they travel eighteen miles at night while carrying a forty-pound rucksack."

"That sounds really hard." Brandi sipped her water.

"We made it a lot harder than that. Each successive test we gave them had a longer distance with less time to complete it. The final test was a forty-mile march with a forty-five-pound rucksack over rough terrain. We called it 'The Long Walk.'"

"Forty miles? That's crazy."

"The distance wasn't the main problem."

Brandi tilted her head. "What was the main problem?"

"The time."

"How much time did they have?"

"We didn't tell them. Uncertainty is difficult for people to handle if they're not mentally tough. Mental toughness is more important than physical toughness. I've seen some of the biggest, most athletically gifted men on the planet fail because they didn't have toughness here." Jack tapped his head.

Brandi nodded. She checked Billy, who still grazed the grassy patch. "Can you watch Billy? I have to pee."

"Sure."

She walked about thirty yards away and squatted behind a thick Hickory tree. She returned to the fallen oak and the grassy patch. Billy still grazed, but Jack was gone. Brandi surveyed the forest.

"Jack. Jack. Jack!" she called out.

It was dead quiet.

Brandi went to her backpack and noticed that Jack's rucksack was still there. *Maybe he had to take a shit.* Brandi climbed atop the fallen oak and surveyed the forest again, but she didn't see him. "Jack. Jack!"

Still no answer.

Over the next hour or so, she watched Billy graze, and she ate most of her lunch. But Jack never came back. *This is a test. It has to be. He wants me to survive on my own. That's why he took me someplace I've never been before. That's why he hasn't taught me land navigation. He wants me to make a shelter and to find water and food. But why would he just leave? Why wouldn't he tell me?* She remembered something he said right before he left. *Uncertainty is difficult for people to handle if they're not mentally tough.* Brandi stood and said out loud, "Okay. I can do this on my own."

She did a mental inventory of her supplies and tools. Jack's rucksack was packed with his lunch, two more granola bars for snacks, and a full water bottle. *I have enough food and water until at least lunch tomorrow.* Jack also packed a tarp, an axe, a knife, a shovel, a first aid kit, a flashlight, a roll of toilet paper, a metal cup, and a small cast iron pan. He also left his .22 rifle, although Brandi hoped she wouldn't have to use it.

After taking inventory, she made a simple shelter, using the fallen oak as the roofline. She didn't bother digging or insulating the floor as she didn't think she'd need the warmth of the earth, especially considering she had her winter gear. Instead, she cut and collected long branches, leaned a few against the oak trunk, and lashed them together with honeysuckle to form a frame. She draped the tarp over the frame to seal the walls from the elements. Then she collected many more long branches and placed them over the tarp, along with sod and moss for the cracks.

During construction of the shelter, Billy stayed close, but she kept an eye on him. The goat ventured up the slope, following the grass and the shallow stream, but he was easy to spot with his white fur.

The long walls were simple, but the two short walls of the rectangular shelter were more complicated. The wall facing the root ball of the tree was very short, only three feet tall, while the entrance to the shelter was five feet tall. So, Brandi hauled and stacked stone to form the short wall. She filled gaps with sod and moss. She cut the excess tarp to form the opposite wall, which doubled as a door, similar to a tent.

Brandi made a small bed for herself with a wooden frame lashed together with honeysuckle and pine bedding. It wouldn't be comfortable, but it would be better than sleeping on the ground.

Finally, she dug a fire pit, just outside the door to the shelter, and lined it with stones. She dug down about one foot, wanting to be certain her flames didn't touch the fallen oak overhead. Her fires were usually only two feet tall, and with the extra foot, the oak was six feet above.

As the afternoon sun fell from the sky, she called for Billy, who trotted over like an obedient dog. She didn't want him wandering the forest at dusk, as she knew the forest was likely unsafe for him. She locked Billy in his shelter at the farm at night. This was no different. She had never seen a bear in the woods, but she had seen coyotes on several occasions. Brandi's stomach turned. *It's probably more dangerous for Billy out here.*

She made a fire with her flint fire starter, thinking that it would provide a deterrent to any possible predators. She sat by the fire on a log she'd rolled from nearby, eating Jack's lunch for dinner. Billy hovered next to her, begging for food. She gave him a little bread, conscious not to give him too much, as it wasn't good for him.

It was colder that night than Brandi had anticipated. She slept in her winter gear, and Billy snuggled with her. His warm body was a welcome comfort. She listened in the dark, hearing the hoots of an owl, the flashlight in her hand. When she got scared, she flicked it on, illuminating her shelter. Then she flicked it off, not wanting to waste the batteries. She thought about seeing Jack tomorrow morning, showing off her shelter and making him proud. She drifted off to sleep, a small smile on her lips.

Chapter 36

After

The gunshot popped. Scout yelped, quickly limped to the corner of the cabin, and lay on the floor. The dog whined and glared at Brandi.

She winced. "I'm so sorry, boy."

Brandi opened Matt's backpack, noticing a black hoodie inside, along with his shovel, knife, and other items. She shoved the gun into the backpack and raced to the kitchen. She collected various supplies: the whiskey, the bottled waters, and the deer jerky. She thought about something her dad had taught her. She opened the silverware drawer and grabbed all the steak knives. Realizing that the steak knives would make noise in the backpack, she grabbed Matt's hoodie and wrapped the knives in the soft cotton. Then she zipped up and shouldered the backpack. She jogged to the front window and peered outside.

Two men on ATVs parked in the driveway, both wearing those hideous masks with black zippers for mouths. She figured it was Roger and Harold. The ATVs were weirdly silent, like Colton's Tesla. Brandi ran to the back door and slipped outside, shutting the door behind her.

She sprinted into the woods, directly away from the cabin. She thought she had escaped without being seen, but she heard faint voices near the cabin.

"Over there. I think I saw something," Harold said.

Brandi hid behind a tree.

"Where? I don't see anything," Roger replied.

"She must've moved, but I know where she is."

Brandi scanned the forest, searching for a place to hide. She low crawled toward a decomposing fallen tree. She went under the massive oak, crawling as close to the base of the fallen beast as possible. Large pieces of bark littered the forest floor. Small trees, shrubs, and brambles had grown up around the fallen oak, taking advantage of the sunlight from the recently opened tree canopy and providing concealment for Brandi. She rifled through the backpack, finding Matt's Buck knife in its sheath. She set the backpack against the stump and unsheathed the knife. She curled into a ball, making herself small but holding the knife, ready to strike. Whatever happened, she planned to fight. She grabbed a large piece of bark and leaned it against her, camouflaging her further.

Heavy footsteps jogged her way. They stopped very close.

"She was right here," Harold said, sounding like he was only a few feet away. "Fucking cunt."

"Did you see white? Did you see her shirt?" Roger asked.

"I saw something brown, but it looked like a person."

"Could've been a deer."

Brandi was thankful for her muddy T-shirt.

"This is a fucking problem," Harold said.

"We'll find her," Roger replied. "It's a long way to civilization on foot."

"We need another dog."

"I know someone locally with bloodhounds. I can have a dog out here in three hours, maybe less."

"Get the bloodhound. I'll make sure she doesn't use the road."

"What about Matt's body?"

"After we take care of her."

"And Scout?"

"I'll put him down."

"That's not necessary," Roger said.

Harold grunted. "You and Matt were always too fucking soft for this. How do you plan on explaining a bullet wound to a vet?"

"I'll treat the dog."

"Get that bloodhound first."

Chapter 37

Before

Brandi woke to beautiful songs sung by robins and blackbirds. Billy stared at her, as if worried she might be dead. He bleated and nuzzled her. She smiled and petted her friend.

She moved the stone aside that held the tarp door shut, opened the flap, and stepped outside. Billy hopped out and trotted toward the green patch. Charred wood and ash remained in the fire pit. It was cool, but warmer than the previous morning, and cloudless overhead. She checked her surroundings, hoping to see Jack, but she was alone.

He'll be here later. It's a long hike. He should be here by lunchtime at the latest.

Brandi ate a granola bar for breakfast and drank the rest of the water. *The next step is to find safe drinking water.*

Billy grazed from the green patch. She grabbed her shovel, both empty water bottles, and joined her pet goat. A very shallow stream flowed through the green patch. She followed the stream uphill, where it disappeared and reappeared several times. Like she'd done many times before, she found what she thought was the source of the spring. It was here that she dug and created a little well for drinking.

Brandi let the dirt and debris settle, then filled her water bottles. She drank the cold, clean water, smiling to herself. She returned to camp with full water bottles and grabbed Jack's knife. Billy bleated, causing the girl to startle and check on her friend. He appeared normal, but she joined him at the grazing patch. Unfortunately, he'd already eaten much of the chickweed, although Brandi found some more further up hill. She cut the chickweed with her knife and ate the winter annual plant raw. It wasn't filling, but it was quite mild, tasting like lettuce. She ate as much of it as she could before Billy made his way up the hill. It wouldn't be long before there were no edible herbs to eat in the area.

For lunch, she ate half a granola bar and some more chickweed. She wanted to eat the entire bar, but it was the last of her food. She thought she should've rationed her food better. Jack didn't show by lunch, as she had hoped. She wondered if he hurt himself. *Maybe he's injured somewhere in the woods.*

After lunch, she took Billy on the leash, exploring the surrounding areas, searching for other food sources, and Jack. She'd already walked uphill for spring water, so she walked directly downhill from her camp, no more than four hundred yards. She didn't want to get lost. She moved slowly through the woods, letting Billy browse on low branches and herbaceous weeds. Along the way, Brandi collected cleavers, stinging nettles, and wild leeks.

She used her winter gloves to collect the nettles, as the plants had hollow hairs on the leaves and stems, which acted like hypodermic needles, injecting histamine that produced a stinging irritation to the skin.

On the way back to camp, she heard the snap of a twig. She startled, her heart pounding. She scanned the forest but didn't see anything unusual. Whatever it was, it sounded big. Brandi hurried back to camp with Billy in tow. She thought, *I should've brought the .22.*

Back at camp, she grabbed the rifle, checked the magazine, and opened the bolt. No bullet was in the chamber, and there were ten bullets in the magazine. She reloaded the magazine and worked the bolt-action, loading a bullet in the chamber. She double-checked that the gun was on safe. It was. She didn't want an accidental discharge injury, especially in the woods all alone. She wondered if she *was* alone. A shiver snaked down her spine.

Brandi kept the rifle nearby as she boiled the stinging nettles in the metal cup, eliminating the sting, along with the cleavers and the wild leek bulbs, which created a soup with mushy greens. It was packed with nutrients, but it wasn't very caloric. Her soup and final half granola bar weren't a terrible dinner, but she was still hungry.

Chapter 38

After

As their footsteps receded in the distance, Brandi removed the big chunk of bark she had been hiding behind. Pill bugs scurried over her body, searching for decomposing wood. She brushed off the bugs and crawled out from under the fallen oak with the backpack.

Brandi opened the pack, doing a more thorough inventory of her supplies: one Buck knife, one folding shovel, one hoodie with an Atari logo, fifteen steak knives, one Ziploc bag filled with deer jerky, two unopened sixteen-ounce plastic water bottles, one mostly full bottle of whisky, two protein bars, lip balm, a pack of tissues, two stainless steel dog bowls, an empty Ziploc bag with remnants of dry dog food, and a thirty-two-ounce stainless steel water bottle—half full. She repacked her gear, except for the Buck knife and scabbard, which she attached to her belt for easy access. Brandi thought about her next move.

She couldn't go to the road, as Harold said he'd be watching there. She didn't want to go in the direction of Colton's cabin or the one that Matt took her to. So she decided to hike away from the road, deeper into the wilderness. *If I don't find help, they'll eventually catch me with that dog. Roger said he'd be able to get the dog in three hours or less. I'll hike as quickly as I can for an hour, but if I*

What Happened in the Woods

don't find anyone, I'll have to find some good terrain to defend. How will I even know if I've been hiking for an hour without a phone or a watch? I guess I'll have to estimate.

Brandi hiked quickly, staying away from any human trails. Along the way, she drank the unopened waters and ate both protein bars. She stashed the trash in her backpack, not wanting to leave any clues to her whereabouts beyond her scent. As she hiked, she saw no signs of civilization, not even a hiking trail. The farther she went, the more she realized she was all alone in the middle of nowhere. Eventually, it would be her and them. She wondered if she could mask her scent somehow. *I can't hide with a bloodhound on my ass.* She did a mental inventory of her supplies. *That might work, but there's only one way to know for sure.*

The terrain steepened, with Brandi hiking slightly uphill. She stumbled upon a narrow game trail, framed with mountain laurels. As she continued on the trail, it narrowed further, the branches of the mountain laurels brushing against her. Her dad spoke to her. *People will take the path of least resistance, meaning a predator will use trails before they walk through brush or through the unexplored wilderness. Use that to your advantage.* Brandi thought, *The dog is gonna lead them here, and they're gonna walk on this trail. Single file too. It's too narrow to walk side-by-side.*

The *whoosh* of rushing water sounded in the distance. She hiked faster, buoyed by the water. She knew if you followed a stream long enough, you were likely to find people. She continued on the game trail for another quarter mile or so, the *whoosh* of water increasing.

The game trail ended, opening to a cliff with a stream twenty feet below. Brandi surveyed the scenic green valley, searching for signs of humanity. She saw nothing but wilderness. A few large boulders sat haphazardly around the cliff. She stared at the boulders, the wheels turning in her mind. She pivoted and checked the narrow game trail. Then she went to the cliff and peered over the edge.

She said aloud, "This is it."

Chapter 39

Before

That night, Brandi lay in her makeshift bed with Billy, her rifle propped against the wall within reach. Coyotes howled in the distance, causing the girl's heart to pound. She wondered if the coyotes could smell Billy. *They're too far away.* The coyotes quieted, and she drifted off to sleep.

Coyotes howled, jolting Brandi from her slumber. She blinked, trying to see in the total darkness of the shelter. She groped about the makeshift bed for her flashlight. The coyotes howled again. They sounded close.

She found the flashlight and illuminated the shelter.

Billy bleated.

"*Shh.*" Brandi grabbed her rifle. She aimed the gun and the flashlight at the tarp door, knowing the plastic cover was no match for a human or a coyote.

After a short time, her shoulders tired, and she lowered the rifle. She listened to the sounds of the forest. The owl hooted. Something small scurried nearby. Then heavier steps. Many steps. Likely several creatures.

Brandi aimed her rifle and flashlight at the tarp door again. She flicked off the safety, her stomach in her throat.

The coyotes howled loud enough that it sounded like they were inside the shelter. Billy bleated and cowered.

She stood from the bed, her nostrils flaring. "Fucking coyotes." She slipped on her boots.

The coyotes yipped back and forth.

Brandi pointed at Billy. "Stay here." She moved the stone aside from the tarp door. She stepped into the night, the barrel of her rifle out front, along with the flashlight.

Five pairs of yellow eyes stared at her, no more than forty feet away. She shouted, "Get the fuck outta here!"

The pack scattered like rats.

Chapter 40

After

Brandi walked along the game trail, carrying the shovel, and finding the narrowest parts of the trail. It was here that she dug four rectangular holes that were about twelve inches deep and roughly the size of a very large boot. The soil was hard, and the folding shovel wasn't a full-sized shovel, so digging was arduous even for these small holes. But she worked at a feverish pace, knowing that time was running out.

She used the sturdiest steak knife to cut into the bottom of the holes and to carve out skinny little slits. She shoved the steak knives into the skinny slits at the bottom of the holes, blade side up. Then she used some of the soil that came out of the hole to pack around the blades for stability. The holes contained four perfectly spaced blades, except for one hole that only had three blades.

She guessed that she'd spent about thirty minutes on each foot trap, which meant she'd been working for about two hours. Additionally, she thought it had taken her about an hour to reach her location. Brandi figured if it took them three hours to get the dog and an hour to find her, she only had one more hour to prepare, and she still had to cover the traps. She wiped the sweat from her brow and thought, *I'm cutting it close.*

Brandi collected small sticks and used them to create a crisscross webbing over the holes. Then she covered the webbing with moss and leaves. The foot traps were obvious if you knew what you were looking for, as the covering of moss and leaves didn't match the game trail exactly. So she spread some more leaves around the game trail to make the traps blend in better.

As she spread the leaves, she heard barking in the distance. Her stomach twisted and her entire body tensed. She bolted to the cliff and her backpack that sat near the edge. She removed her muddy shirt and her sports bra and dropped them on the ground. The barking grew louder. Brandi grabbed the Atari hoodie and the whisky bottle from the backpack. With shaky hands, she doused the hoodie with whisky. She put on the sweatshirt with the hoodie up. Finally, she doused her pants and shoes, hoping to mask her scent.

A high-pitched scream came from the game trail.

Chapter 41

Before

A pack of coyotes picked at a carcass, yipping and growling at each other. Brandi tiptoed toward the scene, barefooted and empty-handed. The carcass was bloody, entrails spilling from the midsection. One of the coyotes moved, exposing Billy's vacant eyes.

Brandi woke, screaming and flailing. Billy bleated, bringing her back to reality. She sat up in bed, her heart thumping in her chest. Billy bleated again, standing next to the door. She slipped on her boots, grabbed her rifle, and joined her friend, petting him.

"You must be hungry," she said, opening the tarp door.

Brandi exited the shelter and squinted into the sunlight. From the height of the sun in the sky and the warmth of the day, she figured it was at least 10:00 a.m., maybe later. After the coyotes had decided to party in her camp, Brandi couldn't sleep until her exhaustion overwhelmed her fear.

Billy trotted to the nearby spring to drink and to eat the green grass and weeds. Brandi followed the goat, scanning the forest for coyotes. A chipmunk scampered about, circling a tree trunk. A red-winged blackbird squawked overhead, annoyed by her presence. A squirrel nibbled on a nut while watching the girl from one eye. Her stomach rumbled, angry at the emptiness. She thought about shooting the squirrel, but she couldn't even aim her rifle at the adorable creature.

After Billy was satisfied, Brandi leashed the goat and explored the forest, searching for food. Like the day before, Billy browsed on bark, low branches, grass, and weeds. She found more stinging nettles, wild leeks, and cleavers. In addition, she collected garlic mustard and dandelion leaves and roots.

While Billy browsed on honeysuckle, Brandi bent over, digging dandelion roots with her shovel. When she stood upright, her vision blurred, and she wobbled, nearly passing out before recovering her faculties.

My blood sugar's low.

A heavy footfall and the crunching of leaves sent a jolt of adrenaline through her veins. Brandi dropped her dandelion roots and grabbed her rifle that was leaning against a nearby tree. She surveyed the forest, rotating 360 degrees. She tilted her head, listening. It was dead quiet.

Brandi grabbed her dandelion roots, smacked them to dislodge clods of black soil, and shoved them into her backpack. She grabbed Billy's leash and hiked toward camp. She thought about her father, annoyed that he had left her in the woods for two days. *How long does he expect me to survive out here by myself? It can't be longer than spring break.* She did the math in her head. *Shit. That could be six more days.*

She cackled to herself and said aloud, "This is my fucking spring break."

Back at camp, she kept Billy tethered to his leash while she boiled her greens and leek bulbs. As she drank her soup, her hand trembled. After downing the soup, she ate every bit of the leftover mushy greens. Then she took the dandelion roots to the stream. She washed the roots in the stream and peeled them as best she could with her knife. From what Jack had taught her, dandelion roots were less bitter if peeled.

Brandi returned to camp and cooked her dandelion roots, which were earthy but quite mild and more calorie dense than her greens.

Chapter 42

After

"Don't leave me," Roger shouted from the game trail. The barking intensified. Heavy footfalls approached. Brandi grabbed the unloaded handgun from the backpack and hid behind a large rock, leaving the backpack and her shirt and bra near the cliff edge.

She crouched behind the boulder, peeking around the corner at the game trail. The bloodhound appeared first, barking and sniffing her scent. Harold fast-walked behind the dog, wearing his mask. He held the leash in his left hand and a pistol in the other.

The bloodhound stopped, sniffed, and barked at Brandi's muddy shirt and sports bra. Harold peered over the edge, likely looking for Brandi's body.

She heard her father's words. *If you're weak, act strong.*

The bloodhound barked at her clothes again. Harold holstered his handgun and picked up the muddy shirt. He said aloud, "Fucking bitch."

"Harry. Help me!" Roger shouted.

Brandi crept quick and quiet from her hiding spot, her empty handgun expertly trained on Harold, using the two-handed grip her dad had taught her.

"Put your hands up, motherfucker," she said with all the confidence she could muster.

His right hand twitched near his holstered handgun.

"Don't even think about it," she said, moving closer, her gun aimed at his center mass. "I'll put three holes in your fucking chest before you even touch it. Put your hands up or you'll end up like Matt."

Harold stared at her through coal-black eyes.

The bloodhound sat before Brandi's shirt and bra, signifying that he had done his job.

Roger groaned and called for help from the game trail.

Brandi spread her feet in a perfect isosceles stance. She dropped her aim to his crotch, lining up the front and rear sights. "Give me a reason. I fucking dare you."

Harold didn't move for a long beat, then he slowly raised his hands to head level.

"Put your hands behind your head."

He placed his palms on the back of his head.

Brandi hesitated.

"What's next, little girl?"

She clenched her jaw, still aiming through her sights. "Use your left hand and toss your gun to me. Nice and slow. Don't make me shoot your dick off."

He moved his left hand from his head across his body to the handle of his gun.

"Keep the barrel pointed down," Brandi said.

Harold retrieved the handgun from his holster.

"Toss it to me."

He tossed it, but very near his right boot. If she were to retrieve the gun, she would be within his grasp and even closer to his boot.

"Put your hand back on your head," Brandi said.

He complied.

Roger moaned in the background. The bloodhound still sat with Brandi's clothes, panting and watching the scene.

Brandi inched a little closer, just out of his reach, her gun still trained on his crotch.

"Turn around."

He hesitated.

"I said, *turn around.*"

He faced the cliff, only a few feet from the edge. The rushing stream cut through the valley below. Brandi inched toward the gun. While he was facing away from her, she reached out with her foot, placing her boot on his handgun. As she pulled his handgun toward her with her boot, he jumped.

Chapter 43

Before

Brandi lay in bed with Billy, holding the flashlight, the shelter pitch dark. Despite the soup and dandelion roots, her stomach felt empty. She had to be careful not to stand too quickly, as she was likely to faint. Her head throbbed.

I need some meat. I have to hunt tomorrow. She thought about the plethora of squirrels she'd seen scampering about the forest. Squirrel soup sounded pretty good.

She thought about hiking out of the forest, but she wasn't sure of the right direction, and in her weakened state, she wasn't sure how far she could go. And what if she got lost? *I should've tried that on day one when I had food. But I thought Jack would be back the next morning. I can't believe he did this to me. One day would've been fine. Maybe two. Three days is too much. It's dangerous. He's fucking crazy. Who the hell leaves their daughter out in the woods with coyotes and bears and fucking serial killers.*

As if on cue, the coyotes howled. Brandi flicked on the flashlight. "I'm done with this shit."

Billy bleated.

She sat up and stood slowly. She petted Billy and said, "Don't worry. I'm done with these fuckers."

Billy stayed in bed, taking Brandi's warm spot.

She slipped on her boots and grabbed her rifle. She moved the rock by the tarp door.

The coyotes barked.

Brandi crept to the doorway. She parted the door like a curtain, shining her flashlight, and placing the barrel of her rifle outside. Like the night before, five pairs of eyes stared back at her. She pressed the button, taking the gun off safe. She aimed at the nearest coyote, lining up the front and rear sights, and fired. The coyote yelped, and the others bolted.

Brandi emerged from the shelter, her flashlight cutting through the darkness. She worked the bolt action, spitting the spent casing, and loading another round. Her beam caught a coyote loping downhill. She gave chase. After a short distance, she found the coyote lying on its side, whining, a red bullet hole in its abdomen. She winced, her stomach turning. The whining intensified.

Tears filled her eyes. She aimed her rifle at the coyote's head and pulled the trigger.

Chapter 44

After

Brandi rushed to the edge, watching Harold smash into the creek, back first, creating a massive splash in the shallow water. She doubted it was much deeper than five feet. Harold hit the rocky creek bottom, then floated near the surface, motionless. The current took his body downstream about twenty yards before he stuck against a large rock.

"*Shit.*"

Brandi grabbed Harold's handgun. She'd never had experience with a Glock, but the semi-automatic pistol wasn't that much different than the Beretta 92. She checked the magazine and the chamber. Both were full. She couldn't find a manual safety on the handgun, like the Beretta, so she figured it didn't have one.

She went to the side of the cliff edge, finding a gentler slope down. Brandi shoved Harold's handgun in her pocket and slid down the steep slope on her butt, using small trees to slow her descent. From this angle, her view of the stream was obscured by shrubs and small trees.

When she reached the valley, she hurried to the stream to confirm Harold's death, but he wasn't there. She peered downstream, thinking that he had become dislodged from the large rock by the current, but she didn't see anything floating in the water.

Then she noticed blood droplets along the narrow shore leading downstream.

Brandi grabbed the Glock from her pocket and followed the blood trail. She listened intently, hearing the *whoosh* of rushing water and the *buzz* of cicadas. As she crept downstream, the rocky shore narrowed further. Trees shaded the stream and grew close to the water's edge. It was here that the blood droplets turned into the forest. Brandi hesitated. The hair on the back of her neck stood on end.

A hawk screeched in the distance.

As she followed the trail of blood with her eyes, a beast crashed through the brambles. She aimed and fired several times as Harold slammed into Brandi, tackling her into the stream. Brandi fumbled the gun on impact. Three feet of water broke her fall, but Harold's massive frame pinned her to the rocky stream bottom. Brandi thrashed and squirmed, desperate for air.

Then he floated, taking the pressure off Brandi and allowing her to surface and stand. She sucked in air, her chest throbbing from Harold's tackle. She scanned the water for the Glock. She spotted the gun and grabbed it, dipping her head back into the water for an instant. When she surfaced, she aimed the Glock at Harold floating face-down nearby. A red cloud surrounded his body. *Is he dead?* She watched him like a hawk, ready to fire at any movement.

The current pushed him slowly downstream. Brandi followed just out of his reach, in waist-deep water. His body drifted into a cluster of large rocks. She watched from ten feet away, the Glock trained on him.

After a minute or so, he hadn't moved. Brandi inched closer, her boots heavy underwater. She reached out and pushed on his shoulder. He didn't react. She poked him again, but he still didn't react. She set the Glock on a nearby rock, but out of Harold's reach, not wanting to submerge the gun underwater again.

Brandi grabbed his upper arm with two hands and turned him over on his back, the buoyancy of the water assisting with the task.

She drew back from the white mask with the black eyes and black zipper mouth. She reached for the mask, her hand trembling. She grabbed the bottom edge of the mask and removed it.

Harold's eyes were beady and too close together, wide open and brown, not black. His stubbly black-and-gray beard didn't appear intentional. Brandi cackled, the spell of the terrifying giant broken.

Chapter 45

Before

The squirrel zipped up the oak tree and onto a fat limb. It sat for a moment, watching Brandi. She aimed and fired. The squirrel scurried up the tree trunk, unharmed.

"Damn it," she said to herself.

It was the fifth shot she'd taken that day, all misses. She had tried to kill four squirrels and one rabbit. She needed some meat. She had briefly considered eating the coyote, but they were known to carry diseases and parasites. She did haul the carcass farther away from camp so as not to attract predators.

Brandi checked on Billy. He was about fifty yards away, tied to a tree, browsing on raspberry brambles. She removed her knit cap and itched her scalp, running her fingers through her greasy hair. She stretched the collar of her fleece and dipped her nose inside, catching a whiff of her body odor. *I seriously need a shower.*

She replaced her knit cap and crept through the forest, slow and silent, her rifle in hand. She spotted another squirrel in the distance. It held a nut in his little paws, gnawing away at his meal. Brandi thought the little guy was adorable, eating almost like a person.

She inhaled and aimed her rifle, lining up the front and rear sights. She flicked off the safety and fired. The squirrel fell to its side and shook as if it had been electrocuted. Brandi approached the dying animal. She thought about shooting it again, but she only had two bullets left. Thankfully, it stopped moving.

Brandi took the squirrel carcass and Billy back to camp, grabbing some nettles, garlic mustard, and cleavers along the way. She skinned and gutted the squirrel, diced it into bite-sized pieces, and cooked it in her soup.

The squirrel soup was quite tasty, but she was disappointed by the small amount of meat that the animal yielded.

That night, Brandi woke to the sound of heavy footsteps. Much heavier than a coyote, more like a person, like a *man*. She imagined being in the woods with a man. She thought about what Jack had said to her. *Do you know how many young girls are assaulted, raped, and murdered?*

Brandi flicked on the flashlight and grabbed her rifle. Billy lifted his head but then settled into her warm spot. She moved the rock from the tarp door, making it easy for someone to enter. She crouched by the end of the bed, propping her rifle on the bed frame and aiming at the tarp door. *If anyone comes for me, I'll be ready.* She only had two bullets left. It was doubtful she could take down a deer with two .22 rounds, much less a person. She would have to make her shots count.

She listened and waited all night for a man who never came.

Chapter 46

After

Brandi searched Harold's pocket, thinking she might need to use his car to get the hell out of the woods. She found two keys on a keychain that read Blevins and Associates. They resembled house keys, with the word Schlage embedded in each key. She shoved the keychain into her pocket.

Then she grabbed the Glock from the large stone and remembered Roger. *Shit.* She went back to the steep slope and used the small trees to help her ascent. A dull ache came from her chest as she grabbed the trees. It took her several minutes to reach the cliff, her feet squishing in her boots, and her wet clothes stuck to her body.

The bloodhound approached Brandi, wagging his tail. She avoided the dog, not sure if he was trained to bite.

Brandi crept down the game trail, the Glock out front, and her senses on high alert. She didn't see it, but she had assumed Roger was stuck in a foot trap. If that was true, *was he still stuck?* Brandi heard him moaning before she saw him. Around the bend, she spotted Roger, his right foot stuck in a trap. He knelt on his good leg, his head down, and his hands gripping his injured lower leg. His mask lay on the ground beside him.

As Brandi appeared, Roger reached for the gun on his hip, but the young woman fired twice. One shot missed, but the other hit him on his right shoulder, causing him to drop his gun.

Roger grabbed his shoulder and said, "God damn it; that hurts."

Brandi crept closer, her gun trained on the center of his chest. She kicked his gun off the game trail, out of his reach.

"I need to go to the hospital," Roger said.

Brandi peered into the hole. The four steak knives had impaled his foot, all the way through, the tips of the blades sticking out of his shoe. He had hit the trap perfectly. Thankfully, he had been wearing thin-soled hiking shoes and not boots, otherwise it might not have worked. She stepped back and lowered the Glock. "It's always about your needs, isn't it? You needed to play these fucked-up games with my life. You needed to drug me and rape me."

"Rape?" Roger held out his hands. "I was good to you. I never hurt you. I thought we had something."

"You're literally sick."

"I'm not him. You have to see that. I never wanted Harold to hurt you. I begged him not to hurt you. Please Brandi. If you leave me out here to die, you could go to prison."

She aimed the Glock at Roger's chest. "I don't see any police officers around."

Roger showed his palms. "Wait! Brandi, please don't."

"Don't worry. It'll all be over soon." She fired into his chest, pulling the trigger in rapid succession, gunshots *popping*, and shell casings ejecting from the chamber. She fired until she ran out of ammunition, and the slide locked back on the Glock.

Roger slumped forward, motionless. Brandi tossed the Glock aside and spit on his dead body.

Chapter 47

Before

Like the night before, Brandi woke to heavy footfalls. *Did I hear that, or was it a dream?* She flipped on her flashlight, illuminating the shelter. The beam was noticeably dimmer than the night before. Billy bleated.

"*Shh.*" She tilted her head, listening.

A twig snapped, sending a shot of adrenaline through her body.

Brandi climbed out of bed, slipped on her boots, and grabbed her rifle. Billy snuggled into her warm spot. She moved the stone away from the tarp door, making it easier for whoever was out there to enter her ambush. Then she took her position behind the bed, her rifle resting on the frame, and aimed at the tarp door.

Over the next hour, Brandi listened and waited, but she didn't hear the heavy steps. Her flashlight beam dimmed further, the batteries nearly depleted. She flipped off the flashlight, sure that she'd turn it back on if she heard the man again.

Maybe it was nothing. Maybe I was dreaming. But that branch snapped. It could've been a deer or something. But deer run in herds.

Brandi's eyelids were heavy. She shut them, feeling the tug of sleep. She opened them, but the interior of the shelter was pitch black. She flipped on the weak beam of the flashlight, illuminating the shelter. Her eyes closed again. She opened her eyes and slapped her face, trying to hold her eyes wide open. The girl put both hands on her rifle and aimed at the tarp door again, listening for the man.

A while later, her vision blurred. Her eyelids were too heavy to resist. After staying up most of the night before, she knew sleep was inevitable. *I'm being paranoid. There's nobody out there.* She leaned her rifle against the wall and climbed back into bed, next to Billy's warm body. She thought, *I'll wake up if I hear something.*

Brandi drifted off to a deep sleep.

Her bedroom door opened, and a large man appeared in the doorway. She covered her head with her blanket. The man crept to Brandi's bedside. He stood over her, his breathing raspy. The girl trembled under the covers, her eyes sealed shut. She braced herself, expecting the man to remove her covers, but he simply picked her up, covers and all, and carried her from her bedroom.

Barking woke Brandi. She sat up in bed, her heart racing. Dim light came from the corner of the shelter, where the tarp had been parted. It was then that she noticed Billy wasn't there. She sprang from her bed, grabbed her rifle, and bolted from the shelter.

A short distance away, four coyotes surrounded and fed on a carcass with white fur. Brandi aimed her rifle in their direction and fired wildly. The coyotes scattered. She ran to Billy, or more accurately, what was left of him. Billy's neck was bloody. Chunks of flesh had been eaten from his thigh, shoulder, and rump. His blue eyes were wide open.

Brandi sank to her knees and sobbed.

Chapter 48

After

Brandi left Roger's body. She glanced over her shoulder not to see the man she'd killed but to see if the bloodhound was with her. It was gone. She figured it had been scared by the gunshots.

A few minutes later, panting and paw steps came from behind her. Brandi pivoted. The bloodhound trotted to her, wagging his tail. He was a large dog with a black-and-tan coat, massive droopy ears, to go along with his droopy face, and bloodred eyes. Brandi bent down and petted the dog, needing his comfort and willing to risk being bitten. But the bloodhound didn't bite. He licked though. She hugged the dog around his neck and cried. Her body convulsed with her sobs, but the dog didn't pull away.

Brandi stopped crying and let go of the dog. As she did so, she noticed his collar. It read, *Fred*. She thought about returning him to his owner, but there was nothing else written on the tag.

Brandi stood, petted his head, and took his leash. "Let's go, Fred."

The young woman walked the bloodhound back the way she came to the best of her recollection. Over an hour later, she found the cabin with the red door, the nearest neighbor to Colton's luxury cabin. By this time her clothes were mostly dry, although her feet were still damp. She thought about taking the gravel access road toward civilization, but she knew it was a long way to the main highway, at least ten miles. She didn't think she could make it without food and water, so Brandi and Fred hiked a little over a mile to Colton's cabin.

When she arrived at the cabin, the sun was high in the sky. Brandi guessed it was around four in the afternoon. She checked the detached three-car garage. The garage doors were locked, and the keys she'd taken from Harold didn't work. She peered into the garage window, spotting two vehicles inside—a Mercedes G-Wagon and a Cadillac Escalade. *Are those Harold and Roger's cars, or Colton's?* She had assumed Colton only had the Tesla, but she didn't know that for certain.

"Shit," she said aloud. "I forgot to check Roger's pockets for keys."

Fred whined.

Brandi patted his head. "Don't worry. We'll figure it out."

They went to the side door of the cabin. She tried the door, but it was locked. Schlage was written on the deadbolt. Brandi remembered that the keys in her pocket had the same moniker. She tried the keys, and one of them fit, turning the deadbolt, and letting them inside.

Brandi shut the door behind her and inspected the keys in her hand. *Are these Colton's keys?* She examined the Blevins and Associates keychain. *I think Colton's last name was Ellis. But that doesn't mean anything. People have keychains from businesses.* A scale was embedded in the Blevins and Associates logo. *It looks like a lawyer's office or something. Maybe it's Colton's lawyer? Or maybe this isn't really his house? He could've been renting it, pretending to be a big shot.*

Brandi and Fred went to the kitchen. The muffins, pastries, and fruit from that morning still sat on the center island. She found a bowl in the cupboard and gave Fred some water. She guzzled several glasses of water herself. Once her thirst was quenched, Brandi grabbed the meat and cheese from the refrigerator and the crackers from the cupboard. She ate grapes and cheese-and-cracker sandwiches. She fed Fred most of the ham.

"I'm gonna get a dog when I get home," Brandi said to Fred. "What do you think about that?"

The bloodhound inhaled the ham, unconcerned about her musings.

"Then I'm gonna get a job at Starbucks. I heard they like pay for college. Maybe I'll take classes online or something. I'm gonna get my shit together. You'll see."

After their little feast, Brandi searched the cabin for keys, while Fred followed her around. She searched most of the lower floor, finding nothing, until she ventured down the hallway to the bathroom. She didn't expect to find keys in the bathroom, but she checked anyway. Nothing. She walked to the only other door on that hallway, the one that resembled an outside door. The deadbolt was labeled *Schlage*.

Her heart rate increased as she tried one of the keys from the Blevins and Associates keychain. It turned. She pushed inside, leaving the key in the deadbolt, and flipped on the light. Her eyes bulged. Fred meandered, his toenails tapping on the black tile. The walls were bloodred. Brandi entered, slack-jawed. A metal-framed bed with cuffs dominated the room. Whips, ropes, and chains hung neatly from one wall. A large wooden X was affixed to another wall, complete with metal cuffs at each corner. A chain was attached to a thick metal beam overhead.

Brandi imagined being attached to the chain with a dog collar. She shivered at the thought. She stepped across the room, pausing when she felt something odd underfoot. It was a drain.

Tools and a workbench sat in the far corner. Various pliers and a few hammers hung on a pegboard. Boxes of differently sized nails sat on the worktop. A massive metal wheel sat against another wall, on a track. Straps and cuffs were arranged on the wheel to fit a person. She imagined being strapped to the contraption and rolled upside down.

Brandi pivoted and shook her head, trying to drive the image from her mind. When she turned, she noticed a doorknob. If she hadn't seen the knob, she might've missed it, as the bloodred door blended with the walls almost perfectly. She opened the door. It was mostly dark, but she could tell it was a home theater. She flipped on the dim lights. Perfect for watching a movie.

Four plush leather chairs faced a massive screen. The walls were pitch black. Fred inspected the theater. One wall had shelving filled with DVDs, remotes, and a DVD player. Brandi ran her fingers over the titles, which appeared to be random. She pulled one DVD, *A Serbian Film*, which featured two angry male faces on the cover, one of them with a red filter. She skimmed the description on the back. It was a horror movie about a porn actor who was an unwitting participant in a snuff film. She placed the DVD back on the shelf and grabbed another.

The cover for *Cannibal Holocaust* featured the reflection of a dead woman on a video camera lens. She picked another. *Guinea Pig: Flower of Flesh and Blood*. Another horror movie. This one was about a man who drugged, tortured, and likely killed a young woman. The description was careful not to give away the ending. Brandi's stomach turned. She thought, *They literally tried to do that to me*. She tossed the DVD on the floor. It landed with the cover facing up, showing the severed head of a young woman.

Brandi regarded the extensive collection of horror DVDs for a long moment. Then she reached into the shelf and pulled a heap of DVDs onto the carpet. She stepped on the DVDs, the plastic cracking, and kicked them aside. She pulled more DVDs off the shelves, dumping them on the carpet until there was only one left. The final DVD stood against the far wall of the built-in bookshelf. It was titled *Funny Games*. The cover image featured a young man peering over his shoulder with a smirk, as if saying, *Watch this*. Brandi stared at the image, clenched her fist, and punched the DVD. Her straight right cracked the plastic and slammed the DVD against the end of the bookshelf, creating a hollow thud.

Brandi tossed the DVD on the floor and inspected the end wall of the wooden bookshelf. She tapped on it with her knuckle. It sounded hollow. She hit it harder with the base of her palm. The wood moved a fraction of an inch. She inspected the edges, noticing a tiny gap at one end. She gripped the tiny gap with her fingertips and slid open the secret door, which was about one foot tall and three feet long.

Behind the secret door was another bookshelf filled with DVDs, but these weren't slasher flicks. They were homemade DVDs labeled by numbers and letters: 1A, 1B, 1C, 1D, 2A, 2B, 2C, 2D, and all the way to 13D. She retrieved the first one, 1A. Brandi inserted the disc into the DVD player, playing it on the big screen.

A blonde woman fought with Roger, smacking him, screaming, going ballistic. Roger's sunglasses were askew. He wore a baseball cap. Roger called for help. A petite man wearing a black ski mask entered the room. *Matt.* They restrained the young woman, and Roger injected her with something. Brandi assumed it was the same drug concoction Roger had used on her.

Once the blonde was incapacitated, Roger removed her clothes and raped her. But to Roger, it wasn't rape. He caressed the woman and kissed her softly. He talked to her as if she were conscious. He told her how beautiful and special she was. He told her how he was falling for her. Matt sat in the corner, almost out of the picture, pleasuring himself.

Brandi stopped the video, loaded 1D into the DVD player, and pressed play. It was the same blonde from 1A, although she was battered and barely recognizable. She hung by her wrists from the ceiling. Harold was nude except for his hockey mask. Tears filled Brandi's eyes as she watched. Harold whipped the blonde until she was bloody. He bound her to the bed and raped her with a blade to her throat. The blade wasn't for compliance. It was for fear. He sliced her carotid artery, blood spraying as he spasmed. Brandi turned away from the screen, nauseated.

She stopped the video and wiped the tears from her face. *That would've been me.* She glanced at the videos, figuring they must've recorded her with Roger both times and with Harold on that cabin floor. She retrieved 13D, the final disk on the shelf. Brandi played the DVD, but it was blank. So she played 13C. She watched herself beg Roger not to do it.

Brandi stopped the video, not wanting to see what happened after he drugged her. If she hadn't killed them, she would've starred in 13D, which would've shown her death, like the twelve other women on that hideous shelf. She snatched 13A and 13B from the shelf, intent on destroying the videos of her.

Fred barked.

Chapter 49

Before

Brandi salvaged what she could from Billy's carcass. She sat before the fire, eating goat meat, her eyes glassy. She wore Billy's collar around her right ankle, over her boot.

After eating her fill of meat, she carried what was left of Billy away from camp, and she buried him. She marked his grave with a small stack of stones.

Brandi stood over his grave and said, "I'm so sorry, Billy. It's all my fault. I never should've moved that rock. I never should've brought you out here. You were such a good friend to me. You deserved better." She swallowed the lump in her throat and trudged back to camp. It was the first time in five days that her stomach was full.

It was only midday, but Brandi entered her shelter, lay in her makeshift bed, and cried herself to sleep.

Brandi woke with a sucking breath. Heavy footsteps approached her shelter. She grabbed her rifle and burst from the shelter, ready to fire.

A man showed his palms and said, "Don't shoot. It's me."

Brandi lowered the rifle.

Jack smiled. "It's over. You passed with flying colors. I'm so proud of you."

The girl tossed aside the rifle. "Fuck you. Billy's dead because you *left* me out here. He got eaten by coyotes."

Jack approached his daughter. "I'm sorry. I didn't think that would happen, especially with you killing one."

She cocked her head. "Wait a second. How do you know about that?"

"I was keeping an eye on you."

She narrowed her eyes. "That was *you* sneaking around and scaring the shit outta me."

"I wasn't trying to scare you. I was making sure that you were safe."

"Where the fuck were you this morning then?"

Jack dipped his head. "I'm sorry about Billy."

"I hate you."

Chapter 50

After

Fred barked and exited the theater. Brandi followed the bloodhound, the hair on the back of her neck standing on end. The side door opened. Fred exited the torture chamber, trotting toward the intruder.

Brandi retrieved the Buck knife from the scabbard at her belt and hid behind the door to the torture chamber.

"Hello? Uncle Harry? Are you here?" he called out.

She recognized Colton's voice. All the pieces of the puzzle locked together. She gripped the knife, thinking, *He's part of this. He literally lures the women.*

Fred barked in the living room, not aggressively.

"Did Matt get a new dog?" Colton asked. Then he called out again, "Uncle Harry? Is anyone here?"

Brandi imagined Colton seeing the mess she made in the kitchen, then eventually finding the open door to the torture chamber. She stood behind the door, her back against the wall, gripping the Buck knife.

Footfalls came from the hallway. Colton paused by the torture chamber door, no doubt wondering why it was open. Brandi heard rustling, followed by *chick-chick*, which she imagined was Colton racking the slide and chambering a round in his handgun. She saw the barrel of the handgun first, followed by Colton's hand, arm, and body.

As soon as he passed, Brandi took two quick steps and plunged the Buck knife into Colton's back, all the way to the hilt. He whirled to her and fired wildly, the *pops* deafening in the soundproofed space. Brandi and Colton fell to the ground at the same time. White hot pain along with blood streamed from the young woman's left thigh. She dragged herself across the floor, desperate to escape him. She dragged herself down the hallway, crawling, her injured leg useless.

Brandi glanced behind her, expecting Colton to emerge from the torture chamber to finish her off, but he didn't. She left a trail of blood along the hallway hardwood. She felt woozy. *I'm losing too much blood.* She removed her belt. Brandi made a loop with the belt and passed it down through the buckle, creating a double loop. Then she put the double loop over her boot and up her thigh, above the wound. Brandi cranked the tourniquet, grunting at the pain and pressure.

She thought the blood had stopped flowing. Colton groaned and wheezed. Brandi dragged herself back to the torture chamber, hoping Colton was incapacitated so she could take his phone. She peeked into the bloodred room.

He lay on his side, the knife still in his back, his gun on the tile next to him, but not in his grasp. She crawled toward him, dragging her bad leg. He wheezed, blood on his lips. He spotted Brandi and grasped the gun, but before he turned the gun on her, she wrenched it from his weak grasp. Colton coughed from the effort. Bright frothy blood spewed from his mouth, likely originating from his lungs.

Brandi tossed the gun aside and stared into his bulging eyes. "You're dying, Colton."

"Help me." He coughed more blood.

She checked his body, noticing the imprint of his phone on his back pocket. Brandi retrieved the phone, pressed the little button on the side to wake it up, and noticed there were no bars. She tried to open the phone, but it required a password.

"What's your password?" she asked.

Colton grunted and gurgled, blood bubbles coming from his mouth.

"If you want me to help you, I need your password," Brandi said.

He quaked with the death throes. Then he stilled.

Brandi shook him. "Colton. Wake up."

He didn't move.

"*Shit.*" She wasn't sure if she needed to open his phone for the Tesla to work.

Chapter 51

Before

Brandi gave Jack the silent treatment on the ride back to the farm. As soon as Jack parked, the girl exited the SUV and slammed the passenger door. She stalked to the farmhouse and entered through the front door. She followed the smell of cooking chicken and rosemary to the kitchen.

Mrs. Hunt opened the oven and checked her roasted chicken. Brandi stood in the kitchen with her arms crossed over her chest.

Mrs. Hunt shut the oven, turned to Brandi and crinkled her nose. "You need a shower, young lady."

"Do you know what he did to me?" Brandi asked.

Mrs. Hunt sighed. "I thought you'd be more appreciative upon your return."

Brandi drew back. "You *knew?*"

The side door opened and closed.

"If thou faint in the day of adversity, thy strength is small," Mrs. Hunt said.

"What the hell are you talking about?" Brandi asked.

Jack entered the kitchen.

"The Old Testament is full of wisdom," Mrs. Hunt said.

Brandi glared at her grandmother, then her father. "As soon as my mom gets out, I'm *gone*. You people are *seriously sick*."

Chapter 52

After

Brandi shoved Colton's cell phone into her pocket and dragged herself back to the hall. Fred appeared. He barked at the young woman, as if encouraging her. Brandi pulled herself along the hardwood, a sharp throbbing pain coming from her left thigh. She dragged herself through the living room, Fred barking his encouragement along the way.

At the side door, she sat upright, reached for the door handle, and opened it. Then she dragged herself outside, followed by Fred. Thankfully, the Tesla was parked very close to the cabin. At the driver's side door, she sat up, her back against the car. She grunted and pushed herself upright on her good leg. She pushed the embedded handle, and the door popped open an inch, then she opened it wide.

"That's a good sign, Fred," Brandi said.

Fred wagged his tail, his head cocked.

"You wanna go for a ride?"

Fred must've understood that as he brushed past Brandi, rubbing against her wound and sending a shooting pain through her leg. He hopped into the Tesla and settled into the passenger seat.

Brandi grimaced and recovered from the wave of pain. She put her back to the open door and sat using her good leg. She hit her head on the top of the door frame as she dropped into the seat, but she didn't notice that pain. Now she sat in the seat sideways, both of her feet on the driveway. She moved her right leg into the car with ease. Then, she grunted and helped her left leg into the car with her hands.

She sat in the driver's seat and shut the door. The car smelled like Colton's cologne. It triggered Brandi's gag reflex. She powered down the windows, letting fresh air and birdsong inside. The car was already on, the screen showing all the options. Brandi pictured Colton driving the car, trying to remember what he did. She pushed the gear on the steering column upward, but nothing happened. A message on the screen appeared, telling Brandi to put her foot on the brake.

Brandi depressed the brake and pushed up on the gear. The back-up camera showed on the tablet screen. She moved her right foot from the brake to the accelerator, and the car motored backwards, sounding like a spaceship. She turned, backing the car into the front yard. She braked and then pushed down on the gear, putting the EV into drive. Brandi pressed the accelerator a little too hard. The car lurched forward, causing Fred to whine.

She let off the accelerator, righted the EV, and glanced at her companion. "I'm sorry, boy."

Brandi drove away from the luxury cabin to the access road. She turned on the road and headed back to civilization, each bump and divot sending a shooting pain radiating from her thigh. She glanced down at her leg, noticing that her boot was covered in blood. She wondered if she had tied the tourniquet tight enough.

As she drove down the road, her vision blurred. Despite this, she kept the car pointed forward, her foot on the accelerator. Fred barked. The edges of her blurry vision blackened. Fred barked again and again. Then those black edges expanded until there was nothing but darkness.

Chapter 53

Before

Brandi lay in bed, hugging her stuffed golden retriever, and staring out the window at the sunrise. Her bedroom door opened, followed by clomping steps.

"Get up. You need to do your chores," Mrs. Hunt said.

The girl didn't move.

Mrs. Hunt half-circled her bed, blocking the sunrise with her large frame. "I said, get up."

Brandi sat up and set her stuffed animal aside. "Isn't gluttony a sin?"

"Excuse me, young lady?"

"Gluttony? Isn't that being a big fat ass, like you?"

Mrs. Hunt grabbed Brandi by the elbow and yanked her from the bed. They stood toe to toe. The older woman bent down, close enough to smell the coffee on her breath. "You will *not* talk to me like that in my own home."

The girl raised one side of her mouth in contempt. "Fat. Ass. Bitch."

Mrs. Hunt reared back and slapped Brandi across the face. "You are Satan's child."

Brandi touched her stinging cheek.

"Do your chores, *now*."

Brandi clenched her fist and threw a perfect right cross—just as her dad had taught her—that connected with her grandmother's jaw. Mrs. Hunt fell awkwardly, hitting the side of the bed before falling to the floor in a heap.

Jack entered Brandi's bedroom. "What the hell's going on?"

Mrs. Hunt groaned.

Jack rushed to his mother and knelt next to her. "Are you okay?"

"I think so."

"What happened?"

Mrs. Hunt pointed at Brandi. "She hit me! It was a cheap shot."

The girl walked over her bed to get away from them.

"Where do you think you're going?" Jack said, his voice booming.

Brandi faced her father, the bed acting as a buffer. "She literally deserved it. She wanted the smoke, so I gave it to her."

Jack helped his mother to her feet. "I don't care what you think your grandmother did; there is *absolutely no excuse* for hitting her. What is wrong with you?"

Brandi puckered her face, as if she'd eaten a lemon. "What's wrong with me? What's wrong with *you* and your *crazy* mother?"

"She needs to be disciplined, *physically*," Mrs. Hunt said to Jack.

Brandi's eyes widened.

Mrs. Hunt crossed her arms over her chest, like she'd just played her trump card.

"Let me handle this," Jack replied.

Mrs. Hunt smirked. "Handle it then."

"Alone."

"Not after she hit me."

Jack raised his voice. "She's my child. I *will* talk to her. *Alone.*"

Mrs. Hunt huffed and marched away.

Jack went to Brandi. "What happened?"

The girl shook her head. "It doesn't matter. I'm so done with you people."

Jack exhaled. "Look. I'm sorry about putting you through all that in the woods. I wanted you to learn something about yourself."

"Like what? That I hate you?"

"That you're stronger than you think. I wanted to build your confidence and mental toughness. You can't do that by taking the easy way out of everything."

Brandi held out her hands. "So you just leave me out in the woods to starve? Make me eat my best friend? What the fuck?"

"I'm sorry that happened. It's a good lesson, though—"

"Don't even."

"You're missing the point."

"What's the point? That you're a psycho just like my mom said."

Jack winced. "The point is that you survived. The point is that you're strong, competent, and mentally tough."

Brandi shook her head again.

"How about this? I'll do your chores today; we'll have breakfast, and then we'll go to the woods for your final lesson."

The girl laughed, but she didn't sound happy. "You can't be serious. There's no fucking way I'm going into the woods again."

"You need to learn land navigation."

"There's no way in hell I'm hiking forty miles."

"It's only a ten-mile course."

Brandi crossed her arms over her chest. "I don't care how far it is. I'm literally *done*. As soon as I turn eighteen, I'm outta here. I never wanna see you again."

Chapter 54

After

A dog barked like crazy. An excited voice played somewhere above her consciousness. She was hoisted from the car and placed on a bed. The dog still barked.

The roar of an engine came, the bed bumpy. The dog barked again. Shade and sun passed over her body. She was floating now, moving so fast.

More voices came from above, sounding even farther away.

Everything went black again.

Chapter 55

Before

Brandi lay in bed, fully clothed, listening to Jack groan and thrash through their shared wall. When he quieted and his breathing regulated, she exited her bed. She retrieved her backpack from the closet, which had already been packed with clothes and toiletries. Then she tiptoed across the hardwood floor to her bedroom door.

She turned the knob and opened the door. The hinges creaked. Brandi froze, wearing her backpack, her heart thumping in her chest. She expected Mrs. Hunt or Jack to emerge from their rooms to stop her, but they didn't.

She crept down the stairs, through the dark kitchen, and to the back door. She grabbed her boots and opened the door, letting in the cool breeze. Her body buzzed as she glanced over her shoulder. Nobody was coming for her. She left the old farmhouse.

Outside, Brandi slipped on her boots and tied her laces, her hands unsteady. Under a bright moon, she walked down the gravel driveway toward the narrow country road. As she turned onto the road, she smiled to herself.

Brandi hiked along the roadside for a few miles before she tried hitchhiking. She worried that if she hitchhiked close to the farmhouse, she might be seen by some nosy neighbor. She figured the farther away she was, the less likely that was to occur.

An SUV motored her way. Brandi moved to the edge of the road and held out her thumb, but the SUV blew past. Shortly thereafter, a pickup truck with fog lights rumbled her way. She held out her thumb again, and again the truck blew past. But this time, immediately after the truck drove by, the brake lights flashed and the truck pulled over.

Brandi fast-walked to the passenger side door. Her stomach fluttered as she stood on the running board and peered into the open window.

A middle-aged man grinned from the driver's seat, his teeth stained yellow. "Where you headed?"

"Franklin City," Brandi said.

"I'm headed toward Franklin. Hop in."

She narrowed her eyes, noticing the tattoo on the man's neck, the fork-tongued serpent peeking out from his collar.

"C'mon, girl. You in or out?" the man asked.

Brandi glanced down the empty road, then she opened the door and slid into the seat.

The man held out his large hand. "I'm Tank."

Brandi shook his hand. "I'm, uh, April."

"All right. Let's get it." Tank put his truck into gear and spun the rear tire, kicking up sod and dirt from the roadside. As they drove toward Franklin City, Tank glanced at Brandi. "What's a pretty girl like you doin' out by yourself at this hour?"

"I'm meeting a friend," she replied.

Tank nodded with a smirk on his face. "A friend, huh?"

"Yeah. A friend."

"I bet this friend's a young man."

Brandi blushed. "Maybe. Maybe not."

"Ain't none of my business."

"You're right. It's not."

"You're lucky I picked you up. Lots of creeps out here at

night." Tank winked at Brandi, then turned his attention back to the road.

She glanced at the passenger door, noticing it was locked. The man must've locked it.

"You hear about them missin' girls?" Tank asked.

"You talking about the girl that worked at Walmart?" Brandi asked.

"And the one that worked at Arby's."

"That's old news."

"He took another girl yesterday. She worked at Dunkin' Donuts. Her name was Vicki something. You hear about her?"

The hair on the back of Brandi's neck stood on end. Tank referred to this Vicki person in the past tense. "How do you know she was killed?"

Tank turned his truck onto US-422. "I don't know that she was. I'm just assumin'. They never found the other ones."

"Maybe they just ran away."

Tank shook his head. "Naw. If it was one girl maybe, but this is three now. Shit, could be more than three. I think we got a serial killer livin' 'round here." Tank stopped at a red light.

Brandi unlocked her door.

The light turned green, and Tank gunned the engine, driving through the intersection.

She edged closer to the passenger door, gripping the door handle.

"You all right over there?" Tank asked.

"I'm fine," Brandi replied.

"I shouldn't be talkin' about serial killers. Here you are in some stranger's truck. I like to watch true crime shows. You ever watch *Forensic Files?*"

"No."

"I like figurin' out the mystery. I'm pretty good at it."

"Who do you think's killing the girls around here?"

"I wish I knew. There ain't much to go on, except the girls are teenagers, and they work low-pay jobs. I think whoever's doin' this is offerin' 'em money. That's how he gets 'em to go with 'im. It's always the same sad story. Predators preyin' on the weak."

Brandi nodded. "You should tell the police."

"I doubt they'd give a shit what I think." Tank pointed at his windshield. "We're gettin' close to Franklin. Where do you want me to drop you?"

"You know Clayton Corner?"

Tank glanced at Brandi with a furrowed brow. "That ain't exactly a nice neighborhood."

"I'm meeting my friend there. I go there all the time."

The man grunted and turned his truck onto Fourth Street. "All right then."

He made the next left onto Clayton Street. The row homes were dark and dilapidated. Various groups of young men hung out on porches and corners, many drinking alcohol, some smoking.

As they neared the intersection of Clayton Street and Corner Place, Brandi pointed at the sidewalk and said, "You can drop me up here."

Tank double-parked next to an old Honda.

"Thanks for the ride," Brandi said.

"Be careful, April," Tank replied.

Brandi exited the truck and went to the sidewalk. She continued toward Clayton Corner. Tank watched Brandi until someone honked at him, causing him to drive away. Brandi spotted a man in a hoodie doing a hand exchange with a skinny woman in the alley. The woman limped past Brandi, her meth in a death grip. Brandi did a double take, thinking it was her mother, until the woman sneered back.

Brandi approached the man in the hoodie.

He licked his lips and said, "What's up, girl."

"I'm looking for Damon."

He frowned. "He don't need another hood rat."

Brandi placed her hand on her cocked hip. "I'm *not* a hood rat. We're friends."

"Call him then. Whatcha need me for?"

"I don't have a phone. It's an emergency. *Please.*"

The man exhaled and retrieved a cell phone from his pocket. "You better not be fuckin' with me."

"I'm not. I promise."

The man tapped on his phone and put it to his ear. "Yo, Damon. I got this little girlie here lookin' for you." The man lifted his chin to her. "What's your name?"

"Brandi," she replied.

"Her name's Brandi." The man listened for a moment. "I'll tell her." The man shoved his phone into his pocket. "He said he'll be by in fifteen."

Brandi waited over an hour on the corner, enduring lascivious leers from drunk and drugged men. She thought, *This is a mistake. I should go back.* But then Damon and his BMW parked along the curb. She grabbed her backpack and hustled to the passenger side door.

Brandi slid into the leather seat, her backpack in her lap, and her gaze on Damon. "Thank you for coming," she said.

"What's up, shorty?" Damon asked.

"I need a place to stay, just for a little while. Until I can figure some shit out."

"I got you."

Damon drove Brandi back to his house, which was a brick rambler with a big yard, about ten miles outside of Franklin City. A black SUV was parked in the driveway. The bay window was lit from the inside.

"Is someone here?" Brandi asked.

"My boys. Eddie and Tony. C'mon." Damon grabbed his keys and exited his BMW.

Brandi exited the BMW, carrying her backpack. She surveyed the house, her eyes settling on the plethora of garden gnomes.

"What?" Damon asked.

"Is this really your house?" she replied.

"Yeah. It was my grandmother's, but she died last year. Left it to me."

"Did you like your grandmother?"

Damon nodded. "I loved her."

"I hate my grandmother."

"Damn. That's cold."

Brandi shrugged.

He gestured with his chin. "C'mon."

Brandi followed Damon into his house. Eddie and Tony sat on the couch in the living room surrounded by faux wood walls and mustard-colored carpet. Brandi recognized both men: Eddie, a weaselly little man with big ears, and Tony, the chubby Italian with acne scaring. Eddie vaped marijuana, while Tony played a first-person shooter game. Two handguns and beer cans were scattered about the coffee table.

Eddie grinned at Brandi, showing his crooked teeth. "What's up, jail bait?"

Tony chuckled.

The girl dipped her head.

Damon put his arm around her. "Don't listen to him. He's fuckin' with you."

Eddie expelled marijuana vapor. "Sorry, baby. Don't mind me. I'm fucked up."

Damon led Brandi down the hall to a small bedroom decorated with flowers: floral wallpaper, pictures of flowers on the walls, a floral print comforter on the bed, and fake flowers in a vase on the bedside table, and another on the dresser.

"You can stay in here," Damon said.

Brandi set her backpack on the bed. "Thank you. I'm gonna get a job, and then I'll find an apartment or something."

Damon nodded, his gaze crawling over her.

The girl averted her eyes, embarrassed by her work clothes and boots. "I know I look like a farmer."

"You look beautiful. Those clothes can't hide that."

She blushed.

Damon took her hand. "C'mon. Lemme show you my room."

He led Brandi to the master bedroom at the end of the hall. He flicked on the lights, then dimmed them to a warm yellow. The room didn't match the grandma décor of the rest of the house. A large circular bed dominated the room, and faced a massive television mounted on the wall. Everything was black, white, or metallic.

"Your room's nice," Brandi said.

Damon shut the door, but not all the way. He motioned with his finger. "C'mere."

Brandi did as she was told, her heart thumping, and her hands shaky.

He wrapped his arms around Brandi, and kissed her open-mouthed. It was rougher than Brandi liked, but she reciprocated. His hands roamed under her T-shirt and sweatshirt. His breathing intensified. He undid her bra, and his hands ventured underneath, touching her breasts, his fingers squeezing her nipples. Damon tugged at her sweatshirt. Brandi lifted her arms, letting him remove it.

He undid the fly of her canvas pants and plunged his hand between her legs. Brandi gasped and moaned.

"You like that, don't you?" Damon whispered in her ear.

Brandi nodded.

The bedroom door opened, causing Brandi to startle and backpedal from Damon. Eddie and Tony entered the bedroom with shit-eating grins on their faces. She zipped up her pants.

"You startin' without us?" Eddie asked.

Brandi backpedaled away from the men.

"What's wrong, baby?" Tony asked. "You don't like us?"

"She thinks she's too good for us," Eddie said.

Brandi looked at Damon, pleading with her eyes. "I don't wanna..."

"Did you think you could stay here for free?" Damon asked.

"I'll give you money," Brandi replied.

"How much you got?"

"I'll get a job and pay you back."

The men cackled.

"She thinks you're Bank of Fuckin' America," Eddie said.

Brandi reached behind her back and fastened her bra. "It's fine. I'll leave."

"You're already here," Damon said. "You can't come here and not pay. That ain't how it works."

Damon approached her, showing his hands. "Don't worry, shorty. They'll be nice."

Eddie and Tony followed Damon. Brandi's back was against the wall. Over Eddie's shoulder, she saw a man dressed in all black. Her gaze ruined the ambush. Eddie glanced over his shoulder just as Jack's fist connected with his jaw. Eddie fell like a sack of potatoes.

"What the fuck?" Damon said, rushing to his bedside table.

Jack stepped over Eddie, his elbows covering his face. Tony threw a right cross, but Jack turned, his punch glancing off Jack's left elbow. As Tony followed through with his errant punch, Jack caught Tony's forearm in the crook of his right elbow. At the same time, Jack pushed on Tony's elbow with his left forearm.

There was an audible *crack* as Tony's arm was snapped like twig.

Tony squealed, and fell to his knees. Jack kicked him in the face, knocking him unconscious.

Jack sidestepped Tony, headed for the boss. Damon whirled from his bedside table, pointing a handgun, causing Jack to stop and show his hands.

"Who the fuck are you?" Damon said, aiming his gun at Jack's face.

Jack stared at the gun.

Damon's finger was on the trigger.

"Don't shoot him," Brandi said.

Damon glanced at the girl for a split second, and in that split second, Jack used his left hand to move the gun to the right; at the same time, he dodged his head out of the line of fire. Also, at the same time Jack grabbed Damon's wrist with his right hand. The opposite force of Jack's hands caused the gun to rotate, breaking Damon's grip and breaking his trigger finger, as it was bent inside the trigger guard.

Damon screeched in pain. Jack took the handgun, dropped the magazine, and racked the slide, a round ejecting from the chamber. Jack hit Damon in the face with the handgun, sending him to the floor, where Jack continued to beat him. Damon's beautiful face was a bloody mess.

Damon no longer tried to block the blows.

"Jack. Jack! Stop!" Brandi yelled.

Jack reared back for the death blow.

"Stop!" she yelled again.

Jack's shoulders slumped.

"Is he dead?"

Jack shoved the gun in his pocket and put his gloved fingers to Damon's neck, checking for a pulse. "He's alive." Jack stood and grabbed Brandi by the elbow. "We need to go. Where's your backpack?"

"It's in the other room."

"Get it."

Tony and Eddie stirred on the floor.

Brandi swiped her sweatshirt from the carpet and hurried to the guest bedroom for her backpack. Jack followed her. On the way out, Jack swiped the handguns on the coffee table, leaving the full magazines and ejecting the chambered rounds.

On the ride back to the farmhouse, Brandi cried.

Jack said, "What the hell were you thinking? What did I tell you about doing stupid things with stupid people in stupid places?" He waited for a reply that never came. "God damn it, Brandi. Those men would've raped you and turned you out. You would've been working the streets for them. Is that what you want? To be a prostitute?"

"No."

"If you keep this shit up, you'll be in prison or dead by the time you're twenty-one."

"*You* should be in prison."

Jack shook his head. "Maybe I should."

Brandi sniffed and wiped her face with her sweatshirt sleeve.

Jack turned his SUV onto US-422 unnecessarily hard, the tires squealing.

"How did you find me anyway? Were you following me like a psycho?"

Jack glanced at his daughter, then back to the highway. "There's a tracker in your backpack."

"A *what?*"

"A tracking device. It's glued to the inside of your backpack pocket."

Brandi rifled through the small pocket on her backpack, feeling a little disc, barely bigger than a watch battery. She ripped the device from the glue and chucked it out the window. "My mom was right about you. You're literally crazy."

"I put it there so I could keep you safe in the woods. You're lucky I forgot to remove it."

"Fuck you, *Jack.*"

Chapter 56

After

Her bedroom door opened, and a large man appeared in the doorway. Brandi covered her head with her blanket. The man crept to her bedside. He stood over her, his breathing raspy. The girl trembled under the covers, her eyes sealed shut. She braced herself, expecting the man to remove her covers. But he simply picked her up, covers and all, and carried her from her bedroom.

Brandi woke with a start. Her vision was blurry; her mind was hazy. Her left thigh pulsed with a dull ache. She lay on her back in bed. Her vision focused. She scanned her surroundings. A television sat dormant in the upper corner of the room. The shades were closed. It was a hospital room with dim lighting. A divider curtain separated her from another patient. Her right arm was hooked to an IV. Cool oxygen flowed into her nose from the nasal cannula. She lifted her covers and her hospital gown. Fresh bandages covered her breast, sternum, and left thigh. Angry purple bruises covered her upper chest. She figured that was from Harold tackling her.

She glanced to her left. Mrs. Hunt slept in a chair, looking old and disheveled. As if she sensed Brandi, the old bag stirred in her seat and opened her eyes. She locked eyes with her granddaughter and nearly shot out of her seat.

"You're awake," Mrs. Hunt said, approaching Brandi's beside. "How are you feeling?"

"What happened?" Brandi asked, her voice raspy.

"You were shot in the leg. They had to operate on you."

"Am I okay?"

Mrs. Hunt nodded. "Praise God."

Brandi stared at her grandmother for a beat. "Why are you here?"

Mrs. Hunt cleared her throat. "I know you probably don't want me here, but I'm all you have, and you're all I have."

The young woman shook her head. "Go away."

Mrs. Hunt winced as if she'd been slapped.

"*Now.*"

"I'm sorry for how I treated you," Mrs. Hunt said.

Brandi clenched her jaw.

"I was too hard on you. I didn't show you any love. I didn't show your father any love either. I know I'm partly to blame for what he did. That's my cross to bear."

Through gritted teeth, Brandi said, "I don't want you here."

Tears filled Mrs. Hunt's eyes. She went to her chair, grabbed her purse, and retrieved a letter from inside. She held up the letter to Brandi. "Your father left this for you before he..." She set the letter on Brandi's lap. "I'll let the nurse know you're awake." Mrs. Hunt left the hospital room.

Brandi checked her bed and the bedside table. On the bedside table, she found a controller attached to a cord that appeared to be an adjustment for the bed. She fiddled with the controls figuring out how to set herself in a comfortable sitting position. She inspected the envelope. *Brandi* was written on the outside in her dad's sharp, blocky handwriting.

The light brightened. A doctor and a nurse entered the hospital room. Brandi was thankful they were both women, especially if she had to be examined.

The doctor smiled and said, "Hi, Brandi. I'm Dr. Lee. How are you feeling?"

The nurse checked her vital signs.

"My leg's a little sore, but I think I'm okay," Brandi said. "Is my leg gonna be like, the same?"

"You should retain full function of your leg, but you'll need physical therapy."

The nurse left the hospital room.

"How did I get here?" Brandi asked.

"A park ranger found you," Dr. Lee replied. "Actually, that's not entirely accurate. A dog found the park ranger and led him to you, if you can believe that."

Brandi beamed. "His name's Fred."

"He's a very special dog, and you're very lucky to be alive. When you came in, you had extremely low blood pressure. It didn't help that your blood type is O negative."

"What's wrong with O negative blood?" Brandi asked.

"There's nothing wrong with O negative blood, except that it's rare. Only 6.6 percent of people are O negative, and that's the only type of blood you can receive. We had enough to stabilize you, but not enough for what you needed. We're not a very big hospital, and there's been an ongoing shortage across the country. Sadly, people aren't donating as much as they used to. Thankfully, your grandmother's O negative."

"She gave me blood?"

Dr. Lee smiled. "She sure did."

Chapter 57

Before

It was a perfect fall day, the sun warm and the sky bright blue. Brandi sat on a plastic chair behind The Tasty Chicken—a local fast-food restaurant—tapping on her new phone. She wore black pants and a blue polo with the cartoon chicken on her right breast. Brandi and her coworkers often took their breaks behind the building when the weather was nice, sitting in one of the sun-bleached lawn chairs.

Brandi scrolled on Instagram, stalking April and Hanna's profiles. They had graduated from Franklin High School four months ago. Their profiles were littered with smiling pictures of the best friends at Penn State. Brandi had graduated too. By the skin of her teeth. After Billy had died, she stopped doing anything. She didn't do her chores or her schoolwork. She didn't even read about animals. Mostly, she had counted down the days until she could leave Jack and Mrs. Hunt.

Jack knew he was wrong for what he did to Brandi in the woods. He had apologized several times. And the way he beat up Damon and his crew was literally insane. Brandi thought they would've let her go, but her psycho father appeared out of nowhere like a ninja. Now she had to avoid Clayton Corner.

When Brandi turned eighteen, shortly after graduation, Jack

was released from his child support burden by the court. But Jack still sent his monthly payment. Brandi figured it was because he felt guilty about what he did in the woods and at Damon's house, although he had never apologized for what happened at Damon's. Jack had reiterated his offer to send her to college with his GI Bill, but she didn't want to go to school anymore.

A car horn honked.

Brandi looked up from her phone.

A white Hyundai with a dented hood and rust spots parked in a nearby space.

Brandi stood and marched toward her mother's car. She opened the passenger door and slid into the cloth seat. "You're early," she said.

Her mother's shift ended an hour after Brandi's, so she had expected to wait for her mother to pick her up like usual.

"I'm not workin' there anymore." Kathy put the Hyundai into gear.

Brandi turned in her seat toward her mother. "You *quit?*"

Kathy drove toward the parking lot exit. "You don't understand, baby. I stuff fuckin' envelopes all day. It's the worst job in the entire world."

"You need a job for your parole."

Kathy turned onto US-422. "Don't worry, baby. I'll get another job. A better one."

Brandi crossed her arms over her chest. "You should've gotten this *better* job before you quit."

Chapter 58

After

Brandi opened the letter from her father. As she unfolded the tri-folded piece of paper, a picture fell to her lap, face-down. A date was scrawled on the back, 6-25-2005—her first birthday. She glanced around the hospital room, as if it was a hidden treasure. Apart from the patient on the other side of the curtain, she was alone. She grasped the corner of the picture, flipped it, and held it up. Her mom and dad sat on a couch, with Brandi in their lap. Kathy beamed for the camera, appearing young, healthy, and beautiful. Jack grinned like a lucky man. Brandi was a chubby toddler, also smiling, wearing a frilly white dress.

She placed the picture inside the empty envelope and read the letter.

Brandi,

If you're reading this, I'm not around anymore. I hope you understand that my death was my choice alone and has nothing to do with anyone but me. It was my own failings as a human being that led me here.

I'm sorry for everything. I know my apology doesn't undo the hurt I've caused you. I screwed things up so very badly. When I hit your mother, she didn't want to see me anymore, and she didn't want me in your life either. She was right to want that. I couldn't control my anger.

At the time, I made a deal with your mom. I gave her full custody of you. I agreed to pay child support and stay away from both of you. In return, your mom refused to testify against me. She could've ruined my military career and sent me to prison if she wanted to. That was the deal I made.

Hitting your mother was the biggest mistake of my life—not because of how it affected me, but because of how it affected you. I should've taken responsibility for what I did. I should've gone to prison and given up my military career. Instead, I took the selfish route. I gave up you.

I wish I would've done things differently. I wish I would've been there when you needed me. I wish I could do it all over again. I wish I had another chance. I'm out of chances, but you're not.

I may not have been there, but I know you. Deep down, I know you. I see so much of myself in you. You're a fierce warrior, but you need to be pointed in the right direction. You need purpose. The adults in your life, myself included, have failed to guide you toward a virtuous purpose. Instead, we put that responsibility squarely on your shoulders with zero guidance.

I am sorry for that, but I am confident that you will find your purpose in life, and you will do great things, whatever you decide to do. I saved some money for you, and you still have my GI Bill. I'd like for you to use the money to go to school and to fulfill your dreams.

I know I never said it, but I love you with all my heart.
Dad
P.S.-Your mom and I were deeply in love when we had you. We have always loved you, regardless of our failings as parents. I enclosed a picture that I think shows that.

Tears slipped down Brandi's cheeks.

Chapter 59

Before

A KNOCK CAME TO THEIR TRAILER DOOR.
"Could you get the door," Kathy called out from her room.
Brandi exhaled and stood from their ratty couch, her phone in hand. She trudged to the front door and opened it. Two skinny men appeared, grinning, showing their black teeth—her mother's old meth head friends.
"Brandi. Long time no see," one of them said.
Brandi guarded the doorway. "What are you doing here?"
"Just hangin' out," the other one said.
"Hey, guys," Kathy said over Brandi's shoulder.
Brandi pivoted to her mother, her eyes narrowed, and her mouth puckered.
"What?" Kathy asked.
"You know what." Brandi went to her room.
As the men entered the trailer, one of them said, "*Damn*, Kathy. You're lookin' good."
Brandi slammed her bedroom door. She crawled onto her mattress, opened IG, and scrolled, sure that everyone's life was lit. Someone else knocked on the front door. Kathy greeted another former friend and welcomed them into their trailer. Less than a

minute later, there was another knock. Then, they stopped knocking and just came in.

Classic rock pumped into the air. Skunky marijuana wafted through the vents. Voices multiplied and grew louder. Brandi thought, *It's just weed*. But then the sweet smell of meth wafted into her room. She stood from her mattress and exited her room, her jaw set tight.

She waded through the party crowd and spied her mother smoking with her skinny friends. Brandi marched to the kitchen. Kathy saw her coming and quickly passed the meth pipe.

"What the hell are you doing?" Brandi said, glaring at her mother.

Kathy giggled.

"You have a drug test. They'll send you back to prison."

"Don't worry, baby," Kathy said. "It's on Wednesday. I'll be good by then."

"Ice only stays in your system for like three days," one of the meth heads said.

"What's wrong with you?" Brandi asked.

Kathy rolled her eyes like a surly teenager. "Relax. I'm just smokin' a little weed."

Brandi shook her head and left the trailer.

Chapter 60

After

A nurse approached Brandi's hospital bed. "There are two state troopers here to see you. Do you feel up to talking?"

The young woman nodded, knowing they would eventually come for her. "It's fine."

"I'll send them in." The nurse left.

Two uniformed troopers entered the hospital room and marched to Brandi's bedside. One trooper was tall and fit, with an olive complexion. The other was short and stocky, with a ruddy complexion. They both had military style haircuts.

The shorter trooper said, "Brandi Hunt?"

"Yeah," she replied, sitting up.

"We're investigators from the Pennsylvania State Police. I'm Trooper Evans, and this is my partner, Trooper Brooks." Evans gestured to the taller man. "We'd like to ask you a few questions."

"Okay."

"Is it okay if I record?" Trooper Evans asked.

Brandi shrugged. "Go ahead."

Trooper Evans tapped on his phone, then set it on the overbed table, near her. Trooper Brooks moved to the opposite side of the bed. Brandi suddenly felt trapped, flanked by the troopers, the phone recording her every word.

"Can you tell us how you got to the cabin at 1528 Parkland Road?" Trooper Evans asked.

Brandi told them about her meeting with Colton and his subsequent invitation. She told them about the photo shoot at the cabin and in the woods and his disappearance.

"What happened after Colton disappeared?" Trooper Evans asked.

Brandi continued with her story. The troopers asked clarifying questions as she went, but they mostly let her tell her story. Until she told them about killing Roger.

"Did you think Roger posed a physical threat to you when you shot him?" Trooper Evans asked.

"Yes," Brandi replied with a furrowed brow.

"But you said he didn't have a weapon at the time," Trooper Brooks said.

Brandi scowled at Brooks. "Yes, but... I was scared."

"He was also immobilized by your trap," Trooper Evans added.

She turned her scowl on Evans. "Yes, but..."

"You could've walked away, but you didn't."

Mrs. Hunt marched into the hospital room. "*What* is going on here?"

Trooper Brooks held out his hand to the older woman like a stop sign. "This is a police interview, ma'am. You need to leave."

Mrs. Hunt took a wide stance, as if rooted in her spot. "I will do *nothing* of the sort. You will *not* interview my granddaughter without her attorney present."

"Ma'am. We're simply getting the facts of the story."

"Don't you *dare* play me for a fool. I know *exactly* what you're doing. You're fishing."

"There are four dead men," Trooper Evans said, now facing Mrs. Hunt. "Brandi needs to answer our questions."

"Is she under arrest?" Mrs. Hunt asked.

The troopers glanced at each other.

Evans said, "No, but—"

"If she's not under arrest, you both need to leave," Mrs. Hunt said.

The troopers glanced at each other again.

"And another thing." The older woman pointed at Trooper Evans. "If you think you're going to charge my granddaughter with anything, you can forget about plea deals. We will go to trial and we will expose *you* and everyone involved. The whole world will know how the state police is prosecuting the victim and the hero who did *your* job for you. I heard they killed at least twelve young ladies. Where were you then?"

"Ma'am. All we care about is the truth," Trooper Evans said.

Mrs. Hunt shook her head, her mouth puckered in disgust. "If you cared about the truth, you would quit your job because you're obviously not very good at it. My granddaughter had to save *herself* from those devils, and you have the audacity to treat her like a criminal. Not on my watch." Mrs. Hunt pointed at Evans and Brooks. "You are not welcome here. *Leave.*"

"Ma'am—"

"*Now.*"

Trooper Evans grabbed his phone from the overbed table, and the two troopers headed for the exit. Mrs. Hunt followed them out of the hospital room, still lecturing.

"Don't you *ever* talk to my granddaughter again without her attorney. You should be giving her a medal, not the third degree. You two should be *ashamed* of yourselves."

Mrs. Hunt returned to Brandi's bedside, dropping her purse on the nearby chair. "Make sure you don't talk to them without your attorney."

"I have an attorney?" Brandi asked.

"Yes, you do. I don't think you'll need him, but if you do, I have him on speed dial."

Brandi smiled for an instant. "Thank you."

Mrs. Hunt nodded. "How are you feeling?"

"Not too bad. I don't know if it's the drugs, but my leg feels a little better today."

"You think you're up for another visitor?"

"Depends on the visitor."

"He's at the nurse's station. I wanted to make sure you were feeling okay before I brought him in."

Brandi tilted her head, intrigued. "Who is he?"

Mrs. Hunt gave her granddaughter a rare smile. "It's a surprise."

Brandi frowned. "I think I've had enough surprises."

"I think you'll like this surprise. I'll be right back." Mrs. Hunt left the hospital room.

Shortly thereafter, she returned with Fred, who wore a vest labeled *service dog*. As soon as Fred recognized Brandi, he wagged his tail so vigorously that his midsection twisted back and forth. He rushed to the young woman, his toenails tapping the linoleum.

Brandi leaned over her bedside and petted him. "It's Fred!"

Fred put his front paws on her bedside. She hugged him, then petted his head and droopy ears with both hands.

Brandi looked at Mrs. Hunt. "He's a service dog?"

The older woman smirked. "He is while he's in the hospital."

Brandi laughed.

Fred nudged Brandi's hand with his nose, urging her to continue with the pets.

Brandi petted him again, her attention still on Mrs. Hunt. "Did the owner let you bring him in?"

The older woman shook her head. "You're his owner if you want to be."

"What? How?"

"I heard through the grapevine that the local bloodhound man wouldn't claim Fred as his own. The police think he's worried about getting into trouble, but they couldn't prove he was his dog, so poor Fred ended up in the pound. I busted him out. I figured you might want him. If you don't, I'll keep him for you."

"What about Scout? There was a golden retriever." Brandi dropped her gaze. "I had to shoot him. I don't know if he died."

237

Mrs. Hunt winced. "I'm so sorry. I can call the lady at the pound. See if anyone brought in a golden retriever."

Brandi nodded.

Mrs. Hunt retrieved her phone from her purse, tapped on the screen, then put the phone to her ear.

"Hi, Lucy. This is Doris Hunt. I was in this morning to adopt the bloodhound." Mrs. Hunt paused for a moment. "I was wondering if you had anyone bring in a golden retriever with a recent gunshot wound." Mrs. Hunt listened for the response.

Brandi watched her grandmother, searching her facial expressions for clues, but the older woman was pokerfaced.

"Thank you very much." Mrs. Hunt disconnected the call. "She said someone dropped off a golden retriever with an injured hind leg on Monday."

Brandi touched her chest and exhaled. "Is he okay?"

"She said he should be fine. One of the volunteers wants to adopt him if nobody else does."

She nodded.

"I have room on the farm for another dog."

Brandi shook her head, her eyes downcast. "I don't think he'll ever trust me after what I did."

Mrs. Hunt stepped closer to her bedside. She placed her hand atop Brandi's. "I understand."

Brandi raised her gaze to Mrs. Hunt. "Thank you, Grandma."

Chapter 61

Before

Under the moonlight, Brandi slowly swayed back and forth on the swing, her feet pushing and dragging the playground wood chips. *She's so fucking stupid. Hanging out with stupid people, doing stupid things. She'll get arrested. That'll be her stupid prize. I bet she fails her piss test.* Brandi shook her head and thought, *I don't even care anymore.* That was a lie.

Rowdy voices approached the playground. Three teen boys in hoodies and skinny jeans and two teen girls. Brandi wiped her eyes with her sleeve.

"Check her out," one of the boys said.

"What's she doing?" one of the girls asked.

"Hey, you on the swing," one of the boys called out.

The group snickered.

"What are you doing out here by yourself?" the boy asked.

Brandi stood from the swing and brushed past the high schoolers.

"So weird," one of the girls said.

Brandi went home, pleasantly surprised that the party appeared to be over. The cars were gone and the house was quiet. She entered the trailer. The place still smelled like weed and meth. Trash and beer cans littered the living room and kitchen. She walked down the hall to her bedroom. She opened the door, her room smelling like sex and body odor. Two beer cans and a used condom littered her floor. She recoiled in disgust.

"*Mom.* Someone had sex in my room!" Brandi called out as she went to her mother's room and opened the door. Her mother lay in bed, on her back, passed out. "Did you hear me? Your meth head friends had sex in my room."

Kathy didn't stir.

Brandi marched to her bedside and yelled in her mother's face. "Your loser friends had sex in my room."

Kathy still didn't stir.

A meth pipe sat on the floor next to her outstretched hand.

Brandi shook her mother. "Wake up. Wake up!"

Kathy didn't move.

Tears filled Brandi's eyes as she violently shook her mother. "Wake up. Wake up you stupid bitch. Wake up!"

Brandi paced in front of her trailer, waiting for the police. Her eyes were red and itchy, but they were dry—all cried out.

It took the police an hour to finally appear.

The police officer asked her questions that she'd already told the 911 operator, but Brandi answered obediently. She didn't have the energy for attitude.

Then he asked, "Is there someone I can call for you? Family?"

Brandi drew her eyebrows together. "For what?"

"Support."

"There's nobody."

Chapter 62

After

Fireworks popped and flashed on the television screen. The Washington DC crowd waved thousands of little American flags. Brandi sat up in her hospital bed watching the Fourth of July celebration, but she thought about her recurring nightmare. Fred yawned. Grandma groaned and stood from her seat.

"I should go back to the hotel," Grandma said. "We're way past visiting hours, and Fred needs a walk."

Fred whined in agreement.

Brandi nodded, her eyes unfocused. "Okay."

"What's wrong?" Grandma asked.

Brandi turned her gaze from the television to her grandmother. "It's literally stupid."

"What is it, dear?"

"I've been having trouble sleeping."

"I can ask the nurse to give you something—"

"No, I don't want any more drugs."

"Okay. What do you need then?"

Brandi took a deep breath. "I've been having this weird dream. I'm really young, and some guy shows up in my room and takes me away. It sounds stupid when I say it out loud, but it feels like it's literally happening. It's really scary."

Grandma moved the chair next to her granddaughter and plopped down. She sighed and said, "We thought you forgot…"

"Forgot what?"

"I don't like this story, but if you're having nightmares, you should know where they come from." Grandma paused for a moment, likely thinking about how best to present the information. "When your mother first started using, she got involved with some unsavory characters while your father was deployed. When he came back, he found your mother passed out with another man in their bed."

Brandi scrunched her face. "That's why he punched her?"

Grandma shook her head. "No. Your father didn't even wake them up. He went to your room, but you were gone. It had been raining that night, and there were muddy boot prints next to your bed. That's when he lost his temper, but not on your mother. She was too incoherent to talk. Your father nearly beat the man to death until he confessed your whereabouts. Thank God your father found you that night. Thank God you were unharmed."

"Why did they take me?"

"To sell you."

"That's why he hit my mom?"

Grandma nodded. "Your father threatened to take you away from your mother. Then your mother started making threats of her own. They got into a huge argument, and your father lost his temper, and then, well, I assume you know the rest."

Epilogue

"I think I'm fitting in okay," Brandi said into the laptop microphone. "I mean, I know I've done things most people could never really understand, but that's okay. They don't have to understand that part of me, and it's unrealistic for me to expect that anyway."

The middle-aged woman on the screen smiled. "I'm so proud of you, Brandi. You've come a long way in therapy. You've done the work, and it shows."

Brandi smiled back. "Well, I've had a lot of help. You. My grandmother. Fred. My friends."

"We all need help from time to time. That's for sure. Our time is almost up. Are you okay with this time next week?"

"This is perfect," she replied.

Brandi said goodbye to her therapist and shut her laptop. She stared at the picture frames on her desk. One held a picture of her grandmother and Fred. She had wanted to bring Fred with her to Penn State, but it wasn't practical or fair to Fred, who absolutely loved farm life. The other framed photo portrayed her family on her first birthday. She remembered what her dad had written to her. *I am confident that you will find your purpose in life, and you will do great things, whatever you decide to do.*

She set her laptop aside and opened the thick textbook titled *General Veterinary Anatomy*. As she turned to her assigned reading, she thought, *I'm trying my best, Dad.*

A knock came to her door.

"Come in," Brandi called out.

One of her roommates entered her bedroom, her face twisted in concern. "Um. You're on Netflix."

"Really?"

"I'm pretty sure it's you."

Brandi stood from her desk and followed her roommate to the common area. Her two other roommates sat on the couch, the screen paused, showing the title screen—*Girl in the Woods*. Brandi *had* been contacted by Netflix, but she'd declined to be involved with the production, even though they'd offered one million dollars, just as she'd declined every other offer. She didn't want to be defined by what happened with those psychopaths in the woods. Brandi's roommates made room for her on the couch, but she decided to stand. A roommate pressed Play on the remote.

Pictures of Harold in a suit with his family appeared with a dramatic voice-over. "Harold Blevins was a prominent defense attorney, known as Dirty Harry for defending the most heinous sex offenders. Dirty Harry had a deadly secret." A surgery recreation was shown. "His secret was exposed while under anesthesia during a knee surgery performed by his childhood best friend, orthopedic surgeon, Dr. Roger Lafferty." Images of Roger appeared on the screen, wearing his white doctor's coat and his arm around his trophy wife.

Brandi clenched her fists, her fingernails digging into her palms. She soothed herself, thinking, *They're literally gone. But you survived. They can't hurt you ever again. You made sure of that.*

"Dr. Lafferty never thought he'd meet someone like him; that is someone who needed to possess young women." The documentary cut to a recreation of Harold and Roger talking in his doctor's office. "A few weeks after the surgery, Harold met with Dr. Lafferty in his office for a checkup. It was here that Dr. Lafferty took a chance, telling his friend about his forbidden needs and desires."

Drone footage appeared of the luxury cabin in the woods. "This heart-to-heart between friends led to an invitation to Harold's luxury cabin in the Pennsylvania wilderness." A recreation of Harold and Roger talking at the cabin was shown. "It was here that the friends developed the rules they would follow to satisfy their needs, avoid prosecution, and profit from their crimes. Despite their collective intelligence and power, they had several impediments to making their evil plans a reality."

Images of Harold and his wife appeared. The picture split in two. "Harold's wife had recently filed for divorce, and Dr. Roger Lafferty had been sued for malpractice." Court documents showing the malpractice case flashed on the screen. "Both Harold and Roger were also known as big spenders, with expensive cars, mansions, and exotic vacations." The documentary cut to images of their materialism. "Harold and Roger needed cash to maintain their lifestyles, and they needed help satisfying their dark needs. Specifically, they needed someone to lure the young women, and they needed someone with IT skills and intimate knowledge of the dark web to raise the needed cash."

Images of Colton flashed on the screen. "Harold had always been close with Colton Blevins, seeing much of himself in his mischievous nephew." Pitt campus appeared. "When Colton was accused of raping a classmate at the University of Pittsburgh, it was Uncle Harold who defended him successfully in criminal court, although he was found guilty by the university and summarily expelled."

They cut to a beautiful brunette. Her name, *Amber Rains, University of Pittsburgh*, appeared at the bottom of the screen. "He definitely charmed me," she said. "I really liked him. Everyone did. He was like the guy that had everything going for him. But when I told him no, it was like he'd never heard the word before."

A recreation of Colton talking and laughing with a young woman appeared. "Colton was a handsome young man and the perfect bait for the young women desired by Harold and Roger. Harold knew his nephew had the looks and the lack of morals for the job."

Promotional footage from Platinum Models, Inc. played on the screen. "Colton developed various ruses to pick up young women, but he found his greatest success targeting low-wage workers. He presented himself as the President of Platinum Models, Colton Ellis. The real President of Platinum Models is C. Howard Ellis, a gentleman in his sixties, whose image was conveniently not pictured on the website. Colton's prey would likely search the website and conclude that it was a legitimate business, and that Colton was in fact the president. Colton brought his uncle and Roger many young women, and he was paid handsomely for his services."

The documentary cut to pictures of Matt with Scout, smiling and showing his gap. "Harold Blevins had successfully defended IT engineer, Matthew Cunningham from stalking and indecent exposure charges, and they'd developed an unlikely friendship." A picture of Harold and Matt standing on a lookout, wearing their hiking gear, appeared on the screen. They almost looked like father and son, with Harold likely outweighing Matt by one hundred pounds.

"Like Harold, Matt had dark secrets and dark proclivities." They cut to a hooded figure typing. "Matt's IT skills and proclivities led him to the dark web, where he was addicted to rape pornography. It was through Matt that Harold Blevins and Doctor Roger Lafferty accessed the dark web and profited from their evil deeds by selling rape and snuff films."

Pictures of Roger and Harold flashed on the screen, smiling for the camera, amber-colored drinks in hand. "These men formed the perfect team, but there were disagreements. Roger was a power rapist who used minimal force to rape. He believed that the young women wanted him and even loved him."

A middle-aged blonde appeared on the screen, her face blurred. "Jane" spoke with a digitized voice. "We were in med school together. I thought we were friends, but Roger wanted more. He tried to kiss me one night, but I rejected him. He seemed fine. We never talked about it. I didn't want to embarrass him any further. We went back to being friends, and everything seemed normal. After a big test, we went out for drinks. I got really wasted, but I only had two beers. I'm pretty sure I was drugged. I woke up in Roger's bed wearing my underwear and nothing else. Roger said that I had taken off my clothes, and nothing had happened, but I could tell something had happened. I was so ashamed and afraid. I never went to the police... but I wish I had."

The documentary cut to pictures of Harold Blevins. "Dirty Harry was a sadistic rapist who enjoyed torturing and eventually murdering his victims. His proclivities clashed with Roger, who wanted to possess his victims longer, to even love them, but Harold couldn't resist torturing them beyond repair."

Pictures of all four men flashed on the screen. "Despite their differences, they had successfully lured a dozen women into their deadly web. They had no reason to think number thirteen would be any different. To these evil men, Brandi Hunt was just another young woman struggling in a bad economy." A three-year-old IG selfie of Brandi wearing tiny jean shorts and a tank top appeared. She'd titled the post *Last First Day of School*.

Brandi cringed at her former cry for attention.

"But Brandi Hunt was different." They showed The Tasty Chicken. "She was an unassuming cashier at a fast-food restaurant in Franklin, Pennsylvania, but these predators had no idea that they had lured a young lady with training in survivalism, marksmanship, self-defense, and even guerrilla warfare." The documentary cut to pictures of Jack in his Army uniform. "Brandi's late-father, retired First Sergeant Jack Hunt, was a highly decorated veteran and a member of Delta Force, a special mission unit tasked with the most complex, covert, and dangerous missions..."

Brandi pivoted and started to leave the common area.

One of her roommates called after her, "Where are you going?"

Brandi said over her shoulder, "I know what happened."

She continued to her bedroom. She opened her desk drawer and retrieved several books, exposing her holstered Glock 19. She clipped the holster to her belt and covered her handgun with her flouncy fleece. Brandi strapped her purse across her chest and left her bedroom.

When she entered the common area, one of her roommates paused the documentary, and they all turned to Brandi.

One of them said, "You're a badass."

"Damn right she is," another roommate said.

"I'm gonna go for a coffee," Brandi replied.

"Do you want company?" one of her roommates asked.

Brandi shook her head and glanced at the television screen. The documentary still had an hour left. "I'll be back in an hour or so." She left the apartment.

Brandi ambled on a campus sidewalk, just after dusk, a cool breeze tousling her hair. Lampposts at regular intervals illuminated the sidewalk with circular beams of light. She passed a rectangular metal post labeled EMERGENCY. A blue light that resembled those on a police car sat atop the post. If she were in trouble, she could push the big red button on the contraption, and theoretically, campus police would ride to the rescue. She thought, *A person could be killed in a fraction of a second. Beaten in seconds. Raped in a minute. How long will it take for campus police to arrive?*

She neared a large man sitting on a bench, his hood up. The man followed Brandi with his gaze as she walked by. Her heart rate was steady. She didn't worry about the man on the bench. She knew the likelihood of attack was low, and even if she were attacked... *it wouldn't end well for him.*

Want to discuss our books with other readers and even the authors?

JOIN THE AETHON DISCORD!

Thank you for reading What Happened in the Woods

We hope you enjoyed it as much as we enjoyed bringing it to you. We just wanted to take a moment to encourage you to review the book. Follow this link: **What Happened In The Woods** to be directed to the book's Amazon product page to leave your review.

Every review helps further the author's reach and, ultimately, helps them continue writing fantastic books for us all to enjoy.

ALSO BY PHIL M. WILLIAMS:
WHAT HAPPENED IN THE WOODS
DEATH DO US PART

You can also JOIN our non-spam mailing list by visiting www.subscribepage.com/aethonthrillsnewsletter and never miss out on future releases. You'll also receive three full books completely Free as our thanks to you.

Facebook | Instagram | Twitter | Website

Want to discuss our books with other readers and even the authors?
JOIN THE AETHON DISCORD!

Looking for more great Thrillers?

A home invasion ends in murder. Was it a burglary gone bad, or was it personal? *Mild-mannered professor, James Harris, met his future wife, Rachel, when she was a student in his class. Despite her age, she was more an adventurous vixen than an innocent schoolgirl. They hid their illicit affair until Rachel graduated, and then James made her an honest woman. Rachel was the town it girl. The woman who all the men wanted and who all the women wanted to be. Even when she manipulated men for personal gain, they smiled and came back for more. But Rachel set aside her immature past to become a brilliant psychologist, who treated the most violent offenders. All that beauty. All that intelligence. All gone. Taken from the world during a brutal home invasion. James could've stopped the attack. He could've at least tried, but he froze. The police and Rachel's family suspect there's more to the story than James is telling. All James knows is what he heard while he hid. The conversation between Rachel and the home invader leaves more questions than answers.* Did Rachel know the home invader? Was it one of her psych patients? Was it an obsessed ex-boyfriend? Am I next? **James must answer these questions before he joins his dearly departed wife in this unputdownable crime thriller full of twists from bestseller Phil M. Williams that will keep you guessing until the very end. Grab your copy today and find out the truth!**

Get Death Do Us Part Now!

From desk agent to unexpected field agent. The safety of the world hangs in the balance. *Kate Malone is an intelligence analyst specializing in Russian military and politics. When asked to debrief a Russian defector in Paris, she considers it just another routine assignment. Routine becomes chaos and leads to a desperate chase through the capitals of Europe... With no training as a field operative, Kate must learn the ways of a spy even as Russian agents hunt her down. Failure could lead to another world war, but success depends on survival. And in the world of international espionage, survival is never guaranteed.* **Experience a gripping tale of international intrigue and espionage perfect for fans of Tom Clancy, L.T. Ryan, and Saul Herzog. Join Kate as she must leave the safety of her agency office behind and face the dangers of life as a field agent.**

Get Too Soon A Spy Now!

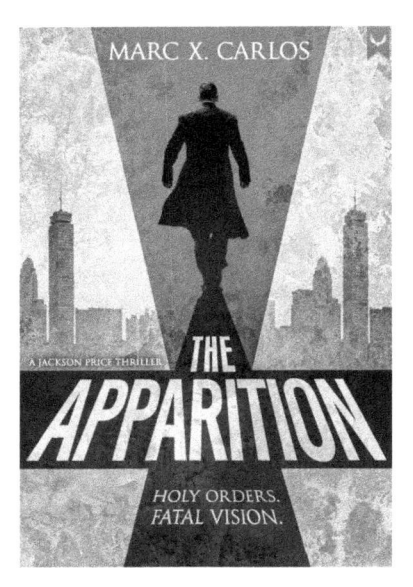

The truth shall set you free. But for one young lawyer, it might just cost him his life... *A popular priest is accused of a horrific assault and tied to the murders of two other women. Jackson Price and his mentor race to uncover the motives of his accuser. At the same time, detectives uncover a checkered past of inappropriate behavior with women and mental health issues. The case may hinge on the truth of an apparition and the impact it has on everyone involved. As the case races through the criminal justice system, Jackson finds himself caught between reality and the delusions of a killer. One could end his short career; the other could end his life. Strap in and follow the investigation to the thrilling end!* **The Apparition is a gripping psychological legal thriller with high stakes suspense and vivid courtroom drama. From debut author Marc X. Carlos, it's inspired by one of his real cases as a career criminal defense attorney with extensive experience in high profile crimes, courtroom technique and crime scene investigation.**

Get The Apparition Now!

For all our Thrillers, visit our website at www.aethonbooks.com/thriller

For the Reader

Dear Reader,

I'm thrilled that you took precious time out of your life to read my novel. Thank you! I hope you found it entertaining, engaging, and thought-provoking. If so, please consider writing a positive review on your favorite retail site. Five-star reviews have a huge impact on future sales. The review doesn't need to be long and detailed if you're more of a reader than a writer. As an author and a small businessman competing against the big publishers, I greatly appreciate every reader, every review, and every referral.

If you're interested in receiving two of my novels for free and/or reading my other titles for free or discounted, go to the following link: http://www.PhilWBooks.com. You're probably thinking, *What's the catch?* There is no catch.

If you want to contact me, don't be bashful. I can be found at Phil@PhilWBooks.com. I do my best to respond to all emails.

Sincerely,
Phil M. Williams

Gratitude

I'd like to thank my wife for being my first reader, sounding board, and cheerleader. I struggled with the complexity of this plot and bored her with endless possibilities of where to take the story. Her support, patience, and unwavering belief in my skill as an author were integral to the creation of this story. Her only complaint was, "Do we have to talk about murder right before bed?" I love you, Denise.

I'd also like to thank my publisher Aethon Books, and their staff. Thank you to Rhett for believing in this story when it was simply an idea: A young couple goes to the woods and the boyfriend disappears. Thank you to my editors, Jakub Dunski and Jennifer Ehrhardt. They did a fantastic job making sure the manuscript was error-free.

Thank you to my mother-in-law, Joy, one of the best nurses on this planet. She is always gracious with her time and extremely knowledgeable about all things medical.

Thank you to my beta readers, Ray and Ann. They're my last defense against the dreaded typo. And thank you to you, the reader. Without you, I wouldn't have a career. As long as you keep reading, I'll keep writing.

About the Author

Phil M. Williams is the author of thirty books primarily in the thriller genre. His thrillers span many subgenres, such as: murder mysteries, political, domestic, dystopian, legal, psychological, and technothrillers. His stories often feature regular Joes and Janes in extraordinary situations that are ripped from today's headlines.

If you'd like to read two free thrillers, go to http://PhilWBooks.com.